PRAISE FOR *DEATH*

"*Death Valley Duel* is a taut, smart, an
keep you spellbound. Scott Graham has written a love letter to the California desert, and to parenthood, and to the athletes who push themselves past limits most of us cannot even imagine. This novel is a steady, dangerous, and addictive race toward justice."

—NINA DE GRAMONT, *New York Times* bestselling author

"Move over, Chuck Bender, because it's Carmelita Ortega's turn. Fans of Scott Graham's novels will relish in watching one of their most adored characters take center stage. By turns a life-and-death thriller and a fascinating examination of endurance sports, *Death Valley Duel* is an adrenaline-soaked journey through one of the most forbidding and alluring places in the United States. Expertly paced and compelling, you'll find it hard to put down."

—C. MATTHEW SMITH, *Twentymile*

"The latest installment in Scott Graham's National Park Mystery series will not disappoint. *Death Valley Duel* is a propulsive, page-turning murder mystery with an environmental cold case at its core that asks thoughtful questions surrounding water rights and American colonialism that keeps it from being just another whodunit. I found myself reading into the early hours of the morning, compulsively devouring this dynamic novel."

—MOLLY IMBER, Maria's Bookshop

"A twisty thriller that promises an epic race to the finish."

—CLAIRE KELLS, *Forgotten Trail*

PRAISE FOR SCOTT GRAHAM'S NATIONAL PARK MYSTERY SERIES

"Terrific."

—C.J. BOX, *New York Times* bestselling author

"Filled with murder and mayhem, jealousy and good detective work—an exciting, nonstop read."

—ANNE HILLERMAN, *New York Times* bestselling author

"One part mystery, one part mysticism, one part mayhem—and all parts exciting."

—CRAIG JOHNSON, *New York Times* bestselling author

"One of the most engaging mysteries I've read in a long while . . . delivers it all and then some."

—MARGARET COEL, *New York Times* bestselling author

"Lush descriptions of natural beauty and twisted false leads create an exciting, rewarding puzzle."

—*PUBLISHERS WEEKLY*

"As always, the highlight of Graham's National Park Mystery Series is his extensive knowledge of the parks system, its lands, and its people."

—*KIRKUS REVIEWS*

"A winning blend of archaeology and intrigue,
Graham's series turns our national parks into places of equal parts beauty, mystery, and danger."

—EMILY LITTLEJOHN, *Shatter the Night*

"Engrossing . . . a glorious portrait of one of the most compelling landscapes on earth. Graham clearly knows the territory.
A topnotch read."

—WILLIAM KENT KRUEGER, *New York Times* bestselling author

"Stunning setting, intriguing plot, and likeable characters."

—ANDREA AVANTAGGIO, Maria's Bookshop

"Only a truly gifted novelist is able to keep a reader turning pages while imparting extensive knowledge about the people, the landscape, and the park system. Scott Graham proves yet again that he is one of the finest."

—CHRISTINE CARBO, *A Sharp Solitude*

"Graham has a true talent for allowing his readers to feel almost as if they were trekking the park themselves."

—*MYSTERY SCENE MAGAZINE*

"A multilevel mystery that plumbs the emotions of greed and jealousy."

—*THE DURANGO HERALD*

"A beautifully balanced book, incorporating intense action scenes, depth of characterization, realistic landscapes, and historical perspective."

—*REVIEWING THE EVIDENCE*

"Only the best novelists have the gift of propelling readers into the middle of artfully crafted adventures . . . Scott Graham once again proves he belongs in the very first rank."

—JEFF GUINN, *New York Times* bestselling author

"An extraordinary ride! You know when a reader says they couldn't put the book down? *Yellowstone Standoff* is one of those rare books . . . a tour de force."

—WIN BLEVINS, *New York Times* bestselling author

"Get ready for leave-you-breathless high country southwestern adventure."

—MICHAEL McGARRITY, *New York Times* bestselling author

DEATH VALLEY DUEL

Also by Scott Graham
in the National Park Mystery Series

Canyon Sacrifice

Mountain Rampage

Yellowstone Standoff

Yosemite Fall

Arches Enemy

Mesa Verde Victim

Canyonlands Carnage

Saguaro Sanction

DEATH VALLEY DUEL

A National Park Mystery
By Scott Graham

TORREY HOUSE PRESS

Salt Lake City • Torrey

This is a work of fiction set in a real place. All characters in this novel are fictitious. Any resemblance to actual events or persons, living or dead, is entirely coincidental.

First Torrey House Press Edition, June 2024

Published by Torrey House Press
Salt Lake City, Utah
www.torreyhouse.org

International Standard Book Number: 978-1-948814-94-2
E-book ISBN: 978-1-948814-95-9
Library of Congress Control Number: 2023936532

Cover art by David Jonason
Cover design by Kathleen Metcalf
Interior design by Gray Buck-Cockayne
Distributed to the trade by Consortium Book Sales and Distribution

Torrey House Press offices in Salt Lake City sit on the homelands of Ute, Goshute, Shoshone, and Paiute nations. Offices in Torrey are on homelands of Southern Paiute, Ute, and Navajo nations.

To Kirsten, Mark, Will, and the entire dedicated team at Torrey House, with gratitude

PROLOGUE

The rattlesnakes were restless.

Twisted around one another in the cramped cage he carried on his back, they filled the night air with the buzzing menace of their rattling tails.

A week ago, he'd used reptile tongs to gather the snakes—Mojave greens, the most venomous rattlesnakes on earth—from their den while they dozed through the cool months of winter and early spring. He'd filled the cage with as many of the rattlers as he dared. Now, trapped in their tight confines, they flung themselves against the walls of the crate, making him lurch from side to side as he hauled them through the night.

The load was heavy, the distance to his destination great. But the reward, necessary after all these years, was worth every stride he took, every jerky sway, every stumble in the darkness.

The eastern sky was growing gray with dawn when he arrived. The snakes balled themselves together in the center of the crate, their looped bodies tensed, as he lowered the enclosure to the ground. He set the cage at the side of the drainage, aimed the screen door back the way he'd come, and heaped dirt and rocks over all but the doorway, hiding the crate's presence in the bottom of the ravine. Straightening, he faced down the dry stream bed and imagined the scene to come with unbridled euphoria.

He would unlatch the screen door and leap back. For a long second all would be still, the silence of the night broken only by the drumbeat of approaching footsteps from lower in the drainage. Then, sensing their freedom, the rattlesnakes would shoot out of the cage, writhing and wriggling.

The snakes would slither off into the desert in all directions. But they would travel only a short distance before responding to the threatening vibration of the footsteps by spinning themselves into tight coils, heads up and tails stiff.

He shivered with delight, savoring the vision of the Mojave greens poised and waiting in the darkness, venom glands engorged and fangs armed, ready to attack their oncoming human prey.

PART ONE

"It's the same game: get me water first. The hell with the other people."

—River's End: California's Latest Water War

1

"Move into the light, Carm!" Rosie Ortega demanded of her older sister Carmelita in the predawn darkness. "You have to."

Carmelita flinched at Rosie's command. Perched on the edge of her folding camp chair in the Mt. Whitney trailhead parking lot, she leaned forward, cinching the laces of her neon purple trail-running shoes.

Standing next to her, Chuck Bender stiffened. He raised a hand in warning to Rosie, who squatted in front of Carmelita with her cell phone aimed at her sister. The last thing Carmelita needed right now, in the tense final minutes leading up to the start of the Whitney to Death 150 ultra trail running race, was Rosie's phone camera shoved in her face.

Carmelita had asked Rosie to film, edit, and post footage online of her preparation for and participation in the Whitney to Death 150. Set to begin in just a few minutes, the annual running competition across the eastern California desert from Mount Whitney to Death Valley was widely considered one of the toughest footraces on earth.

Rosie, who had just turned fifteen, had taken on the role of Carmelita's personal filmmaker with her usual gusto. Over the months leading up to the race, she'd captured hours of footage with her cell phone camera of seventeen-year-old Carmelita training for the competition in and around their hometown of Durango, Colorado. She had produced rough-cut videos from the footage and uploaded them to the internet as the April race approached. The videos featured her distinctively raspy voice as she praised Carmelita's work ethic and quiet confidence.

"I'm not moving," Carmelita told Rosie without looking up. She bent farther forward in her seat, presenting the back of her head to Rosie's upraised phone, and continued tightening her shoes.

By Chuck's count, this was the sixth time Carmelita had loosened and retied her laces while seated in the chair, a show of nerves that, though notably uncommon for her, was fully justified this morning.

The Whitney to Death 150 followed rugged hiking trails and old mining tracks eastward from Mount Whitney, at 14,505 feet the highest point in the lower forty-eight states, to Badwater Basin in the heart of Death Valley National Park, at 282 feet below sea level the lowest point in all of North America. In the decade since the race's inception, barely one in five runners had completed the entire one-hundred-fifty-mile race in the allotted fifty-hour time limit. The other four out of five racers either dropped out or failed to finish in time, victims of the brutal nature of the competition—unrelenting heat and lack of shade during daylight hours and brutally challenging terrain at night.

Last fall, Carmelita had proposed to her mother, Janelle, and Chuck, her stepfather, that she apply to compete in the race and had asked them to serve as her support crew if she was accepted. When they had questioned her about the wisdom of attempting the Whitney to Death 150 at her young age, she had convinced them she possessed the two key attributes required for the competition: the willpower to complete the long training runs necessary over the months leading up to the race, and the mental fortitude needed to keep going when the going got tough, as it inevitably would, over the course of the run. She also promised them that if the race ultimately proved too demanding, she would drop out before she did any permanent damage to her body or psyche.

A staffing shortage at Durango Fire and Rescue, where Janelle worked as a paramedic, had forced her to stay in Colorado and pick up vacant shifts rather than travel to California to serve on Carmelita's support crew. In Janelle's absence, Carmelita had recruited Janelle's younger brother Clarence and his girlfriend Liza to crew for her along with Chuck and Rosie.

As Rosie reported in the videos she filmed and posted, Carmelita's training for the Whitney to Death 150 had proceeded smoothly, a steady accumulation of miles throughout the winter on snowy trails in the San Juan Mountains surrounding Durango. Perhaps because of the gritty appeal of the unvarnished videos Rosie produced, or the refreshing positivity of her behind-the-scenes narration, the short films proved popular online, with each newly posted video gaining hundreds of new followers for Carmelita's social media channels.

Carmelita had begun tapering her training mileage four weeks ago, harboring the strength and stamina she'd developed over the preceding months for the formidable endurance test ahead. She'd been remarkably upbeat two days ago, when she and Chuck had spent the day together surveying the race route by car, while Rosie, Clarence, and Liza remained in Whitney Portal Campground, the starting point of the race beneath the towering east face of Mount Whitney.

Now, in the dark parking lot, Chuck bit down on his lower lip, his nerves jangling, as Carmelita retied her shoes yet again in her seat beside him. Her fixation this morning on her laces concerned him. On top of the immense physical challenge presented by the Whitney to Death 150, the psychological pressure of the competition was enormous as well.

"But you *have* to move," Rosie said to Carmelita, extending her phone closer to her sister. "It's too dark where you're sitting. Nobody will be able to see you."

With her free hand, Rosie tucked an unruly lock of her dark curly hair beneath the stretchy strap of her headlamp. In the chilly mountain air, her round cheeks, visible in the downward cast of her headlamp beam, were tinged with red.

Carmelita's hair, as dark as Rosie's but smooth and straight, was gathered in a ponytail at the back of her neck. The flexible band of her headlamp held her beaming light in place on her forehead over her backward-facing running cap. The light illuminated her thin forearms and delicate fingers as she worked on her shoes.

Opposite her, a floodlight on a portable tripod cast a glowing circle of light on a patch of the otherwise unlit trailhead parking lot adjacent to the campground. The steep winding road up Portal Canyon from Owens Valley ended at the paved lot, where the main hiking trail to the summit of Mount Whitney began.

"You've tied your shoes, like, a million times," Rosie said.

Carmelita hunched her shoulders and continued fiddling with her laces.

Chuck drummed the back of her nylon seat with his fingers, his thumb hooked over the chair's aluminum frame. He was lean and fit from his decades of work on archaeological digs, though as he neared his fifties, his close-cropped brown hair was flecked with gray, and with each passing year, the crow's feet extending from the corners of his eyes and mouth cut deeper into his sun-burnished skin. In the cool early morning, he wore a fleece jacket, loose cotton pants, and lightweight hiking boots.

"Please, stop that," Carmelita scolded him.

He jerked his hand away.

Rosie chortled. She wore black sweats, running shoes with marshmallowy soles like her sister's, and a bright yellow fleece top. "Geez, Dad. You're more nervous than Carm is."

"He *should* be nervous," Liza said. She zipped closed one of the many pockets on the custom-made running vest Carmelita would wear during the race, its compartments filled with snack food, packets of energy gel, and soft plastic bottles filled with fruit-flavored electrolyte drink. A whitewater river guide in her late twenties based out of the northern Arizona city of Flagstaff, Liza had gravitated to the position of chief gear wrangler for Carmelita in Janelle's absence. "You should be nervous, too, Rosie. We all should be."

"Well, *I'm* not," Carmelita said.

Her confident tone reassured Chuck. This was the Carmelita he knew, the Carmelita who had trained hard and well for the race and was ready for whatever was to come over the next fifty hours.

She snugged the laces tight on her shoes, sat up straight in her seat, and slapped her bare thighs below her running shorts. Looking directly into the lens of Rosie's phone camera, she said, "Let's do this, shall we, peeps?"

She rose from her chair and faced the lighted circle of pavement. Marian and Doug, the founders of the Whitney to Death 150, scurried back and forth beneath the floodlight, clipping quarter-sized GPS trackers to the shirts of racers gathered in the parking lot. The couple organized and directed the race each year. Both Doug and Marian—known to racers only by their first names—were portly and gray-haired, well past middle age. They were rumored to work for the Los Angeles Department of Water and Power, the largest employer in rural Owens Valley, two hundred miles north of Los Angeles.

Ten years ago, so the story went, the two had dreamed up the Whitney to Death 150 as a diversion from their tedious engineering jobs in the sparsely populated valley, where the utility company shunted snowmelt water flowing off the east side of California's Sierra Nevada mountain range into the concrete-lined Los Angeles Aqueduct, which transported the liquid gold south to the LA metropolitan area.

Marian and Doug had organized the initial race far from the public eye, with no website, press releases, or official sign-up forms. The first competition, on the demanding route they laid out over isolated public lands between Mt. Whitney and Death Valley, had attracted only a handful of racers via word of mouth. Over the ensuing years, Doug and Marian had continued to host the Whitney to Death 150 each spring, with no overt publicity or special-use permits from federal land agencies. They had maintained the small size of the race, capping the number of accepted applicants at around forty.

Despite its small size and stealthy presence on the ground, the Whitney to Death 150 was hugely popular on the internet. Each year, more and more fans from all around the world tracked the racers' progress throughout the competition, wagering massive amounts of money on competing runners through online betting sites.

Chuck squeezed his watch, lighting its digital face. 4:45 a.m. In fifteen minutes, the runners gathered for this year's race would set out. No noisy blast from a starting gun would mark the 5 a.m. start of the competition. Rather, the runners would simply jog out of the parking lot and descend Portal Creek Trail away from Mount Whitney, beginning the hundred-and-fifty-mile trek to Badwater Basin—which, if fit and fortunate enough, they would reach two long days and nights from now.

Having read and reread all the online postings about the race he could find, Chuck knew that as soon as the racers left the parking lot, Marian and Doug would toss the floodlight in their car and drive down Portal Canyon Road to the broad flat floor of Owens Valley. After passing through the small town of Lone Pine, they would await the racers' arrival at the first of the race's four check-in points set at roughly thirty-mile increments along the race route. The initial check-in point, which also served as a rest and refueling stop for competitors, was situated in the middle of Owens Valley at the edge of what once had been Owens Lake. The oval-shaped body of water, several miles across, had dried up a century ago, after the Los Angeles Department of Water and Power began directing the snowmelt water that had sustained the lake into the Los Angeles Aqueduct.

At the check-in point beside the now-dry lake, competitors

would recite their racer numbers to Marian and Doug. They then would spend a few minutes at their personal aid stations, where their support crews would provide them with food and drink, before setting out on the next segment of the race.

Liza squeezed Carmelita's shoulder and handed her the running vest. "You got this," she said.

A member of the Ute Mountain Ute tribe whose homelands lay west of Durango, Liza was stout and brawny, her tattooed upper arms rippling with muscle. Liza's hair cascaded down her back in a long coal-black braid. Despite the morning chill, she wore a tank top and knee-length khaki shorts secured by a wide leather belt with a big metal buckle.

Chuck rested his hand on Carmelita's other shoulder. Her skin was cool beneath the smooth fabric of her long-sleeved running top. "Damn straight you got this," he told her.

Rosie giggled. "Mamá will hear that if I put it in the next post." She rose from her crouch and backed far enough away to capture all three of them with her camera.

"Damn straight she will," said Clarence, standing off to one side. His toothy grin sparkled in the dim light of the parking lot, and his dark eyes gleamed with their customary merriness. His belly overlapped the waistline of his jeans, stretching the fabric of the black T-shirt he wore. His dark shoulder-length hair was tucked behind his ears, which shimmered with thick silver stud earrings.

Clarence's big-heartedness had impressed Chuck when he'd first hired Janelle's younger brother as a dig assistant. Now thirty, Clarence had followed Janelle north from New Mexico to Colorado when she'd moved to Durango with the girls upon marrying Chuck. These days, Clarence continued to work part-time for Chuck and other archaeological firms on digs around the Southwest during the busy summer months, and as a bartender in downtown Durango in the winter.

A short burst of laughter escaped Carmelita's lips, further

reassuring Chuck. She rolled her shoulders, shaking off his and Liza's hands.

"I'm all set," she said, steel in her voice.

In the seven years since he'd married Janelle and become stepfather to Carmelita and Rosie, Chuck had witnessed Carmelita's extraordinary willpower time and time again. He had introduced her to competitive rock climbing when she was twelve, two years after he'd joined the family. Through a combination of tremendous natural ability and extreme competitiveness, Carmelita had ascended to the top ranks of the sport early in her teen years.

Two years ago, at fifteen, she'd taken up running on trails around Durango to cross-train for her weekend sport-climbing competitions. She'd been captivated by the extreme challenge of ultra trail running over the months that followed, leading her to propose applying for the Whitney to Death 150.

Chuck had suggested she compete in shorter ultra races, in the fifty- to hundred-mile range, before attempting what was widely considered one of the most challenging competitions in the ultra-running world. But Carmelita had reminded him she had competed in top sport-climbing events at the very beginning of her climbing career and had notched a string of podium finishes in the process.

"I did fine against the best climbers right from the start. I'll be fine going up against the best trail runners, too," she told him.

Chuck had assured Janelle it would be okay if Carmelita completed only a portion of the race. "There's nothing wrong with a DNF," he said.

"A DNF?" Janelle asked.

"Did Not Finish. DNFs are considered perfectly acceptable in ultra racing—especially for the Whitney to Death 150 with its astronomical DNF rate."

Though Chuck had told Janelle a DNF was a logical expectation for Carmelita in her first attempt at the Whitney to Death

150, it turned out her training-run times compared favorably with those posted online by other runners accepted for the race, including the times posted by Margot Chatten, the only other teenage runner in the competition.

Margot was a trail-running phenom from San Francisco who had won a number of ultra races around the West the previous year, and who, at seventeen, was the same age as Carmelita. Margot's promotional videos, posted after each of her victories, were slickly produced, complete with catchy background music and high-tech graphics. Her videos invariably featured Rick Chatten, her father and coach, humble-bragging about his daughter's exploits after each of her races. Rick, Chuck learned online, had left a high-tech job in the Bay Area and was devoting himself full-time to his daughter's trail-running pursuit.

In the predawn darkness, Carmelita tugged on her vest, clipped its straps over her narrow chest, and strode toward the circle of light. Chuck followed her across the pavement, along with Rosie, Clarence, and Liza. Just as he entered the light behind Carmelita, the hum of an idling car engine sounded behind him. Glancing over his shoulder, he spotted a car rolling quickly toward them through the darkness with its headlights off.

"Look out!" he yelled.

He grabbed Rosie's arm and yanked her out of the path of the oncoming car. She stumbled and fell to her knees, her phone clattering to the pavement beside her.

The vehicle, a minivan, struck Carmelita's folding camp chair. The chair crumpled beneath the car's front bumper. Chuck tugged Carmelita away from the minivan, which rolled past them and into the light, shoving the crushed chair along with it.

The vehicle headed straight for Marian and Doug. Marian screeched and leapt out of the car's path. Doug was facing away from the vehicle, however, and it plowed into him from behind. He bounced off the front of the car and sprawled across the pavement.

The minivan clipped the floodlight with its front bumper and came to an abrupt halt. The floodlight fell across the roof of the vehicle and the winked out in a shower of blue-white sparks.

"Doug!" Marian shouted in the sudden darkness. "Oh, my God! *Doug!*"

2

Two days before the race, while scouting the 150-mile route in advance of the competition, Chuck had driven with Carmelita to the long-abandoned Wildrose charcoal kilns in Wildrose Canyon.

The rock-walled canyon cut deep into the Panamint Mountain range in Death Valley National Park. The jagged peaks of the Panamint Range rose high above Badwater Basin, forming a stark rampart on the park's west side. The difficult crossing of the Panamints would come on the second night of the Whitney to Death 150, near the end of the competition.

Chuck stopped at the first of the ten kilns lined along the road in the bottom of Wildrose Canyon and climbed out of the big crew cab pickup that served as his work truck and the Bender-Ortega family road-trip vehicle. Carmelita hopped from the passenger seat, her feet crunching in the gravel beside the truck.

Since morning, they'd driven roads that followed as closely as possible the mostly backcountry route of the Whitney to Death 150. Leaving Portal Campground, they'd crossed Owens Valley, passed by the Cerro Gordo and Coso Mountain ranges on the east side of former Owens Lake, and traversed the desert plain that separated the Cosos from the Panamint Mountains, in the process crossing the boundary, marked only by a small sign, into the national park. They'd passed no one on the winding dirt road up Wildrose Canyon, and the Wildrose kilns were deserted as well.

The midafternoon temperature was above ninety degrees. Hot air lifting off the flat expanse between the Coso and Panamint ranges funneled past them and on up the canyon.

The torrid breeze ruffled Carmelita's long hair. "Whoa," she exclaimed, slipping a loose strand behind her ear with her finger. She faced the line of kilns, the Panamint Mountains looming beyond.

Chuck stood with her before the beehive-shaped structures, their arched ground-level doorways staring back at him like black cyclops eyes. The kilns, twenty feet high and constructed of brick and mortar, appeared out of place here in the rugged desert backcountry.

The odd structures, far from any towns, were worthy of Carmelita's exclamation. But when Chuck glanced at her, he saw that she wasn't looking at the kilns. Rather, she was gazing open-mouthed at the Panamint Mountains, peak after vertiginous peak studding the horizon at the head of Wildrose Canyon.

"They're so big," she said. "They're so *out there*."

He lifted his eyes to the mountains and nodded in agreement. "The Whitney to Death 150 is as remote as ultra races get. There aren't any sport climbing walls out here, that's for sure," he said, referring to the fiberglass walls adorned with molded plastic holds used for the sport climbing tournaments Carmelita regularly competed in.

"That's why I want to do it," she said, setting her hands on her hips. "It's one hundred percent legit."

"You don't have to, you know. That'd be fine with me. With your mom, too."

She directed a withering look at him. "Thanks for the vote of confidence."

"I'm offering you just the opposite—a reality check. That's part of why we drove out here today."

She dropped her hands to her sides. "I get it. I know you want me to see for myself what I'm getting into." Her eyes returned to the mountains. "But still—*whoa*."

He pointed at the tallest of the Panamints, a massive hunk

of bare gray rock lit by the afternoon sun. "That's Telescope Peak. It's more than eleven thousand feet high. The race route crosses the range just north of it." He aimed his finger at a tight V between the summit of Telescope Peak and the next mountain to the north. "Through that notch right there."

He lowered his finger, pointing at the dirt track continuing up the canyon from the kilns.

"From here—just like on the maps I've been studying for the last six months straight—you'll follow the road for another mile to an old silver mine. The road ends there. You'll go straight up to the notch from the mine during the second night of the race, climbing the cliff faces on the way," he said, mentioning the series of short rock faces topped by ledges that runners were required to surmount on the way to the notch marking the Panamint divide. The crossing of the divide via the notch comprised one of the race's two notorious off-trail sections.

"From what I've read, I'll be able to see the notch above me the whole time, so at least I won't get lost."

"Even in the dark, do you think?"

"It should be visible against the stars."

Chuck nodded and continued his narration of the race route. "From the top of the divide, the route follows Golden Staircase Trail, one of the least used trails in the park. It's at the end of a long dirt road out of Badwater Basin, so hardly anybody ever hikes it."

"At least it'll come at the end of the race, when I'll be heading for the finish line."

"If you get there in time—no later than 7 a.m., fifty hours after the start."

"*When* I get there in time, you mean." Carmelita's mouth lifted in a determined smile. "In first place."

Chuck grinned at her. "You don't need any extra vote of confidence from me, that's for sure."

Her walnut eyes sparkled. "From you, I just need a reality check." She turned to the high peaks. "Which, honestly, I appreciate." She looked at the kilns. "So, what are these things?"

An hour later, Chuck knelt inside the first of the kilns lined along Wildrose Canyon Road, his headlamp glowing on his forehead and a surgical mask covering the lower half of his face. He grasped a metal trowel in his hand.

Over the preceding sixty minutes, he'd advanced from the doorway deeper into the kiln, shuffling on his knees from sidewall to sidewall and forward to a point nearly halfway across the ash-covered bottom of the structure. As he went, he scooped small mounds of ash off the floor with the blade of his trowel, sifted the ash with his fingers while inspecting it in the light of his headlamp, then deposited the ash back on the ground and lifted another scoopful.

The air in the kiln was thick with floating particles of ash and smelled of charred wood. The temperature inside was stiflingly hot. Sweat plastered his T-shirt to his back and beads of perspiration dripped down his forehead.

Only a small amount of light filtered into the cavern-like interior of the structure through the kiln's two openings: the waist-high doorway behind him and a small square aperture in the roof. The roof opening had allowed smoke to escape when the kiln had been used to create charcoal out of juniper wood harvested from the previously forested walls of the canyon.

Chuck searched for telltale chunks in the mound of ash he scooped onto his trowel blade. Seeing none, he returned the ash to the floor and scooped another bladeful from a spot a few inches away from the previous scoop.

The process of inspecting the ash as he advanced across the floor of the kiln was slow and tedious, but the sense of anticipation he felt at what he might discover if he just kept working remained as fresh as always. At the beginning of his career, he'd assumed the keen sense of anticipation he felt each day he worked in the field would diminish over time and eventually disappear altogether. But the captivating sense of possibility had never waned, leaving him as eager to begin work each day as when he first began his career as an independent archaeologist twenty-five years ago.

This afternoon in Wildrose Canyon, his sense of anticipation grew increasingly pronounced as he neared the center of the kiln—the location most likely to harbor what he sought.

He inched forward on his knees, dug his trowel blade into the ash, lifted it, and—

"Find anything?" Carmelita asked from the doorway.

He wrenched his hand in surprise, sending the scoopful of ash flying into the air. The ash dissipated, forming a murky gray cloud. He looked back at her. She knelt in the open doorway, silhouetted by the bright sunlight outside. "Not yet. I have a good feeling, though."

"You always say that."

"If you're not a hopeful archaeologist, you won't be an archaeologist for long."

"I can see why. You're in here in the dark, broiling in the heat, choking on all the dust—looking for what, exactly?"

"I'll know it when I find it." He waved his trowel around the inside of the kiln. "I'd like to finish up in here today. It's the first in the line, which makes it the most likely candidate. But I'll need some more time, if that's okay with you."

"No problem. I still need to stretch."

She'd gone for a jog while he worked in the kiln.

"How was your run?"

"I kept it slow and easy, a little ways up and back, just enough to stay loose. I'm saving everything I have for the race."

She left the doorway and Chuck returned to work, scooping ash from the floor, sifting it, and returning it to the ground.

He repeated the process for another ten minutes until, at

nearly the exact midpoint of the kiln, he lifted a bladeful of ash, sifted it with his fingers, and there, resting in the gray particles—

He held his breath, his eyes wide.

A tan-colored object poked from the mound of ash near the tip of his trowel blade.

His heart raced, hammering in his chest.

Still holding his breath, he lowered the trowel to the floor, plucked the item from the ash, and brought it close to his eyes. He exhaled in elation. The object was exactly what he'd hoped to find, exactly where he'd hoped to find it.

He crawled out of the kiln and stood up, the object clasped in his hand.

At the truck, Carmelita balanced on one foot, her other foot on the rear bumper and her leg extended, stretching her hamstring. She lowered her foot to the ground and pointed at his curled hand. "Find something?"

He tugged his mask below his chin and drew a long breath of clean outside air into his lungs. "Yes."

She approached him. "And…?"

He opened his hand to her.

"Oh…my…*God*," she whispered. "That is sooo incredible."

From lower in the canyon came the sound of an automobile grinding its way up the gravel road toward the kilns. Chuck closed his fingers over the object as the car came into view.

It was a minivan.

3

Racers and crew members shrieked in the predawn darkness of the Mt. Whitney trailhead parking lot, their cries loud in Chuck's ears. They converged on the accident scene along with Chuck, the girls, Clarence, and Liza.

The minivan's headlights came on, illuminating Doug lying on his stomach in front of the halted car.

Before Chuck reached Doug, two male runners—a broad-chested man wearing a lightweight nylon sun hoodie, and a skinny racer in black shorts and a white singlet—helped him turn over and sit up on the pavement.

"Owww," Doug moaned, rubbing his lower back. "It hurts so bad."

"Thank God, you're not dead," said the thin runner crouched beside Doug. He wore a white ball cap over his short bleached-blond hair.

"I feel like I could be," Doug said, grimacing.

"Is anything broken?" the hooded runner asked, his bass voice resonating from deep in his chest.

"I don't think so," Doug replied.

The driver's door to the minivan opened and a man stepped out and peered down at Doug. It was Rick Chatten, Margot's father.

"Jesus!" Rick exclaimed. He was short and stocky with wiry brown hair. He spun, looking all directions. "You," he snarled at Chuck, his face darkening. "This is all your fault. *You* did this."

Chuck stepped back. "What are you talking about?"

Rick dropped to his knees beside his car and peered beneath it. "I *knew* it." He glared up at Chuck while aiming a finger beneath the minivan. "Look at this."

Chuck knelt next to the car. Rick directed his phone light under the vehicle. Liquid dripped from a point near the junction of the front axle and passenger-side wheel, puddling on the ground.

"That's brake fluid," Rick said.

"Yep," said Chuck, climbing to his feet. "Did you have it checked out, like I told you?"

Rick stood up. "Everywhere I tried was closed."

"Then whose fault would you say this *really* is?"

Rick locked eyes with Chuck. "You're the one who yanked it off the rock."

Chuck pointed at the folding chair pinned beneath the front bumper of the car, his anger flaring. "You smashed into the chair my daughter was just sitting in. You could've killed her. You almost killed Doug. And *you're* trying to blame *me*?"

Chuck raised his arm and cocked his fist. Before he could flatten Rick's nose, however, the thin runner who'd come to Doug's aid stepped between him and Rick, facing Margot's father.

"You *idiot*," the runner snapped at Rick. "What were you thinking, blasting across the parking lot like that?"

"I was just turning around to be ready to head down the canyon after the start of the race," Rick said, "but the brakes went out and the damn thing took off on me."

"It was an accident, Kelsey," Doug told the racer from where he sat on the pavement. "It's almost start time. You need to get ready."

Kelsey flicked his hand and stomped out of the light.

Rosie grasped Chuck's still-raised arm from behind. "Don't be nuts, Dad."

Rick sneered at Chuck. "Gonna do what your kid tells you?"

Chuck allowed Rosie to pull his arm down. Thanks to

Janelle's ongoing tutelage, he was getting better at shrugging off those who antagonized him. It had been a long time since he'd decked someone, or even threatened to do so—though maintaining his poise in the face of people like Rick still wasn't easy.

He turned to Clarence and Liza. "This is Margot's father, Rick, the guy I told you about. We met at the kilns."

Liza looked Rick up and down. "Do you suffer from any sort of seizure disorder?"

Rick recoiled. "No, no. The brakes went out on me, that's all." He pointed beneath the car. "There's a leak. I'll get it repaired in Lone Pine."

She stepped past Rick and stopped before Doug. In the glare of the minivan headlights, the hooded runner helped the race organizer to his feet.

"Thanks, Domenico," Doug said.

"How are you doing?" Liza asked him.

Doug massaged his back, his face pale. "I'm all right. Just banged up."

Rick extended a hand to him. "Hey, there, man. Sorry about that."

"Don't touch me," Doug warned.

The passenger door to the minivan opened and a man in his early twenties climbed out holding a video camera. He rested the camcorder on the roof of the car, preparing to film the exchange between Rick and Doug.

Rick wheeled on the young man and slashed his finger across his neck. "Cut it, Carl."

"But you told me you wanted everything," Carl said.

"Not this!"

"Whatever you say, boss." Carl plucked the camera off the roof of the car. "Margot?" he called into the darkness. "Where are you? Margot?"

Margot's squeaky voice came from the shadows. "You can film me all you want, Carl."

She brushed past the cameraman and entered the light. A collective intake of breath sounded from the racers and crew members gathered in front of the minivan. Over a revealing two-piece outfit that looked more like a swimsuit than a running ensemble, Margot wore a thin cloak made of a sheer fabric that glittered in the headlights. The transparent garment floated around her body, shimmering as she walked.

"Dad!" she exclaimed, stopping before Rick. The cloak settled against her hips like a dragonfly folding its diaphanous wings. "Are you okay?"

Carl aimed his camera at the pair.

"I'm fine, sweetie," Rick said to her. He jabbed a thumb at Doug. "He's okay, too."

"That is so weird," Margot said to Doug. "Dad, like, never messes up when he's driving."

Chuck clamped his mouth shut, recalling what had happened two days ago in Wildrose Canyon.

Rick swung his arm in an arc, taking in Doug, the minivan, and the smashed chair beneath the car's bumper. "This was all beyond my control, sweetie," he said to Margot.

"Of course, it was," she said. She checked the bulky GPS watch strapped to her thin wrist. "My gosh!" she exclaimed. "Only five minutes to go!"

She pirouetted away from her father, her robe winking in the light, and disappeared into the darkness.

In the parking lot, Carmelita canted her body forward while keeping her heels on the ground, stretching her achilles tendons before the race. Around her, racers adjusted the straps on their running vests and centered their headlamps on their foreheads. Their crew members massaged their necks and shoulders and spoke encouragingly in their ears.

Margot's father retrieved the toppled tripod and held it out to Doug and Marian. The broken floodlight dangled from its end. "I'll have my people reimburse you for this."

Marian yanked the mangled light from his grasp. "Just stay the hell away from us," she said.

"Three minutes!" Margot cried from the shadows. "Dad! Three minutes!"

"On my way," Rick called to her, departing in the direction of her voice.

Marian glowered after him.

Carmelita turned to her. "Could I get my tracker from you?"

The race organizer shook herself. "Of course."

She pulled a pair of numbered plastic disks from one of the voluminous exterior pockets on the navy cargo pants belted around her plump waist. The disks were an inch across. Short metal spikes extended from their backs.

"Only two more to go," she said.

She held one of the disks up to the number printed on the sticker affixed to the right leg of Carmelita's shorts. The number thirty-two was printed on both the sticker and disk.

"Racer number thirty-two and tracker number thirty-two," Marian announced. "We have a match."

She pressed the metal spikes protruding from the disk through the bottom hem of Carmelita's shirt and attached the disk through the fabric by pressing a spring-loaded clasp over the spikes. She gave the disk a firm tug and told Carmelita, "You're all set."

She held up the final disk. "Seventeen!" she called out. "Last one. Isn't that you, Astrid?"

"Yes, ma'am," said a booming voice from the far side of the parking lot. "That'd be me."

Carmelita looked on, fingering the disk attached to her shirt, as a burly female runner strode to the front of the mini-van. Astrid's pale thighs, as big around as fire hydrants, gleamed like ivory in the headlights. A tangle of frizzy brown hair hung at the back of her head, secured by a thick rubber band. Her running top, stretched tight over her wide shoulders, and shorts were light tan, the color of desert sand.

Astrid drew herself up and stood stiffly before Marian. She saluted the race organizer, her arm bent at her elbow and her fingers pressed to her forehead. "Number seventeen reporting for duty, ma'am," she barked, staring past Marian into the darkness.

"At ease, soldier," Marian said. She grinned. "You never give it a rest, do you?"

"No, ma'am." Astrid held her poker face a moment longer, then guffawed, her cherry-red lips glistening in her milky face, and slapped hands with Marian.

Marian attached the final GPS tracker to the hem of Astrid's shirt. "Go get 'em, trooper."

"Yes, ma'am," Astrid said. She spun on the balls of her feet and marched away.

Still smiling, Marian turned to Carmelita. "Astrid's a Marine. An actual, honest to God, enlisted member of the US Marine Corps." She shook her head. "It takes all kinds, I guess."

"You mean," said Doug, "we *attract* all kinds."

"Thirty seconds!" Margot called from the darkness.

Marian's smile disappeared. "That's not how we do it," she said to Carmelita. "We let the start happen organically."

Around the parking lot, headlamps lit up on foreheads, clicked on by racers. The white lights were joined by the glow of cell phones held aloft by crew members.

"Ten!" Margot called out. "Nine! Eight! Seven!"

"Shut up," Marian muttered, just loud enough for Carmelita to hear.

"Six! Five! Four!" Margot cried.

Marian tsked.

"Three! Two! One! *Go!*" Margot screeched.

Carmelita remained in place as the rest of the runners jogged across the parking lot to the trailhead, their headlamps glowing. For months, she'd anticipated this moment, when she would wait at the starting line and begin the race a minute or two behind her fellow runners, feeling her way into the competition from the back of the pack.

But she hadn't anticipated Rick would mow down Doug with his car before the race.

Crew members filmed the departing racers with their upraised phones. The competitors left the parking lot and headed down Portal Creek Trail one after another. In seconds, they were gone—all except Carmelita, who stood in front of the minivan with the two race organizers and Chuck, Rosie, Clarence, and Liza.

"What are you waiting for?" Chuck asked her, clearly aghast.

She faced Doug. "Are you *sure* you're all right?"

"Sure, I'm sure," he said.

"He really sent you flying."

"It wasn't any fun, I'll say that."

Marian grasped Carmelita's arm. "You're even nicer in person than you were online."

"Online?" Chuck asked.

"Doug and I have gotten to know your daughter pretty well over the last few months," she explained to him. "She asked us lots of questions. Good ones."

Doug nodded and looked at Carmelita. "We'd have a lot more successful finishers if everyone asked us as much about the race as you did." He glanced at his watch and said to her, "Speaking of which, it's now forty-nine hours and fifty-nine minutes to the cutoff."

"You're certain you're okay?" Carmelita asked.

He put his hand to his back. "Nothing a little ibuprofen won't take care of. I'll see you at the first check-in. Now, *git*."

Satisfied, she clicked her headlamp off, then on again, a quick equipment check. Unlike the white lights of the other racers, her headlamp glowed purple, matching her shoes, through a film of lavender plastic she'd glued over its lens. With a wave to everyone, she jogged across the pavement and started down the trail. The purple beam of her headlamp flickered off the trunks of the pine trees that grew thick and tall in the Portal Canyon, well behind the white lights of the other runners weaving through the forest below her.

"Go, Carm, go!" Rosie shouted down into the woods from the parking lot above, triggering a smile from Carmelita as she began the race's steep initial descent to the mouth of the canyon.

4

Two days before the race, the minivan rolled to a stop in front of Chuck and Carmelita in Wildrose Canyon.

The words “Team Chatten” were painted across the hood of the car, and a life-sized photo of a young female runner wearing a sport-bra top and bikini running shorts was silkscreened on both sides of the vehicle. Taken from ground level, the photo accentuated the runner’s bare legs. Stenciled beneath the picture in large block letters was a website address: *margotchatten.com.*

The minivan sat well above the roadbed on oversized wheels and tires. Chuck studied the oddly raised vehicle. Though the big tires provided several inches of added ground clearance, the car’s spongy factory-installed shock absorbers and leaf springs, visible at the back of the wheel wells, had not been replaced as part of the retrofit.

Two people exited the minivan—a short man with brown hair in his forties, and the blond teenage girl whose picture emblazoned the sides of the car. The man wore black sneakers with thick white soles, mauve shorts, and a fitted T-shirt that hugged his upper body, while the girl wore cork-soled sandals with leather straps, denim shorts, and a cropped top that revealed her toned midriff. The man and girl eyed the line of kilns and spine of mountains beyond, then turned to Chuck and Carmelita.

“Rick Chatten,” the man said, introducing himself without extending his hand.

“I’m Margot,” the teenager said. Her voice was high-pitched. She looked at Carmelita. “I know you, don’t I?”

"The same way I know you," Carmelita said. "From our social media."

"Your vids are good," said Margot. "I love how jerky they are. They've totally got the down-and-dirty vibe going for them."

"That's one way to put it," Rick said. "Another is 'amateur.'" He turned to Chuck. "Do you produce them for her?"

Before Chuck could answer, Carmelita narrowed her eyes at Rick and said, "My sister shoots and edits them."

Rick kept his gaze on Chuck. "I bet you're here for the same reason we are."

"Maybe so," Chuck said, tucking his closed fist behind his back.

Margot rocked her head back and forth, loosening her neck. "We're checking out as much of the race route as we can." She tilted her head at the mountains and said to her father, "The crossing looks totally gnarly, Dad."

"You won't have any problem with it, sweetie," Rick assured her. He turned to Chuck. "Are you heading on up the road?"

"It's only maintained as far as the kilns. I've heard it gets pretty rough beyond here."

Rick gestured at the minivan's oversized wheels and tires. "That's why I had this thing jacked up."

"Those will help." Chuck did not add that despite the minivan's increased clearance, its springy factory suspension would likely lead to trouble on the unmaintained section of road higher in the canyon.

Rick turned to face the historic brick structures. "There's more of these things than I thought there would be. Then again, they had to build enough of them to achieve their ROI, didn't they?"

"ROI?" Chuck asked.

"Return on investment."

Chuck glanced at the bare canyon walls above the kilns,

where thousands of juniper trees, felled to feed the ovens, once had stood. "They kept cutting until there were no trees left."

"They did what they had to do. It would've been all about their P and Ls—their profit and loss statements." Rick pointed at the bed of Owens Lake, a massive oval, half green and half brown, visible far to the west between the canyon walls in the middle of Owens Valley. "Just like that lake."

"*Former* lake," said Chuck. "It won't be coming back anytime soon, either, just like the junipers, no matter how much water they try to refill it with."

"Who's 'they'?" Margot asked.

"The Los Angeles Department of Water and Power. A hundred years ago, they cut off the snowmelt water running from the mountains to the lake. They tried to refill it a while back, after environmentalists sued them, but the lakebed wouldn't hold water. When the lake was full, its clay bottom acted like a giant pool liner. But not anymore. They're trying other ideas these days to keep the dust storms from kicking up." Chuck pointed at the distant lakebed. "See?"

The southern half of the oval was green with plants, while the northern half was a brown expanse of bare soil cut by long straight lines. The two halves were divided by a dirt road that ran across the middle of the former lake.

"The race crosses the lakebed on the road between the planted and unplanted halves," he said. "On windy days, it's like the return of the Dust Bowl on the northern half of the lakebed. When the wind blows really hard, the air in Owens Valley is more toxic than anywhere else in North America."

Margot raised her eyebrows at Carmelita. "We'll be sucking that stuff into our lungs."

"Only if it's windy, sweetie," Rick told her. "You'll be fine. All you have to do is look straight ahead and—" He stopped in the middle of the sentence.

"—put one foot in front of the other," she finished dutifully.

"That's a girl," he said. "It'll be just like the Great Salt Lake 100."

"In Utah?" Chuck asked.

"We won the junior division last year," Rick boasted.

"We?"

"Er, Margot. The Great Salt Lake 100 starts in Salt Lake City, goes around the north end of the lake, and finishes way out on the Bonneville Salt Flats. There's some serious wind and dust out there."

"You'd think the finish would be back in Salt Lake City instead of out in the middle of nowhere."

"The race is put on by a bunch of wacko environmentalists. They know a good photo op when they see one, I'll give them that much. They put up a big, blue, inflatable arch with the words 'Save the Lake' on it for the racers to run through at the finish line. The blue arch, the white salt flats, the green mountains behind—I have to admit, it's pretty impressive." Rick paused. "Actually, Kelsey McCloud is one of the people who puts it on."

"Kelsey?" Carmelita said. "Isn't he…?"

"That's him," said Rick. "Kelsey McCloud has won the Whitney to Death 150 the last three years in a row. He's a goddamn machine. Then again, he's never faced Margot before."

"Dad," Margot said with an embarrassed giggle.

"Kelsey is from Salt Lake City," Rick continued. "He didn't even run in the Great Salt Lake 100 last year because he was so busy putting it on with all of his enviro buddies. They started the race to call attention to the drying up of the lake. The finish out on the salt flats is all about the photo op. They post pictures of every finishing runner online and try to get the runners to re-post them on their social media accounts. The race has gotten really big, really fast. And, of course, the betting numbers have followed."

"Betting?" Chuck asked.

"Uh-huh. The people who run the Great Salt Lake 100 get a piece of the action. Still, their numbers don't come anywhere near the numbers for the Whitney to Death 150. Everybody knows it's the most heavily wagered ultra race on the planet. That's because it's unofficial—no permits or licenses or anything to put limits on the betting totals. Nobody knows how big the numbers really are, though. Doug and Marian keep all that to themselves." Rick rested a hand on Margot's shoulder. "As for me, I'm putting some serious money on this one right here this year."

"If I even manage to finish," she said.

He gave her shoulder a shake. "You'll knock 'em dead, just like always."

"We'll see about that." She faced Carmelita. "The route comes right past here and keeps going, doesn't it?"

Carmelita pointed up the canyon. "To the end of the road and on up and over the mountains from there."

Rick looked at Chuck. "We should take a closer look. How about you lead the way in your monster truck?"

Chuck kept his fist behind his back. "We're still checking out the kilns."

"We'll see you up there, then."

Rick climbed into the minivan with Margot, gunned the engine, and accelerated up the road.

Chuck turned to Carmelita after the minivan disappeared in the upper canyon. "If it's as rough up there as I've heard it is, he won't make it far."

"Why didn't you stop him?"

"He wouldn't have listened."

"True that."

Chuck brought his hand from behind his back.

"Sooo…" Carmelita said, her eyes on his fist.

He opened his fingers. The pebble-sized object he'd plucked from the ash rested on his palm.

"Is that a rock?"

"In a way, yes—if you consider enamel a mineral, which technically it is."

"Enamel? It's a *tooth*?"

He nodded.

"It's…it's…*human*?"

"Almost certainly." He nudged the tooth with his finger, turning it over on his palm. Roots extended from its base and thin black lines ran up its sides. "It's a molar, from the looks of it."

Carmelita looked at the kiln, her eyes growing clouded. "Somebody died in there, didn't they?"

"Their body was burned in there, at least, it would seem. It'll take more than just this one tooth to say for sure, though."

She peered around the canyon, which was devoid of movement after the departure of the minivan. "How did you know?"

"It's complicated."

"It can't be *that* complicated."

"You've got your race to worry about."

"Right now, I'm way more worried about whoever's tooth that is you're holding in your hand."

"It's eighty-seven years too late for that, I'm afraid."

"What happened here eighty-seven years ago?"

"That's what I've been hired by Tabitha Eddy to find out. She's the executive director of the Native Peoples Foundation. That's her part-time gig. Full-time, she's a professor of Native American Studies at Stanford University. She got her hands on some grant money from the university and hired me to perform a site survey out here for her."

"But you're an archaeologist, not a police detective."

"She tried the police. The local Inyo County Sheriff's Department, to be exact. The National Park Service, too. But nobody was interested after all these years."

"I bet they'll be interested now."

He rocked the tooth on his palm. "Officially, I've been contracted jointly by the Native Peoples Foundation and Stanford to survey the kilns, with the national park's sign-off since the kilns are inside the park boundary. Tabitha suspected I might find something like this in the course of the survey, though." He raised his hand. "See the black lines?"

Carmelita squinted at the molar. "They look like burn marks." She leaned forward and sniffed. "It's scorched. I can smell it."

He sniffed the tooth, too. It smelled like charcoal. "You're right." He closed his fingers over it. "Whoever disposed of the body didn't understand how kilns work. That's what Tabitha was hoping when she sent me out here. Kilns aren't furnaces, they're ovens. The Wildrose kilns were designed to cook wood slowly, transforming it into carbonate, which basically is high-grade charcoal. The low front doors and small openings in the roofs limit the amount of oxygen inside and maintain a slow, steady, low-temperature burn. The kilns heated the juniper wood harvested here in the canyon just enough to turn it into carbonate that was then burned at super-high temperatures in the blast furnaces of the silver refinery in the town of Keeler, on the edge of Owens Lake. Back when Owens Lake was a lake, that is."

Carmelita looked from Chuck's closed fist to the kiln. "You're saying whoever disposed of the body thought the kiln was an incinerator, but it wasn't."

"Right. Their fire didn't do the job they thought it would. I'm guessing they put the body on a pile of wood inside, set the wood on fire, and left, thinking their work was done."

"But it wasn't."

"Not entirely. Charcoal kilns are designed to remain below

1,000 degrees Fahrenheit. Human bone turns to ash right around that temperature, but enamel doesn't burn until it reaches 1,800 degrees."

"Which explains why you found the tooth."

"And why I wouldn't be surprised to find residual pieces of bone, too."

"Or another tooth."

"Or several more."

"How did you know which kiln to search?"

"I figured they'd have stopped at the first kiln they came to. They'd have been in a hurry. They were getting rid of a body, after all, and they didn't want to get caught."

"They *thought* they were getting rid of a body."

Three honks from a car horn sounded from higher in the canyon. After a beat of silence, three more honks echoed off the walls of the gorge.

Carmelita stared up the road past the kilns. "Threes."

Chuck nodded, already moving toward the big pickup. "SOS."

5

Chuck watched with the others until Carmelita's purple headlamp disappeared among the trees as she descended into the depths of Portal Canyon, trailing the pack of runners after the start of the race. Then he crossed the parking lot to Rick, who was on his hands and knees peering beneath the Team Chatten minivan.

"Do you have anything to wrap the brake line with?" Chuck asked him.

"Uh, no," Rick said, looking up. "I used the emergency brake to stop." He made no mention of the fact that he'd slammed into Doug before managing to do so. "I figure I can use it to drive down the canyon to Lone Pine."

"You won't make it out of the mountains on just your emergency brake. That's why they call it an *emergency* brake."

Rick stood up and brushed his hands on his shorts. "What the hell am I supposed to do, then?"

"I've got a roll of duct tape in my truck. That should get you to Lone Pine. But it won't last the whole race. You'll have to do what you should have done two days ago: get the line fixed in town."

"Fine," Rick said, biting off the word.

Chuck retrieved the duct tape from the diamond-steel truck-bed toolbox bolted behind the cab of the pickup. Lying on his back, he wrapped the sticky gray tape around the fracture point in the brake line. He tugged Carmelita's camp chair from under the bumper and directed Rick to pump the brake pedal, building up the pressure in the car's brake lines, then drive forward a few feet and punch the brake pedal again. The vehicle came to an abrupt stop when Rick did as Chuck instructed, indicating there was sufficient fluid and pressure in the brake lines for him to safely descend Portal Canyon Road.

Rick steered the car out of the parking lot, heading down the canyon. The other crews in their vehicles—an assortment of pickup trucks, sedans, and SUVs—along with Marian and Doug in their big, white, unmarked SUV, were already descending the road ahead of Rick.

Chuck jogged to the pickup, tossed the roll of tape and Carmelita's chair in its bed, and hopped behind the wheel. Rosie, Clarence, and Liza took their seats and he pulled out.

Portal Canyon Road clung to the side of the canyon high above Portal Creek. Several hundred yards ahead, the crew vehicles wove down the road in a snaking line, their headlights painting the walls of the gorge with swathes of light as they rounded each bend.

Chuck whipped around the tight curves, gaining on the line of cars. Rosie, Clarence, and Liza looked out the side windows at the runners, whose headlamps flickered amid the trees below as they ran down the trail next to the creek.

The road descended to the mouth of Portal Canyon, where the tight gorge opened onto the flat floor of Owens Valley. Chuck slowed and turned from the pavement onto a dirt track leading to Portal Creek Trail. The procession of vehicles continued on the paved road toward Lone Pine.

"We're the only crew heading over to the trail," he noted to the others.

"We're the only crew with a runner who has never competed in an ultra race before," said Clarence.

They planned to meet and offer encouragement to Carmelita wherever they could along the race route, rallying her spirits as often as possible during the two-day, two-night competition. The dirt track leading from Portal Canyon Road to the trail offered the first opportunity to do so after the start of the race.

According to the rules of the competition, support crews were allowed to meet their runners anywhere along the race route. To assure fairness and accountability, however, crews could supply their racers with food, drink, and replacement items like fresh socks and shoes only at the four check-in points designated by Doug and Marian along the course.

The dirt two-track leading to the trail wound between house-sized granite boulders resting on the valley floor outside the mouth of the canyon. The boulders had been flushed from the gorge by flash floods. Flakes of quartz embedded in the granite sparkled in the truck headlights as they passed the massive chunks of stone.

The track ended beside Portal Creek a hundred yards downstream from the canyon mouth. Portal Creek Trail left the forested gorge and paralleled the gently descending creek across the open floor of Owens Valley. A mile farther downstream, long before the water reached the bed of former Owens Lake, the creek was directed into the Los Angeles Aqueduct and sent south to the Southern California metropolis.

Chuck parked the truck facing the trail and stream. Leaving the headlights on, he climbed out with the others. The creek gurgled over rocks a few feet beyond the path, the water glinting in the headlight beams. Upstream, a headlamp appeared as a runner emerged from the last of the trees at the mouth of the canyon.

"There's the leader," Liza said.

Chuck checked his watch. 5:45. The canyon mouth was four miles from the start, meaning the lead runner was maintaining a swift five-mile-per-hour pace.

"Yippee!" Rosie cheered the runner. She stepped into the lights in front of the pickup and held up her phone, filming the racer's approach. "You're in first place!"

Night was just beginning to give way to day, the stars winking out overhead and the eastern sky turning gray with dawn.

A cool breeze from the mountains eased out of the canyon and spread across the open valley floor, carrying with it the piney scent of the forest.

Chuck savored the fleeting smell of the High Sierra. The remainder of the race would feature the harsher scents of the Mojave Desert—sage and dust and sunburnt sand.

In the dim morning light, he recognized the race leader as Kelsey McCloud, the three-time race winner who'd come to Doug's aid in the parking lot along with Domenico, the hooded runner. Kelsey's racer sticker, affixed to the leg of his shorts, bore the number one, identifying him as the favorite in this year's competition.

"Way to go, Kelsey!" Rosie shouted.

She tracked the lead runner with her phone as he passed through the truck headlights. Captured for an instant in the headlight beams, Kelsey's gait was long and smooth, appearing effortless.

"Thanks, Rosie," he said.

"Sure thing!" she cried after him as he sped away.

"He knew your name," Clarence said.

"Well, sure," said Rosie. "I filmed him and a lot of the other racers in the campground the last couple of days. I had to get to know them to get the good stuff."

"What's the 'good stuff'?"

"Closeups. That's the secret. It's my secret, anyway. And it works. I've proven it. Margot's got Carl filming her and posting up the pro-level videos he makes of her. Plus, she's been out there winning races since last year. But even so, my videos of Carm have gained more followers every time I've posted them than any of Margot's."

"And the secret is closeups?"

"It's a lot more than that, really. But yeah, that's the basis of it all. It's just a matter of knowing how people think."

Clarence shook his head, frowning. "Sorry, I don't get what you're saying."

"People want to know *people*," Rosie explained. "That's what you have to understand if you're trying to get your stuff watched on the internet. There's a reason they call it chasing eyeballs. I mean, think about it—how is it you get to know anybody? By looking them in the eye and talking to them. That's what I did with Kelsey and the others in the campground, and that's what I've been doing with Carm all along. I get in close and let people really see her. She's pretty, everybody knows that. But she's lots more than that, too. She's smart. And she's, like, totally driven. It's the whole package that makes her interesting to people. All I have to do is make sure they get to see how interesting she is beyond just her looks. From that, the viewer numbers follow. That's what I figured out, and it's been working great."

"Close-ups," Clarence repeated.

Rosie nodded. "The way I do it is, I let the camera jiggle a little bit, so the viewer has to work to focus on Carm. Then, as soon as she starts talking, I hold the camera still. She never says much, so when she does say something, people want to hear what she has to say. It doesn't even matter what she says—how she felt on her training run that day, how many miles she ran, what the weather was like, whether she spotted a rattlesnake or heard one rattling along the trail—it's all good when she says it in closeup. Then, as soon as she stops talking, I jiggle my phone again. That lets the viewer know they can relax. Everybody probably thinks I'm messing up by making it jerky, but what I'm really doing is getting the viewers ready to focus back in on Carm the next time she says something." Rosie shrugged. "Carm thinks it's great."

Clarence's eyebrows rose high on his forehead. "That's… that's brilliant."

"Well, yeah, sure." She twisted the corner of her mouth. "Carl is making plain old sports videos about Margot. He has the start of the race, the rest stops during the race, and the end of the race, with Margot raising her arms at the finish line and everybody cheering for her, and then her dad telling everybody how great she did. But people care about sports for the people that do the sports way more than they care about the sports themselves. So that's what I've been giving them—Carmelita the *person*. And, I mean, the proof is in the eyeballs. Carm has never run a single ultra race, but her viewer numbers are right up there with Margot's, the big-time ultra-running star."

"All thanks to you."

She smiled. "All thanks to me."

He looked after Kelsey. "That guy's the real star, isn't he? Three straight wins the last three years in a row. He sure isn't wasting any time right out of the starting blocks, is he?"

"That's because there's no time to waste," Rosie said. "I still can't believe Carm just stood there at the start."

"She was making sure Doug was okay."

"Nobody else did that."

"Nobody else is your sister."

"She's crazy to have done it, though."

"She has to be crazy to want to do this race in the first place," Clarence said, grinning. "Which is probably what makes her so interesting to your viewers—all those closeups you're capturing are of a crazy person. Besides, she told Liza and me she didn't want to get caught up in trying to stick with the leaders at the start of the race."

Liza nodded. "She said she wants to set her own pace. Staying behind for a couple of minutes to check on Doug might've been part of her plan."

Over the following minutes, more runners left the mouth of the canyon. Chuck recognized several top ultra athletes as they ran through the truck headlights.

Matt Sharon, an internationally renowned runner from

Ireland, passed through the lights in second place, less than a minute behind Kelsey. White four-leaf clovers dotted Matt's shamrock-green shirt. A mop of curly red hair flopped around his ears and a reddish-brown beard covered his face.

In third place, seconds behind Matt, came Waitimu Mwangi, a top-level marathoner from Kenya who'd recently switched to trail running, leaving the crowded marathon ranks behind. Waitimu's spindly upper body was balanced over legs as thin as twigs. Despite the chilly morning, his skin glowed with perspiration.

He flashed a broad grin at Rosie as he passed. "Ah-lo, Rosie!"

"Ah-lo, Waitimu!" Rosie cried back.

The first female racer to exit the canyon, in fourth place overall, was Hannah Rinkl, one of the best trail runners in the world. Hannah was a prominent LGBTQ activist. She was as committed to Queer causes as she was to ultra running, using her standing as a top trail runner to campaign for LGBTQ rights. Hannah wore a rainbow-striped shirt, and a pride-flag patch adorned the crown of her cap.

Domenico appeared in his sun hoodie a few minutes after Hannah, running smoothly down the trail. Astrid exited the canyon close behind him, her big arms and legs pumping. She offered a smile and salute to Rosie's upraised phone as she pounded past in her sand-toned outfit.

Margot trailed Domenico and Astrid in sixth place. She bounded lightly down the trail, her stride as loose and relaxed as that of Kelsey.

"Hey there, Rosie!" she called, waving as she passed. Her blond ponytail, poking though an opening in her cap, bounced from side to side at the back of her neck with each step.

"She's right up there with the leaders," Chuck marveled as Margot disappeared down the trail.

"Carm will catch her," Rosie said. "She'll catch everybody, just you wait and see."

—

Wait they did, as runner after runner emerged from the trees and ran through the lights of the truck. Racers in their twenties and thirties passed first, trailing the leaders by several minutes. Older runners followed, making up the back of the pack, their gray hair glimmering in the headlights.

With Waitimu's thin thighs a notable exception, most of the racers' upper legs were strikingly muscular, like those of professional cyclists. The runners wore specially designed running vests similar to Carmelita's, the pockets stuffed with drink bottles and food. Their trail shoes featured inch-thick foam-rubber soles with lugged bottoms.

"Thirty-six," Liza counted off when a woman runner with flowing gray hair walked down the trail, approaching the headlights. "An even three dozen so far."

"Way more than half of them are guys," Clarence noted.

"But three of the top seven were women."

"Which was totally cool to see," Rosie said. "Carm says women are taking over ultra racing. The longer the race, the better they do against men." She looked at the woman who'd just appeared from the canyon mouth. "Except her. She's not even running."

The woman strode steadily down the trail toward them.

"She's moving along pretty well, though," Chuck observed. "I've read that ultra racers use a combination of running, jogging, and speed-walking during races, depending on the route and how they're feeling." He eyed the woman. "If she maintains a three-mile-per-hour speed-walking pace for the whole race, she'll make the fifty-hour cutoff time—just barely, but she'll make it."

"Carm should at least be ahead of her by now, though, shouldn't she?" Rosie asked.

The woman walked with her head down and her eyes on the trail, appearing to be deep in her own mental space barely an hour into the competition. She did not acknowledge the presence of Chuck, Rosie, Clarence, and Liza as she passed through the truck headlights and continued down the path.

Chuck faced upstream, his jaw muscles tight. He checked the time on his phone. "You're right," he said to Rosie. "Carm should have been here by now. She only started a couple of minutes behind everybody else."

"Do you think something's wrong?" Clarence asked.

"This early on, I can't imagine what it could possibly be."

Chuck stared up the creek, willing Carmelita to appear from the mouth of the canyon. She had devoted more than half a year to training for the race. Could it all be unraveling so quickly?

He tapped the face of his phone, attempting to bring up the Whitney to Death 150 real-time race map on its screen. But there was no phone service here at edge of Owens Valley, out of sight of cell towers positioned on ridges above the valley floor, and the map refused to appear.

New to the competition this year, the map enabled anyone anywhere on earth to track the racers' positions on the course in real time via the GPS chips clipped to the racers' shirts. The real-time map represented a significant improvement over past years' races, when the only postings on the race website as the competition progressed were the runners' times at each of the four official check-in points.

"There!" Rosie cried, pointing at the canyon mouth.

Carmelita's purple headlamp appeared among the last of the trees in the canyon, beside the white headlamp of another runner emerging from the forest with her.

"Finally," Chuck said.

But what had held her up until now?

"Carm!" Rosie hollered up the trail as the two lights left the trees together. "Carmelita!"

"Help!" Carmelita yelled back. "Please, help!"

6

The three car horn blasts echoed down Wildrose Canyon past the kilns. Chuck grabbed a clear plastic evidence bag from the supply he kept in the truck toolbox. He shoved the tooth into the protective bag, then into his pocket, and leapt behind the wheel of the pickup. Carmelita dove into the passenger seat. He drove hard and fast up Wildrose Canyon while she gripped the handle bolted above her door, holding herself in place.

The smooth road to the kilns turned into a rough rocky two-track beyond the historic site. They raced up the rutted road, the pickup bucking and bounding over stones fallen from the sides of the canyon and gathered in the twin ruts.

"Is this really necessary?" Carmelita asked, clutching the handle. "I'm sure they're just stuck."

Chuck kept his foot on the gas. "What if they went off the road and rolled? They could be hurt."

He negotiated a series of tight bends in the canyon and emerged onto a straightaway.

"There they are," Carmelita said, pointing ahead through the windshield.

The Team Chatten minivan sat upright in the middle of the road, a hundred yards from where the road ended at the ruins of the old silver mine. The abandoned mine, consisting of collapsed roofing timbers and crumbling stone walls framing the shaft entrance, was at the foot of a steep mountainside rising from the head of Wildrose Canyon to Telescope Peak and the other craggy summits of the Panamint Mountains.

As Chuck drew close in the truck, he saw that the vehicle was stranded, its underside resting on a knee-high chunk of granite. He braked to a stop at the minivan and climbed out with Carmelita. Rick and Margot stood on opposite sides of the car.

"What a waste of money," Rick griped, glaring at his vehicle.

"What happened?" Chuck asked.

"You can see for yourself what happened!" he snapped. "Two thousand bucks to raise this thing up—" he flicked his fingers at the vehicle in disgust "—and this is what happens."

Chuck crouched and peered beneath the minivan. The rock impaled the undercarriage close to the front axle on the car's passenger side. No telltale splashes of oil or brake fluid coated the rocks beneath the vehicle. "You lucked out," he said, rising. "It looks like you missed both the oil pan and the brake line."

Rick glowered at him. "I didn't *miss* anything. I was going around the rock, but the damn car bounced like a ping-pong ball and landed right on top of it."

"Your factory suspension is too soft for roads like this."

Rick directed his ire at the rock-strewn track. "If you can even call this a road." Then he scowled at the minivan. "They told me the bigger wheels and tires were what I needed."

"They should've stiffened the suspension for you, too. Or you could've just gotten an SUV."

"Minivans are the perfect race vehicle—plenty of room on the inside and lots of promo space on the outside," Rick said, pointing at Margot's picture on the side of the car.

Margot turned away from her father and rolled her eyes.

Chuck crossed his arms over his chest, studying the car. "All of the race check-in points are on good roads, so you've got that going for you, at least."

"If I ever get out of here," Rick grumbled. He slapped his phone in the front pocket of his shorts. "I don't have a signal here. Could you drive us back to where I can call for a tow?"

"I think Carm and I can do you one better than that. We can pull your car off the rock if you like."

Rick's eyebrows rose. "Really? That'd be great."

"Assuming we can keep the rock away from your oil pan and brake line, that is."

His brows fell. "Oh."

Chuck retrieved the heavy nylon tow strap he kept in the truck toolbox and slung one end of it around the rear frame of the minivan. Carmelita wrapped the other end around the pull hook welded to the front frame of the pickup.

"Climb into your car and hold the steering wheel tight," Chuck directed Rick. "The wheels will try to turn on you. You'll need to keep them straight."

Chuck reversed the truck, taking up the slack in the strap until it grew taut between the pickup and minivan. He pressed the gas. The truck's rear tires spun for an instant, then caught. The truck surged backward, tugging the stranded minivan with it. Crunching noises issued from beneath the minivan as its undercarriage scraped its way off the rock. After a few feet, the car settled on all four tires, free of the boulder.

Rick hopped out and checked beneath the vehicle. "Still no leaks."

Chuck knelt beside him. "You should head straight to the nearest garage and get it checked out, just in case."

Carmelita freed the strap from the truck and minivan and gathered it in loops while Chuck pulled the pickup to the side of the road.

Rick turned the minivan around and departed back down the canyon with Margot, his eyes straight ahead.

"Not even a thank-you wave," Carmelita commented, looking after him.

"You're Margot's competition. The last thing he's going to do is be nice to us," Chuck said. "Margot seems friendly enough, though."

"He's the problem, not her. They say he's a screamer. He

screams at anybody and everybody during her races and he never stops."

"Somehow that doesn't surprise me."

Carmelita's eyes went to the mountainside rising above the mine at the end of the road. The cliff walls—half a dozen short rock faces, each ten to fifteen feet high—cut across the steep slope in horizontal bands.

Chuck followed her gaze. The race route went straight up the mountainside, forcing runners to surmount the cliff bands one after another. "And you thought you were giving up rock climbing for trail running," he said.

She didn't reply, her eyes focused on the cliffs.

"What are you seeing up there?" he asked.

"The easiest places to climb each face."

"There are easy places?"

She elbowed him, still staring at the cliffs. "Got 'em," she said after a minute.

"Will you still have them in the dark?"

"I'll have my headlamp."

"That'll be enough?"

"Absolutely."

They bounced back down the unmaintained track to the kilns. Chuck climbed out of the pickup and faced the first structure, fingering the bagged tooth in his pocket. "Want to give me a hand?" he asked when Carmelita joined him beside the truck.

"Searching for more body parts?"

"Yes."

"Sure—if you'll explain to me why, exactly, we're out here searching for the burned up pieces of somebody." She pointed at the kiln. "Is that some sort of crime scene in there?"

"We don't know for sure what happened in there."

"You have a pretty good idea, though, from whoever hired you, don't you?"

"From Tabitha, yes, I do," he acknowledged.

"She obviously has some idea of what happened. I mean, she's paying you to do this for her."

"She thought a particular body might be here. And it looks like she was right."

"It just feels like we're desecrating something. You found the tooth. Now we're looking for more of him, or her, or whoever."

"What we're doing here is the exact opposite of desecration. If we can prove someone's body was disposed of in the kiln, we'll have done that person's family a favor. We'll provide closure for them."

"But that's not why you're here, is it?"

"I'm here on behalf of Tabitha and the Native Peoples Foundation, plus Stanford University, which is footing my bill."

"As an archaeologist."

"Correct. If I find anything indicating a crime occurred here, the park service and sheriff's department will take over."

"But you've already found something."

He rested his hand over the tooth, stowed in the front pocket of his pants. "One tooth doesn't a whole body make."

"What does? Or would?"

"Another tooth, or more teeth, or a bone fragment or two. Any and all of which is what we're currently searching for."

"Okay. I'm in. I've never gotten to search for burned body parts before."

Chuck handed Carmelita a trowel and surgical mask, then centered his own mask over his nose and mouth. Stooping, he led the way into the kiln.

Carmelita knelt beside him at the center of the structure. She lifted ash on her trowel blade and sifted through it with her fingertips, as he'd done earlier. Finding nothing, she deposited the ash back on the floor. "Like that?"

"Exactly like that." He lifted a bladeful of ash beside her. "I want to work this middle area of the kiln really well."

"Because that's where you found the tooth?" she asked, her voice muffled by her mask.

He nodded. "Where there's one..."

"...there may be more," she finished.

"How did Tabitha know to send you here?" Carmelita asked after several minutes, lifting more ash on the blade of her trowel and sifting her fingers through it.

Chuck returned a mound of ash from his trowel to the floor. "Do you remember the study I did in Yosemite Valley a few years ago?"

"Oh, yeah. Yosemite was where I started rock climbing. You were studying the Native people who lived in the valley before it was made into a national park, weren't you?"

He nodded. "In the mid-1800s, the Ahwahnechee people, who'd lived in Yosemite Valley for hundreds of years, were forced out of the valley at gunpoint by California militiamen. I studied their displacement from the valley on behalf of Tabitha and the Native Peoples Foundation."

"What does that have to do with Tabitha sending you here?"

"I called her a few weeks ago and asked if she had any work I could do for her while I was out here crewing for you." He tugged his mask higher on his nose. "When I told her I'd be on the east side of the Sierra for your race, she said two words to me: Mono Lake. The lake is just east of Yosemite Valley over Tioga Pass. When the Ahwahnechee were driven out of the valley, they joined the Kootzaduka'a people who lived around the lake. Tabitha is a member of the Kootzaduka'a tribe—also known as the Mono Lake people—who still live around the lake."

Carmelita sat back on her haunches. "I remember Mono Lake from when we were here before. It has rock towers sticking out of it."

"Right. Tufa towers. But they shouldn't actually be visible above the waterline. The towers only form underwater, which is where they still should be. Back in the 1940s, the Los Angeles Department of Water and Power started diverting the water that flowed into Mono Lake. They sent it south through a tunnel to the aqueduct in Owens Valley and on to Los Angeles from there. The lake began to dry up, just like Owens Lake before it. The tufa towers appeared as the surface level dropped. People who'd seen what happened to Owens Lake fought to save Mono Lake before it dried up, too. They finally won—in a manner of speaking. The utility wasn't required to refill the lake, but it was forced to stop draining it any further. Until now, that is."

"Which is where Tabitha comes in. And you."

"Right. With longer periods of drought in the West these days, water is becoming more scarce, and therefore more valuable. Cities are willing to pay big money for new sources of water, whether it's in the form of groundwater, rainwater, snowmelt water, or just sitting in a lake. And wherever there's big money at stake, there's the potential for trouble."

Carmelita pointed at the tooth in Chuck's pocket, her eyes bright above her mask. "Or maybe even murder."

They sifted through the ash together in the kiln for another thirty minutes, the air in the chamber growing increasingly thick with floating particles.

"How's your mask working?" Chuck asked Carmelita. "I don't want your lungs to get mucked up before the race."

"Nothing's getting through," she reported. "If I start to feel anything, I'll get out of here. But I don't want to quit until we find something more. Until *I* find something more." She swept her fingers through the layer of ash covering the floor of the kiln. "Tabitha knows who the tooth belonged to, doesn't she?"

"She has a pretty good idea."

"She must've told you."

"She did." Chuck cleared his throat. There was no reason to withhold the information from Carmelita. "The tooth most likely belonged to a young Paiute man named Russell Raining Bird, who lived in the town of Lone Pine, in the middle of Owens Valley, a hundred years ago. Most of the Paiute people, the original inhabitants of Owens Valley, were forced off their lands by the white farmers and ranchers who took over the valley in the 1800s. Some Paiute families managed to stick around, including Russell's family. Russell loved Owens Lake, just like everybody else from Lone Pine. On Sunday afternoons, the whole town headed down to the lake for fishing and swimming. When the lake started to shrink, the townspeople built a boardwalk out to the receding waterline. They kept making the boardwalk longer and longer. They complained to the utility, of course, but there were a lot more people in Los Angeles than there were in Lone Pine, so no one paid any attention to them. Besides, their complaints were the least of the utility's worries back then, what with the bombings."

"Bombings?"

"The construction of the Los Angeles Aqueduct led to what became known as the California Water Wars. When the utility started taking the water from the creeks, it destroyed the farming and ranching in Owens Valley and put the local workers out of jobs. The locals dynamited the aqueduct over and over—which prompted the utility to hire them to maintain the canal instead of blowing it up."

"What about Russell Raining Bird?"

"He wouldn't give up on Owens Lake. The more the other locals were hired by the utility, the louder he got with his protests. The rest of his family had left the valley by then, and he was one of the last Paiutes still living in Lone Pine. He hired a photographer to take pictures of him parading on the muddy shoreline of Owens Lake in a full-body swimsuit while holding a sign accusing the utility of destroying the lake. When nothing came of that, he reenacted his protest on the sidewalk in front of Los Angeles City Hall. Pictures of his one-man protest in the city were printed in the LA newspapers. In response, the utility sent him a letter offering him a job in the valley at double the salary of any of the other locals."

"A bribe."

"Precisely. But Russell wasn't the bribing type. He showed the letter to anybody and everybody he could find. People were pretty unhappy when they read it—politicians, bureaucrats, and, most of all, the locals in Owens Valley who'd been bought off for a lot less money."

"Let me guess: along about then is when Russell Raining Bird disappeared."

Chuck tapped the tooth in his pocket with his fingertips. "Correct."

Carmelita glanced around the kiln. "After all these years, how did Tabitha find out his body was burned in here?"

"The Inyo County Sheriff's Department received an anonymous letter a few months ago. The letter writer claimed their father had told them years ago on his deathbed that he'd been present when Russell Raining Bird was killed. The writer said they wanted to confess on behalf of their father, and to clear their own conscience, too. The sheriff's department decided there was no point in following up on the letter because no one ever officially reported Russell as a missing person. For all anyone knew, the utility paid him off and he simply left the valley, never to return, which meant there was no cold case for investigators to investigate. But one of the deputies is a friend of Tabitha's and showed her the letter. The deputy figured she'd be interested, considering Russell Raining Bird's Paiute heritage."

"And Tabitha thought the letter was legit?"

"She had no way of knowing for sure, but she decided it was worth following up on. The letter writer claims their father confessed that Russell's body was burned in one of the Wildrose kilns. Tabitha was going to drive out here and poke around on her own at the end of the semester. But when I reached out to her, she secured some grant money from Stanford and contracted with me to survey the kilns instead. Anything I find, as an archaeological field expert, will carry more weight than whatever she might find as an academician."

In addition to the grant money, Chuck had jumped at the contract Tabitha offered him for another reason. When he'd mentioned to Tabitha Carmelita's dream of attending a highly ranked private college like Stanford, Tabitha had told him about a little-known scholarship program for deserving children of Stanford University contractors. Excited as Chuck was about the program, he hadn't yet told Carmelita about it, awaiting the completion of his contract to assure she was eligible to apply for it.

"What's in it for Tabitha?" Carmelita asked.

"It all comes back to Mono Lake," Chuck said. "The Native Peoples Foundation is fighting to protect the lake on behalf of the Kootzaduka'a people who live around it. The lake is sacred to them. Plus, Mono Lake is a critical stopover point for migrating birds. And unlike dried-up Owens Lake, toxic dust storms don't blow off it because it's not fully drained—not yet, anyway."

"I thought you said Mono Lake is protected from being drained any further."

"When it comes to water, nothing is ever *fully* protected. That's especially true of surface water. As far as plenty of people are concerned, Mono Lake is just sitting there waiting to be used up, along with all the water flowing into it."

"Does Los Angeles still want the Mono Lake water?"

"Probably, along every other city in California running low on water—which is just about every other city in the state. For now, Los Angeles is required to maintain Mono Lake at its current level. But what if LA sold its rights to another city? That city could potentially drain Mono Lake while a new round of lawsuits aimed at protecting the lake played out. That's what Tabitha is trying to keep from happening. She and the other Native

Peoples Foundation board members figure the discovery of Russell Raining Bird's body could serve as a wake-up call to everyone who believes Mono Lake is safe after all these years. They believe that if they can prove a Native American was murdered for the water in Owens Lake decades ago, and then publicize the murder as far and wide as possible, that would go a long way toward putting people on notice that Mono Lake remains at risk today."

"You already found his tooth."

"All we need is another piece or two of him."

"Hmm," Carmelita said after a few dozen more scoops, staring at the latest mound of ash on her trowel blade.

A dark gray lump the size of a penny stuck out of the lighter gray mound of ash. She extended her finger toward it.

"Careful," Chuck said. His heart galloped, rattling his ribcage, as he eyed the lump. "I don't think that's a tooth. It's too dark. But the color's right for a bone fragment. If it is, it could crumble with just the touch of your finger. Bones are made of collagen, which turns brittle at temperatures as low as 160 degrees." He patted the floor of the kiln. "Set it down, would you?"

She lowered her trowel to the ground and tugged the blade away, leaving the object protruding from the tiny mound of ash.

Chuck leaned over the lump, aiming his headlamp at it. Tiny fractures covered its surface. The end of the lump was rounded, in the form of a tiny ball.

His heart beat faster. "It definitely looks like a bone fragment. See the fractures? They form on collagen as it heats up. In the process of burning, collagen turns from white to yellow to dark brown. Then, just before it becomes ash, it turns dark gray, just like this," he said, pointing at the lump. "Based on the rounded end, I'd say you found a finger bone."

Carmelita scrutinized the lump. "Poor Russell Raining Bird."

"Whoever killed him didn't stick around long enough to make sure his body burned up completely. That means what we now have here, after all these years—" he waved his hand around the kiln "—is a crime scene."

7

Chuck sprinted up the trail toward Carmelita's purple headlamp and the white light next to it emerging from the mouth of Portal Canyon. Rosie, Clarence, and Liza followed close behind him.

The path wound through sagebrush growing close on both sides of the trail. The sage was silvery green in the dawn light. Its astringent scent prickled his nose as he ran.

"Carm!" he called ahead.

"Here!" she cried.

The headlamps halted at the mouth of the canyon. He directed his phone light at Carmelita as he reached her.

"I'm okay," she said, panting. She aimed her headlamp at a woman beside her. "It's Darlene."

Carmelita supported Darlene with an arm around her waist. The racer wore runner's garb, her numbered sticker on her shorts. She was short and slight, with spiky gray hair peaking from beneath her cap.

Darlene moaned, reaching down to her left side. "My leg."

Rosie halted beside Chuck and aimed her phone light at Darlene. Her shin was bruised and bloodied.

Liza knelt and examined Darlene's left leg in the combined light of the two phones. A cut slashed through the skin of her shin, extending from one side of her leg to the other, midway between her knee and ankle. Blood trickled in matching rivulets from the ends of the wound, soaking into her ankle sock.

Chuck drew a sharp breath, staring at the gash.

Darlene leaned forward and gripped Liza's shoulder. "I don't know what happened."

"I found her on the ground," Carmelita said. "I helped her get out of the canyon."

"You can go ahead and take off now," Darlene told her.

"You're sure?"

Darlene indicated Chuck, Rosie, Clarence, and Liza with a tilt of her head. "I'm good."

"We've got her from here," Liza assured Carmelita.

"Okay." Carmelita pressed a button on her GPS watch, lighting its face. "Four miles down, 146 to go." She waved goodbye to the group and jogged away, the lavender glow of her headlamp adding a purple tint to the sagebrush lining the sides of the trail.

Liza scrutinized the wound on Darlene's leg. Chuck stood back, grateful for Liza's wilderness medical training as a river guide.

"Weird," she said. "It's so straight and clean." She looked up at Darlene. "Let's get you to the truck."

She rose and gripped Darlene's elbow, and they walked down the trail together while Chuck, Rosie, and Clarence lit the way from behind.

"One second, I was moving right along," Darlene recounted, limping beside Liza. "The next, *wham*, I was facedown in the dirt."

They stopped in the glow of the pickup headlights, the creek babbling beside them.

"Janelle keeps a med kit in the truck," Chuck said. "I'll grab it."

"And a seat, please," said Liza.

He plucked Carmelita's battered camp chair from the truck bed, wrestled the chair open, and set it behind Darlene. The injured runner sank into it.

He retrieved the medical kit from the truck and handed it Liza. The kit was the size and shape of a large fishing tackle box. She opened it and took out a pair of disposable latex gloves.

"Let's have a look," she said to Darlene, tugging on the gloves.

She placed her hand on Darlene's knee, bracing the injured leg, and examined the wound. Only a small amount of blood oozed from it.

"It's too uniform to have been caused by a rock or a tree branch," she said. She leaned closer. "Ah-ha."

Chuck peered over her shoulder along with Clarence and Rosie.

"Check it out!" Clarence exclaimed, pointing at the wound.

A dime-sized object protruded from one side of the cut on Darlene's leg. Liza grasped the object and pulled. The object remained embedded in the skin of Darlene's lower leg, and Liza managed only to stretch the end of the wound. Darlene yelped in pain.

"Sorry," Liza said. "Brace yourself. This will only take a second."

She pulled harder. The object came free from the wound, trailing a thin filament behind it.

Liza held the object up in the glow of the headlights. "It's a fishing fly."

The trailing filament—fishing line—led to a fishhook wrapped with black, gray, and white thread, creating a fake oversized insect.

Chuck jutted his chin. "The utility stocks Portal Creek with trout. It's one of the requirements for taking the water—they have to stock all the streams from the mountains to where they're diverted into the aqueduct." He touched Darlene's shoulder. "Someone must have left their fishing line tangled around some trees. The line cut your leg when you ran into it."

"Some *jerk* must've left it," said Rosie.

Liza raised the hook higher. A white spray of fibers rose from the back of the fly above the hook's shaft.

"It's a Parachute Adams," she said. "It's made to look like a mayfly. The fibers on top imitate the fly's wings. Trout can't resist it."

"They can't resist it when it's floating in a creek," Rosie said. "Not when it's wrapped around a tree." She squatted next to Darlene. "That totally sucks, what happened to you."

"I must've gotten off the trail in the dark," Darlene said. "I was right next to the creek when the line snagged me."

"I'm sorry your race is over," said Liza.

"What do you mean?" Darlene bent forward, studying the wound. "It's hardly bleeding." She straightened in her seat and looked out across the valley. In the distance, Lone Pine's compact grid of streetlights glowed like an oasis in the end-of-night gloom. "I've got miles to go before I sleep, lots of them." She looked at Liza. "Slap a bandage on me. I just need to make it to my crew at the first check-in point. They'll take care of me from there."

Liza tilted her head. "You're sure?"

Darlene nodded firmly. "No question."

Liza chuckled. "Fair enough."

Rosie stood up. "I'm glad you're not quitting," she said.

"Never," Darlene replied.

Minutes later, freshly bandaged, Darlene set off down the trail after Carmelita.

Liza peered up the trail in the opposite direction as she stripped off her gloves. No more runners emerged from the mouth of the canyon. "Looks like that's everybody."

Chuck watched as Darlene jogged slowly away beside the creek, limping only slightly. "Lucky for her we came over to the trail from the road."

"I bet she would've made it to the first check-in point without our help," Liza said. "She's pretty tough."

Clarence eyed the departing runner. "Carm would've stayed with her, though, which would've put her even farther behind the leaders than she already is."

"This isn't about Carm competing against the other runners," Chuck said, wagging a finger at Clarence. "It's only about her. The race is a chance for her to test herself against herself, nothing more." He aimed his finger at Clarence's chest. "You'd better not be turning into Rick Chatten on us."

Clarence raised his hands to Chuck. "No way, jefe. Believe me, I have no plans whatsoever to turn into that imbécil." He shrugged. "But you know Carm as well as I do. When has she ever been content to not compete when there's a competition going on?"

"Never," Rosie chirped.

8

It was closing in on noon, the sun high overhead, when Chuck arrived with Rosie, Clarence, and Liza at the first of the four official check-in points along the race route. The initial check-in point was thirty miles from the starting line in Portal Canyon and a few miles from the town of Lone Pine. It was situated at the junction of the little-traveled county road that passed around the shore of former Owens Lake and the single-lane dirt road that cut straight across the shallow lakebed.

Chuck parked the pickup on the shoulder of the deserted county road. Climbing out, he turned a slow circle, getting his bearings.

The view was expansive in all directions. Weeds and bunch-grass grew close to the shoreline of the former lake, giving way to a sea of ricegrass a few inches tall covering the valley floor. The only visible trees were those lining the streets of Lone Pine, forming a patch of dark green a few miles to the north.

The wind, picking up with the rising heat of the day, lifted dust from the parched ground beside the road and spun it into thin whirlwinds that twisted into the cloudless blue sky. The temperature was in the low eighties, comfortable enough for now. But the heat was increasing by the minute, just as it did each day in the eastern California desert, where daily tempera-ture swings ranged up to seventy-five degrees, among the largest twenty-four-hour temperature differentials on earth.

The floor of Owens Valley stretched west to the base of the Sierra Nevada range, where a shadowed V at the foot of the mountains marked the mouth of Portal Canyon. Mount Whitney soared high above the head of the canyon, its summit white with late-winter snow.

The bed of former Owens Lake extended several miles east from the county road. The northern half of the empty lake consisted of brown dirt gouged by bulldozers into deep furrows lined by berms several feet high. The dirt berms were meant to act as windbreaks, holding the surface dust of the lakebed in place. Despite the presence of the berms, however, the morning breeze lifted skeins of dust off the bare half of the lakebed. The dirt particles floated eastward, riding the wind up and over the Cerro Gordo Mountains and on into Death Valley National Park.

In contrast to the dusty northern half of the lakebed, the southern half of former Owens Lake was a lush green carpet of plant growth. Rectangular fields covered the south end of the lakebed, broken by canals delivering irrigation water to the planted fields, which ranged from light to dark green depending on vegetation type.

The one-lane dirt road ran east across the lakebed from the paved county road, between the lakebed's cultivated and uncultivated halves. On the west side of the county road, a signpost marked the end of the trail across the valley from Portal Canyon.

Nothing moved on the trail for as far as Chuck could see, but the race leaders were due to begin arriving at the check-in point soon.

Along both sides of the paved road, support crews were busy setting up aid stations for their racers, erecting portable shade canopies and placing camp chairs and tables beneath them.

Chuck teamed with Rosie, Clarence, and Liza to set up the aid station they would staff for Carmelita, affixing legs to a roll-up camp table and arranging on the table a variety of snack foods and electrolyte drinks. Before the race, Carmelita had said she might want junk food at the check-in points such as a peanut butter and jelly sandwich and potato chips teamed with a sugary drink like high-fructose soda. Or, she'd said, she might prefer easy-to-digest goo, the sugary energy syrup in squeeze packets favored by many ultra runners.

Liza lined up liter bottles of water and powdered electrolyte mix on the table, ready to refill the soft bottles carried by Carmelita in her vest pockets to drink while she ran. Chuck opened the battered camp chair and attached an oversized sun umbrella to its back, providing a shaded seat for Carmelita.

Rosie plopped into the chair. "That looks nice," she said, gazing out at the green fields covering the southern half of the lakebed. "Like a square golf course in the middle of the desert."

"They're using some of the water from the mountains to irrigate half of the lakebed as an experiment," Chuck said, "to try holding down the dust with plants."

Rosie aimed her phone at the dust-filled air above the barren northern half of the lakebed. Filming, she swung her phone to the clear air above the cultivated southern half. "Looks like it's working."

"The dust that rises off the lakebed is filled with toxins like arsenic and lead that have been floating into Death Valley ever since the lake dried up. Environmentalists sued the water company to fix the problem." Chuck pointed at the dust rising above the berms lining the northern half of the lakebed. "The windbreaks obviously don't work." He ticked his finger to the clear air above the cultivated plots. "The plants work great, but they require water the utility would rather send to Los Angeles."

"Well, too bad for them."

"They're trying different kinds of drought-tolerant plants to see which do the best job of holding down the dust with the least amount of water. They're trying buffalo grass, sagebrush, even jimsomweed—which, weirdly enough, seems to be working the best of all."

"Why's that weird?"

"Jimsonweed is poisonous. It's toxic, just like the dust it's meant to control."

"That *is* weird," Rosie agreed.

She rested her phone on her stomach, leaned back in the chair, and extended her legs into the sun from beneath the umbrella. "I'm completely and totally and utterly exhausted," she announced. "I'm going to take a nap while we wait for Carm." She closed her eyes and feigned a snore, sucking air through her nose.

Liza rearranged the food and drink items on the table, setting them close together, then spreading them apart. She caught Clarence and Chuck watching her and gave them an embarrassed smile. "There's no way I can just stand around and wait for her to get here."

"Neither can I," Chuck said. "I think I'll go over and see what Marian and Doug are up to."

"Good idea," said Clarence. "I'd like to know how Doug is doing."

He glared up the road at Rick Chatten, who was assembling an elaborate aid station for Margot with the help of two women and Carl, the young videographer who had emerged from the minivan after the accident at the start of the race. The women had driven to the check-in point in a second vehicle, a sedan with *margotchatten.com* stenciled on its doors.

Rick and the crew members had positioned a pair of head-high, ten-foot-square shade canopies next to the minivan, creating a ten-by-twenty-foot rectangle of shade. Beneath the structures, they had set up a full-size lounge chair and a cot complete with fleece blanket and pillow. The cot and lounge chair rested on a thick Persian rug rolled out on the shoulder of the road. At the edge of the rug, a long folding table was topped with a wide selection of snacks. Two huge ice chests rested beneath the table.

As Chuck looked on, Rick aimed a stiff finger at one of the

chests. "Get it out!" he barked at Carl. "It should be on the table, not in there! It'll be too cold. What do you want her to do, freeze to death when she drinks it?"

Carl leapt to comply, opening one of the chests, removing a bottle of bright pink electrolyte drink, and setting the bottle on the table. Rick turned his back on Carl and stomped over to the minivan.

"Poor Margot," Clarence said, "to have a father like that."

"I hope the crew members are being paid lots of money to put up with him," Chuck said.

"They deserve hazardous duty pay."

Rick climbed into the van through its open side door and disappeared from view.

Clarence rubbed his mouth, staring after Rick. "The more I see of him, the more I wonder about the accident."

Chuck frowned. "What are you talking about?"

"I wonder what he might *really* have been up to this morning." Clarence glanced at Carmelita's chair, its aluminum legs bent and its nylon arms ripped and frayed. "I don't trust that guy," he said, glowering at the minivan. "I didn't trust him before the race, and I trust him a lot less now."

Rosie opened her eyes and sat up in the chair. "Do you think he tried to kill Carmelita just so Margot would win the race?"

"Well…" said Clarence.

Chuck pressed his hand to his forehead. "That's…that's insane."

"Is it? He smashed into Carm's chair right after she stood up from it."

Chuck shook his head, exasperated. "I saw the fluid leaking from the broken line with my own eyes. He didn't have any brakes."

"You said you told him to get his car checked after you helped him when he got stuck."

"He should have had it checked, but he didn't."

"How do you know he wasn't taking advantage of the opportunity to reduce his daughter's competition this morning?" Clarence asked. "The broken brake line offered him the cover he needed. For all we know, he could've cut the line himself and then tried to run Carmelita down."

Rosie stared at her uncle, her mouth falling open. "He tried to hit Carm, but he missed her and hit Doug instead."

Chuck threw up his hands. "Why would he go after Carm? Why wouldn't he go after Kelsey McCloud? Or one of the other top runners, the ones we saw at the front of the pack, like Matt Sharon or Waitimu Mwangi? This is Carm's first race ever. No one even knows who she is, much less if she's any good."

"You said Margot knew who Carmelita was," Clarence pointed out. "It's a different world today, with social media. It's all about your brand, your follower numbers." He directed his square jaw at the minivan and sedan parked bumper to bumper at the Team Chatten aid station, the minivan emblazoned with Margot's leggy likeness and website address, the sedan also bearing her website address. "*That's* what counts these days—clearing everybody else out of your lane. Margot's lane is young female trail runners, and in the Whitney to Death 150, the only other racer competing against her in that lane is Carmelita Ortega."

Rosie's eyes grew big and round. "I bet he wasn't trying to kill her. I bet he was just going to pop her one—" she punched her palm with her fist "—like he did to Doug. Killing her would've been too much. He just wanted to hurt her enough to make her drop out of the race."

Chuck looked from Rosie to Clarence, prepared to disagree. But he hesitated. "Rick *did* say he has some serious betting money riding on Margot," he admitted.

Then he pressed his lips together, silently berating himself. What was he doing, giving even a shred of credence to Clarence's nutty idea?

"No," he said. "You're wrong, Clarence."

He stared at Janelle's brother. Clarence stared back.

Finally, Clarence blinked. "Okay," he said. "I know it's a long shot."

"Aww," Rosie groaned.

"But Rick really did run down Carm's chair," Clarence said. "He really did hit Doug. So we have to keep a close eye on him."

"Totally," said Rosie, scowling up the road at the Team Chatten aid station from beneath the umbrella.

"Fine," Chuck said. He looked at Clarence. "How about if you and I do that right now?"

He and Clarence walked up the quiet county road past aid stations under assembly by other support crews. The stations were similar to Carmelita's straightforward setup, with folding camp chairs, sun umbrellas or single shade canopies, and simple selections of snacks and drinks.

Chuck and Clarence slowed as they walked past the aid station Rick and the other three Team Chatten crew members had prepared for Margot. Rick sat in the middle seat of the minivan, visible through the open side door, staring at a laptop computer propped on his knees. Carl and the two female crew members stood in the shade beneath the twin canopies, their backs to Rick and their eyes on their cell phones.

No telltale brake fluid puddled beneath the van.

"Looks like he tracked down a mechanic in Lone Pine," Chuck said to Clarence, eyeing the dry gravel under the vehicle.

"Or he squirted some fluid under his axle when he got out of his car this morning to make it look like an accident," Clarence countered.

Chuck groaned. "You just won't give it up, will you?"

"Nope."

Beyond the Team Chatten aid station, positioned where the dirt road across the lakebed met the paved county road, the official check-in site consisted of two folding tables set beneath a ten-foot-square shade canopy. The words "Whitney to Death 150" were stenciled on the canopy's nylon roof. Packages of snack food and bottles of soda and electrolyte drink rested on one of the tables beneath the canopy. Two laptop computers and a black receiver box with a shiny silver antenna sat on the other table. Cables ran from the computers and receiver box to a bank of batteries resting on the ground beneath the table.

Staffed by Marian and Doug, the check-in site served as the central meeting place for the race, with support crew members regularly stopping by to learn the latest on the competition from the race organizers.

As Chuck and Clarence neared the check-in site, Doug hoisted a five-gallon insulated cooler from the back of his and Marian's SUV and carried it to the food-and-drink table. He set the cooler on the table, spun it so its spout faced out, and placed a stack of disposable cups next to it. The word "WATER" was stenciled in big block letters on the side of the cooler.

Marian sat at the tech table in a folding chair, typing on one of the laptop computers. She paused to adjust the antenna on the receiver box, then resumed typing.

Chuck and Clarence stepped into the shade beneath the canopy. Chuck tapped the Whitney to Death 150 app icon on his cell phone. Beside him, Marian stopped typing and leaned forward, squinting at her computer screen.

"Can you see the racers?" he asked her while he waited for the race app to load on his phone.

"Yep. You?"

The app appeared on his screen, its background a photo of Badwater Basin in the middle of Death Valley National Park. He tapped the map button in the upper right corner.

When he'd brought up the real-time map on his phone before the race, the route of the Whitney to Death 150 had appeared as a red line zigzagging across the desert from Mount Whitney to Death Valley. With the competition now underway, green dots were superimposed over the red line on the Owens Valley portion of the race route. A blue square marked the site of the first check-in point at the edge of former Owens Lake.

"I've got them, too," he reported to Marian.

"Good," she said. "We weren't sure if the map was working for everyone."

"You two are geniuses," Clarence said to her and Doug, waving his hand at the computers and receiver box.

"Marian's the real genius," Doug said. "She built the real-time program and put it out there for everybody to use. When it comes to computer stuff, I'm just along for the ride." He rested his hand on the water cooler, wincing as he did so.

"Still hurting?" Chuck asked him.

Doug rapped the cooler with his palm, then rubbed his shoulder, grimacing. "I managed to lug this thing over here, but I probably shouldn't have." He glowered at the Team Chatten aid station. Rick had climbed out of the van and was again haranguing his aides. The crew scurried about beneath the twin shade canopies, repositioning the lounge chair and cot in response to his gruff directives.

Chuck resumed studying the map on his phone. One of the green dots was within half a mile of the blue square denoting the check-in point. He turned his phone to Clarence. "The leader's getting close."

"That's Kelsey," Marian said. "You should be able to tap each dot and see the racer number associated with it, then cross-reference the number to the leaderboard."

Chuck tapped the lead dot. The number one appeared, superimposed over the dot in a tiny bubble. He looked out from beneath the canopy. Half a mile away, a tiny figure moved across the grassy plain, approaching the check-in site. "Here he comes."

Marian looked at Doug. "It's showtime, dear," she said, a tremor in her voice.

"Everything will work," Doug assured her. "You've tested it a million times."

"Bettors insist on real-time posting nowadays," Marian explained to Chuck and Clarence.

"So we added it this year," said Doug. "Or I should say, Marian added it. There's a ton of pressure riding on making sure it syncs up okay."

"Don't remind me," said Marian. She frowned at her computer. "Come *on*," she urged it. "Sync, for crying out loud. *Sync!*"

"Easy, dear," Doug soothed her. "It'll work. Just give it time."

"There it is! Whew!" she exclaimed, throwing herself back in her seat. She sank low in her chair, her eyes on the computer. "It's coming over. The numbers look good." She sat up, eyeing the screen. "No, I take that back. The numbers look *great*."

"Racer numbers?" Clarence asked.

"Betting numbers," Doug said. "That's what pays the bills. It's the only way we could possibly pull off the race each year."

"People love it," Marian said. She pointed at the computer. "This year, with real-time added, it looks like they're loving it all the more." She said to Doug, "The big money's still on Kelsey."

"As it should be." He turned to Chuck and Clarence. "Kelsey won almost every ultra race worth winning last year, including ours. He's the man."

"And Hannah is the woman," Marian said. "She won a couple of ultra-ultra races outright last year, races that are two hundred miles long or longer. She beat all the women *and* all the men. That's one of the beautiful things about ultra racing—it's the supreme equalizer. The longer a race gets, the more it becomes about stamina and guts instead of just strength and muscle mass, and that puts women right in the mix."

"Waitimu is the wild card," Doug said. "This is his first year with us."

"Like Carmelita," said Chuck.

"Except Waitimu's got a real shot at winning." Doug looked at Chuck. "No offense, mind you."

"None taken." Doug had no knowledge of Carmelita's pre-race training times.

"Waitimu moved to the US from Kenya a few years ago to train for the Olympics. He's finished in the top ten at the Boston Marathon every year for the last five years. Even so, it's become increasingly clear that a medal performance isn't in the cards for him, so he switched to trail running instead."

"For the money?"

"For the *potential* money. He's got a wife and two little kids."

"We saw him when he left Portal Canyon," Chuck reported. "He looked good. Like he was out for a Sunday jog. He was in third place."

Marian tapped at her computer. "He's in second now," she said. "He just passed Matt."

"The guy from Ireland?" Clarence asked.

Doug nodded and turned to Marian. "Not again."

"Relax. It's early, hon, real early."

"I know. It's just…" He addressed Clarence. "Matt's a crowd favorite. Maybe even *the* crowd favorite. But he always finds a way to screw up. Three years ago, he got dehydrated and had to spend some extra time rehydrating in his aid station and finished second to Kelsey. Two years ago, his car broke down when he was on his way here the day before the race. He was up all night getting it fixed and barely made it to the starting line. He hung in there for most of the race, but he was just too tired to stay with Kelsey at the end. Then, last year, he was in the lead, but he took a wrong turn coming off the Panamint divide and Kelsey passed him and went on to win by less than five minutes." Doug lifted and dropped his shoulders. "Maybe that's why everybody loves Matt so much. He's not the Kelsey robot, winning race after race like some sort of automaton. He's actually human."

"He has a great sense of humor, too," said Marian. "People started calling him The Flake because of all his screwups, so he had his crew serve bowls of corn flakes and milk to everybody at the start of his next race. He posted up footage of the whole thing on his channels."

"Which made everybody love him all the more," Doug said.

"There's plenty of money on him right now. Almost as much as Kelsey." Marian's eyes remained glued to the computer screen. "Domenico's in fourth place," she reported.

Chuck looked up from his phone. "He was in fourth when he left Portal Canyon, too."

Doug nodded. "That's Domenico Lyons."

"He helped you when Rick hit you, didn't he?" Chuck asked. "The guy wearing the hoodie?"

"That's him. He's real quiet. Keeps his hood pulled over his head all the time. He's finished in the top five a couple of years."

"His betting numbers look pretty decent right now," said Marian. "It's fascinating, watching the numbers go up and down."

Chuck frowned. "People can keep betting after the race starts?"

"That's the great thing about an ultra race," she said, nodding. "It's not over in three minutes like a horse race. It goes on and on. People can follow along and bet on their favorite runners for two whole days and nights."

"That's what makes it so addictive," Doug said.

"And lucrative?" Chuck asked.

"For the betting companies, sure. For us, not so much. We only get a tiny slice."

Marian gestured at the computer screen. "The map is clearly helping, though. The numbers keep looking better and better."

"Let's hope it holds," Doug said.

He peered out from beneath the canopy. Kelsey approached through the low ricegrass lining the cross-valley trail, his visage wavering in heat waves, less than a quarter mile from the aid station.

"I've got eyes on him," Doug said to Marian.

"Me, too," she replied, smiling at her computer screen. "The map's working, hon."

"I never doubted you, dear."

Chuck returned his attention to the map on his phone. He tapped the dot denoting the final runner in the race, at the back of the pack, far out on the valley floor. Darlene's number appeared above the dot. Though she remained in last place, it was good to see that she was still on the move.

He tapped the dot ahead of Darlene, in second-to-last place. Rather than Carmelita's racer number, thirty-two, the number twenty-nine appeared over the dot. He tapped the next dot, for the runner in third-to-last place. The number eighteen appeared. He tapped the next dot. Thirty-five.

He swallowed, staring at his phone. When he'd last checked the map, while passing through Lone Pine, Carmelita had been among the last runners in the race, after slowing to help Darlene in Portal Canyon.

But where was she now? Where was number thirty-two?

9

"What now?" Carmelita asked Chuck, staring at the charred finger bone resting in the mound of ash on the floor of the kiln in Wildrose Canyon.

He checked his watch. It was getting late. "We should head back to camp."

Her eyebrows lifted. "You've got to be kidding me."

"I want to get out of the canyon and into cell range to let Tabitha know what we found. She'll be blown away. Besides, even if we leave right now, it'll still be past dinnertime when we get back to the campground."

At the mention of food, Carmelita nodded. In the months leading up to the race, she'd assiduously tracked the timing and calorie count of every one of her meals. She pointed at the bone fragment. "We can't just leave this here, though, can we?"

"The playing field has shifted. With a second find, we have no choice but to back off."

He pulled the tooth from his pocket, took it out of the evidence bag, and rested it in the ash next to the fragment, then snapped pictures of the molar and bone with his phone, its camera flash bright in the dusky light of the kiln.

"Got 'em," he said, checking the pictures on his screen.

He scooped ash off the floor and ladled it over the objects. The human remains disappeared beneath the cascade of gray particles, leaving a low mound of ash in the center of the structure.

"It looks like a tiny grave," Carmelita said.

"Because it is."

—

Chuck called Tabitha as soon as he and Carmelita left the canyon, working his phone with one hand while steering the truck with the other.

Tabitha whooped at his news. Then she quieted. "Russell Raining Bird didn't deserve what they did to him." A beat of silence passed over the phone. "You're sure about what you found?"

"As sure as I can be with only a visual inspection." He pulled to the side of the road and sent her the pictures he'd taken of the objects.

"Unbelievable," she said upon seeing them. "We have to call it in."

He pursed his lips.

"Don't we?" she asked.

From his parking spot on the edge of the road, he looked across the treeless plain that separated the Panamint Mountains from the Coso Mountains. Three days from now, after the climb up and over the Cosos, racers in the Whitney to Death 150 would run across the plain and enter Wildrose Canyon, beginning the final ascent of the race. They would pass the kilns and continue to the old mine at the end of the road. From there, they would climb the low cliff bands above the mine, cut through the notch marking the Panamint divide, and descend the other side, continuing to the finish line in Badwater Basin.

But the racers would complete the race only if Tabitha did not alert officials from Death Valley National Park and the Inyo County Sheriff's Department to the discovery of the body fragments in the kiln. If she reported the find, the officials were all but sure to close Wildrose Canyon Road and shut down the race while they looked into the discovery, ending Carmelita's dream of competing in the race and making her months of training for naught.

Chuck glanced across the passenger seat at Carmelita. It was her desire to participate in the Whitney to Death 150 that had led to his contract to survey the kilns, resulting in the discovery of the human remains. How could he possibly deny her the opportunity to participate in the race?

He pressed his phone to his ear. "To be honest," he told Tabitha, "I didn't think I'd find anything. Certainly not this quickly. Today was supposed to be a cursory look, just to get the lay of the land. But now…" His voice trailed off.

"I'm listening, Chuck."

"Both the sheriff's department and the park service told you they weren't interested in following up on the letter. That's why you hired me to search the kilns instead."

"Correct."

"That being the case, I don't see the need to alert them to the find right away. You deserve to see the remains for yourself first. Once this thing goes public, it'll be a big deal. The whole world will come crashing in, I guarantee it."

"How about if I leave right now to meet you there?"

"Are you in Palo Alto?"

"Yes."

"It's a long drive. It'll be way past dark if you come now. Plus, I've got Carmelita with me. She needs to get back to our campsite to rest up for the start of the race the day after tomorrow."

Opposite him in the truck, Carmelita nodded.

"What do you propose?" Tabitha asked.

Chuck looked through the windshield. The road was empty, as it had been all day. According to the Death Valley National Park website, each year only a handful of tourists made the lengthy out-and-back drive to the historic kilns, which were miles up dead-end Wildrose Canyon on the far western edge of the park.

"The tooth and bone fragment aren't going anywhere. We covered them up, so they're entirely hidden. I'll be coming back to the kilns during the race, tracking Carmelita along the way. The race starts Friday morning, which means the runners will be passing the kilns the next day, on Saturday, late in the day. How about if I meet you there then?"

"Hmm. That works. I'll be able to teach my classes through the end of the week. Plus, that'll give me time to get everything set up at my end. I'll fill in Henry, my department chair, and I'll call an emergency meeting of the NPF board. You're right, Chuck—this will be a big deal. They'll appreciate knowing about it beforehand."

"The more prepared you are to take advantage of what's about to hit you, the better."

"For Mono Lake."

"For every last drop of water still in it," he agreed.

10

Chuck stood next to Clarence beneath the shade canopy at the initial race check-in site, staring at his phone.

"I can't find Carmelita," he said, his concern making his voice quiver.

Marian looked up from her computer. "What do you mean, you can't find her?"

"I keep checking the dots. None of them are her."

"Try the finder function."

"What's that?"

"Upper left corner. Tap the drop-down menu and click the word 'Find.'"

Chuck followed her instructions. A search bar appeared, superimposed over the map on his screen. "Okay, got it."

"Type in her last name."

Marian returned her attention to her computer.

Chuck typed Ortega and pressed enter. A glowing dot changed from green to red almost halfway up in the pack of runners. After a moment, the dot changed back to green and Carmelita's number, thirty-two, appeared over it.

"Got her," Chuck said. "She's passed a ton of people. I can't believe it."

Marian's eyes crinkled as she smiled. "Well, I can. Your daughter's got some serious legs on her. I've been tracking her. She was still at the back of the pack when she got to the mouth of Portal Canyon. She must not be very good at nighttime descents. I can't blame her for that—trail-running downhill in the dark is an acquired skill."

"That wasn't it," Chuck said. "She stopped to help another runner who fell. A woman named Darlene."

"Darlene Roberts?" Doug asked. "Older, short gray hair?"

"That's her. She ran into some fishing line tangled around the trees next to the trail. It cut her shin. She says her crew will fix her up when she gets here. She wouldn't even think about quitting."

"That's Darlene for you. Actually, she's the same as all ultra runners. Pain doesn't mean the same thing to them as it does to the rest of us. They live to suffer."

Marian tapped at her computer keyboard, then leaned forward, staring at the screen. "She's still in last place. She's even behind Hester."

"The woman we saw walking?" Clarence asked.

"That would be her," Marian said. "Hester Baldwin. She speed-walks from the start all the way to the finish. She manages to beat the cutoff time every other year or so, always with only a few minutes to spare. Anybody trailing her during the race is in serious danger of missing the cutoff. That's especially true of anyone trailing her early in the race, when everybody's going fast and building up buffer time for the mountain crossings. Everybody but Hester, that is. She never runs. But she never changes her speed-walking pace, either. She just keeps plugging away for the whole fifty hours." Marian looked out from beneath the canopy. Kelsey McCloud was only a hundred yards from the check-in site. "Time to deal with the front of the pack now." She glanced at Doug. "All set, hon?"

"Ready as can be, dear." Doug pulled a paper cup off the stack on the table and filled it with water from the cooler.

Kelsey jogged up to the check-in site seconds later.

"Number one checking in," he reported to Marian, barely winded, as he entered the shade beneath the canopy.

"Got you," she replied, giving her keyboard a quick rat-a-tat-tat of strokes. "Good first stretch, Kelse."

"Thanks." He accepted the cup of water Doug offered. "Glad to see that you're upright."

"It takes more than a speeding-out-of-control car to keep me down," said Doug.

Marian cocked an eyebrow at the lead runner. "And you think *you're* tough."

Kelsey smiled. "I'm not tough at all. Just stubborn. Very, very stubborn."

He raised his cup to Marian, Doug, Chuck, and Clarence. Turning away, he drank the water while he ambled up the county road to his two-person crew, a man and woman in their mid-thirties, about his age, waiting at the aid station they'd assembled for him on the road's shoulder.

Waitimu Mwangi approached on the trail a moment later. Doug filled another cup with water when the Kenyan runner arrived at the check-in site.

"Number fourteen," he reported to Marian.

"You're doing pretty well for your first ultra race, Waitimu," she complimented him.

He placed his hands together and bowed to her. "Ah, thank you. It is my honor to be here with you today." He straightened. "I am blessed that the sun is shining down on me today. I am blessed that my legs are carrying me forward across the big desert today. And I am blessed, most of all, that my wife, Imani, and my children, Adia and Jelani, are waiting for me at home in this wonderful land that is called America."

"You must really miss them."

"Ah, yes, with a big pain in my heart," Waitimu said, placing his palm flat on his chest. "But I will return home to them very soon." His mouth stretched wide as he smiled. "My children are the most beautiful of all the angels. I am happy now, to be running, but I will be even more happy when I am back home with them once again."

Waitimu accepted the cup of water proffered by Doug. Sipping, he strode down the road to his waiting crew, which consisted of three college-aged youths.

"I like that guy," Clarence said, looking after him.

"I'm glad we accepted his application for this year's race," Doug said, nodding. "He sounded good on paper. He's even better in real life."

Doug filled a third cup of water. "Our race is all about hydration," he explained to Chuck and Clarence, setting the cup on the table next to the cooler. "The runners drink all they can at the check-in points to minimize the amount of liquid they have to carry on the trail. I offer a cup of water to every runner here at the first check-in, to emphasize the importance of maintaining their fluid intake throughout the race."

Matt Sharon, the Irish runner, arrived shortly after Waitimu. Cheers from surrounding support teams greeted his arrival.

"Aren't you the popular one?" Marian teased him as he checked in.

"I'm not sure why," he said with a sad smile. "Everyone loves a loser, I suppose."

"You're not a loser and you know it, Matt," Doug said. "Three second-place finishes in row to Kelsey isn't exactly terrible. You've come close every year. You've pushed him so hard. That's why everybody loves you—they keep believing your year will come."

Matt sighed, his chest deflating. "Maybe this year will finally be the one."

"Chin up, old man," Doug said, adopting a British accent.

Matt's wan smile brightened. "Blimey," he replied, switching from his Irish accent to London cockney. "Stiff upper lip and what d'you say?"

Doug abandoned his attempted accent. "That's exactly what I'm saying."

"You won't hear any whinging from me if I wind up totally knackered and things go pear-shaped for me again this year," Matt assured Doug, continuing his cockney delivery. "You hear me, mate?"

"Loud and clear," Doug said, grinning and handing him a cup of water.

Matt downed the water and set off for his aid station and crew.

"You can see why everybody adores him," Marian said, looking after him.

"The lovable loser," Doug agreed.

"Until, maybe, finally, this year."

"You got that right, mate."

Domenico Lyons came in close behind Matt. He announced his number in his deep bass voice, which emanated like a foghorn from the depths of his hood.

"You're hanging tough," Doug said.

"Thanks." Domenico kept his head down, his face shrouded, as he accepted the cup of water and headed for his aid station and support crew.

"He's a strange one," Marian said. "He shows up every year like clockwork. He hangs with the leaders for most of the race, then fades at the end. Far as I know, he doesn't race in any other ultras except ours. He keeps to himself and hardly posts anything on social media."

"We keep accepting his application every year because he always finishes so high," Doug said. "But we don't really know the first thing about him."

"We do know he helped you when you got hit this morning," said Marian. "He just likes to keep to himself, that's all. Nothing wrong with that."

"You're right, hon," Doug replied. "Nothing wrong with that at all."

Hannah Rinkl coasted into the check-in site a few minutes after the four leading male runners. She'd barely recited her number to Marian, accepted her cup of water from Doug, and departed for her waiting crew when Margot arrived.

The teen runner stated her number to Marian. Unlike the other racers, she waved off Doug's cup of water. "Sorry," she said, covering her mouth with her hand and letting out a nervous giggle. "No, thank you."

"You're sure?" Doug asked.

"Dad told me not to. He's got everything calculated for me, down to the last drop."

Doug lowered the cup to the table. "Okay, then."

He turned to Chuck and Clarence after Margot left for the Team Chatten aid station. "Too bad her dad's not as calculated with his driving."

Chuck watched as Margot lay back on the lounge chair at her aid station, her feet raised. She took deep swallows from the bottle of electrolyte drink Carl had removed earlier from the cooler at Rick's command. One of the two women crew members crouched next to Margot and began kneading her calves. Rick hovered over his daughter, holding out a plateful of snacks—chips, oatmeal cookies, and banana and apple slices. Carl stood back, filming.

Chuck returned his attention to the check-in site as more runners streamed in from the trail. He assessed the racers as they arrived. Considering that they'd just run thirty miles nonstop, they appeared remarkably fresh. They offered warm smiles to Marian as they recited their racer numbers to her, and graciously accepted the cups of water Doug offered them. Several runners grabbed packaged snacks—energy bars, bags of chips, packets of cookies—from the table before departing for their respective aid stations.

"They make it look easy," Chuck marveled during a break between runners.

"For now," said Doug. "But just you wait. Things will begin to get interesting at around the hundred-mile mark. That's when the you-know-what will really start to hit the fan—the blisters, the cramps, the nausea."

"And the hallucinations," Marian added. "Don't forget about them."

Doug tipped his head to her. "As I'm sure you know, we don't allow pacers," he said to Chuck, referring to noncompeting runners allowed to accompany racers during the latter stages of most ultra races, helping them stay on course when their minds began to break down near the end of competitions. "We don't want to make it too easy."

"I don't think you need to worry about that," Chuck said dryly, glancing at the heat waves dancing above the valley floor.

Doug grinned. "We like to think of the Whitney to Death 150 as an individual endeavor, man vs. the elements."

"Or woman," Marian said.

"In place of pacers, our racers often use each other for support along the way, running together for periods of time. But they always break up before the end of the race and duel it out at the finish."

"Have you ever lost anyone?" Clarence asked. "Per the name of your race, I mean: Whitney to *Death*."

"Never." Doug rapped the side of his head with his knuckles. "Knock on wood."

"Most of our runners have been doing this a long time," Marian told Clarence. "When they begin to lose it mentally, they know to slow down until they regain their faculties. If their senses still don't come back, they know to stop."

"Either that," Clarence said, "or they don't have enough strength left to take another step."

Marian chuckled. "There's a lot of that, too, of course. But there's something more. I've witnessed it time after time. When they come into the last two check-in points, the ones who are in trouble have a certain look in their eyes. I can tell the race is over for them just from that look. Invariably, they never leave their aid stations. They sit down and are incapable of getting back up again. It's not their crews telling them to stop, it's their bodies."

"Or their minds," Doug said.

"Or that," Marian agreed.

Chuck looked out at the sun-blasted desert stretching away to the mountain ranges bounding both sides of the valley. Given Carmelita's inexperience with ultra racing combined with her high motivation level, would she really be willing to stop twenty-four or thirty-six hours from now if she needed to?

"But that's still to come," Doug said to Clarence. "At the end of the race. We'll all be hallucinating by then, we'll be so sleep-deprived."

At his aid station, Kelsey stood up from his folding chair and pulled on his running vest. It hung heavily from his shoulders, its pockets bulging. He jogged away from his cheering two-person crew and descended the gentle slope toward the bed of the former lake, running on the dirt road cutting between the bare northern half and planted southern half of the lakebed. Seconds later, Waitimu set out after Kelsey to the cheers of his youthful crew. Soon after, Matt Sharon and Domenico Lyons left their aid stations, cheered by their crews as well.

In less than a minute, the four race leaders were small figures shimmering in the distance as they traversed the empty lake.

Waiting at the check-in site with Clarence, Chuck monitored Carmelita's progress on the real-time map, clicking her green dot over and over again to make her racer number appear on his phone and assure himself she was still on course.

Finally, the moving dot that corresponded with her number neared the blue square denoting the check-in point, and she appeared in the distance, running through the ricegrass.

Emotion flooded Chuck's veins—pride at her accomplishment thus far in the race, relief that she had made it through the initial thirty miles of the competition, and a sharp jolt of trepidation at what she faced in the long hours and 120 miles of running still to come.

She drew closer, her shoulders erect and her arms swinging smoothly back and forth, running comfortably on the trail.

Like the other runners before her, she jogged straight up to the race check-in site.

"Thirty-two," she said, stopping before Marian.

"Gotcha," Marian said.

"Hip, hip!" Doug cheered. "You made it! How are you feeling?"

"Pretty good," Carmelita said. She raised her foot behind her and grabbed her ankle with one hand, balancing on her other foot and stretching her quadriceps, then repeated the movement with her other foot, loosening both thighs. "The real question is, how are *you* doing?" she asked Doug as she accepted the cup of water he offered her.

"I've felt better, I admit," Doug said. "But I'll survive."

"I was worrying about you while I was running."

"Don't you be doing that. You've got yourself to be worrying about."

"I'd rather worry about you than me."

"Well, then, feel free to worry about me all you want. But I'm doing fine, really I am."

Chuck pointed down the road at Rosie and Liza waiting next to the truck. "Ready?"

Carmelita nodded, and he and Clarence accompanied her past the Team Chatten aid station. Margot had departed by now, and Rick, Carl, and the other crew members were busy folding the cot and lounge chair and rolling up the Persian rug.

"Wow," Carmelita said softly, ogling Margot's extravagant station.

"Over the top, if you ask me," Clarence muttered. "Way over."

Rick did not acknowledge them as they passed.

"Whoo-hoo, Carm!" Rosie cheered as they approached, filming with her upraised phone.

Carmelita handed her depleted vest to Liza and sank into the chair beneath the oversized umbrella.

"The shade feels good, doesn't it?" Rosie asked. When Carmelita didn't answer, she continued. "And the chair."

"Let her rest," Chuck urged Rosie.

But Carmelita said, "They both feel good, the chair and the shade."

"I tested out the umbrella," Rosie said. "I took a nap under it. I even practiced snoring, because— "

"*Rosie*," Chuck cautioned.

"She's fine," Carmelita said to him. "It's nice." She looked at Rosie. "It's good to hear your voice."

"Was it lonely out there?"

"Not as bad as I thought. I talked to everybody I passed."

"You sure passed a lot of people. We've been watching you on the map. You're flying!"

"I'm feeling good," Carmelita said. "So far, anyway."

"What would you like to drink?" Chuck asked.

"TrailFire," she said, naming the most popular electrolyte drink among ultra racers. "Por favor."

"Bueno. TrailFire it is." Chuck handed her a bottle of the bright red drink. "What about food?"

"I'm okay for now. I'll eat at the next check-in. That's my plan, remember? Hydration nonstop, solids at check-in points two and four."

"You're sure?"

She rolled her eyes at him.

He raised his hands, smiling. "Okay, okay."

Liza refilled the empty bottles from Carmelita's vest with water and electrolyte drink mix. "Any hot spots? Blisters?" she asked.

"My feet are fine," Carmelita reported between gulps of TrailFire. "My legs feel good, too."

"Your speed shows it," Clarence said. "You passed almost half the pack in the last twenty miles."

"Don't forget your planned pace," Chuck told her.

Carmelita again rolled her eyes at him.

Rosie snickered. "You must be feeling good. You've rolled your eyes at Dad twice now."

Carmelita rolled her eyes at Rosie. Then she smiled. "On that note," she said, standing up and stepping into the sun.

"So soon?" Chuck asked.

"It's a race."

"You said you were going to take it easy."

"I never said anything about taking it easy. I said I was going to set my own pace—which has nothing to do with sitting around doing nothing at the check-in points."

"But you're not doing nothing," Chuck said. "You're resting. You're—"

Clarence directed a sidelong look at him. "She knows what she's doing, jefe."

Rosie aimed her phone at Carmelita. "The sooner you leave, the sooner you'll finish."

"I won't finish for another two days, no matter how fast I go."

"Minus a bunch of hours already today, and a bunch of miles."

"You got that right." Carmelita accepted the replenished vest from Liza and pulled it on. "And…I'm…*outta here*," she announced to Rosie's upheld camera.

"You were never here to begin with," said Rosie. "Just like the wind."

Carmelita jogged across the county road. "See you on the other side," she called over her shoulder as she started down the dirt road to the lakebed.

"Go, Carm, go!" Rosie yelled.

Chuck, Clarence, and Liza joined her, waving and shaking their fists and cheering for Carmelita until she was well out of earshot.

Carmelita was a tiny speck on the lakebed when Chuck checked the map on his phone a few minutes later. A number of dots were crowded close together, unmoving, at the check-in point. Ahead on the race route, dots denoting the first fifteen or so runners moved across the bed of the lake in tiny jerks and starts. He tapped the lead dot. Kelsey's number appeared above it—the repeat winner from Salt Lake City was still in first place. Chuck tapped the second dot. Waitimu's number appeared—the Kenyan continued to trail Kelsey in second place. He tapped the third dot, summoning Matt's number, then the fourth dot, Domenico's.

Well back from the four lead runners, another dot caught Chuck's eye.

A short distance out on the lakebed, behind the dots of the lead runners and Carmelita, a dot denoting one of the racers was not moving. Chuck stared at the dot. It remained motionless on the map. He shook his phone. Still the dot stayed in place.

He looked up from his phone. In the distance, runners were spread along the dirt road, crossing the former lake. A wind-whipped cloud of dust, thicker than the wispy curtains of dirt particles that had risen off the lakebed earlier in the day, enveloped the racers as it swept across the lakebed. The dust cloud dispersed, and the racers reappeared as small spots of motion, their arms and legs churning.

All but one, that is.

Where the motionless dot on the map indicated, a runner stood ramrod straight in the center of the dirt road.

As Chuck watched, the runner toppled forward and landed face-first on the ground.

PART TWO

"The term 'Keeler fog' was coined decades ago for the pervasive, unusually fine-grained, alkaline dust that infiltrates the smallest cracks and contaminates residences [with] particles so small that they can be inhaled deeply into the human respiratory tract."

—Marith C. Reheis, US Geological Survey

11

"Marian! Doug!" Chuck yelled to the race organizers. He pointed at the runner lying in the middle of the dirt road.

Marian and Doug stepped from beneath the race canopy and peered out at the lakebed. Doug's back straightened and Marian's hand went to her mouth. Doug ran for their SUV while Marian looked on, remaining at the check-in site.

Chuck leapt behind the wheel of the truck. Rosie, Clarence, and Liza climbed in with him and he sped down the dirt track, followed closely by Doug. Chuck weaved past racers on the road and skidded to a stop at the downed runner. Liza yanked the medical kit from the back of the pickup and hurried to the runner's side. Rosie raised her phone, filming. Chuck and Clarence stood next to her.

The runner, a man, lay on his stomach, his head to one side and his eyes closed. He was in his forties, with sandy brown hair and a goatee. In the wake of his fall, his singlet and vest were bunched high on his back and his cap was askew on his head. Dust coated his goatee and circled his nostrils. He coughed, lifting a small cloud of fine particles off the ground in front of his face, then drew quick panting breaths.

Liza pressed her fingertips to the runner's wrist and eyed her watch. She frowned as time ticked by. "His heart is racing. A hundred and twenty beats per minute."

The runner rolled to his side and drew his knees to his chest, continuing to cough. His lips and fingers were blue-gray. He threw back his head and wheezed, fighting to inhale, his eyes squeezed shut.

Though the air was clear—for the moment, at least—the smell of dust filled Chuck's nose.

"Oh, my God," Doug exclaimed as he arrived. He knelt next to the fallen runner, opposite Liza. "Joseph!" he cried, squeezing the racer's shoulder.

Saliva dribbled from the corner of Joseph's mouth. His arms shot out from his sides and his hands fluttered. His eyes opened, but only the whites were visible, the pupils rolled back in his head. He continued to take shallow breaths, and his eyes fell shut once more.

A gust of wind blew a dense cloud of dust down the road, engulfing the group. The dust cloud dissipated as quickly as it had arrived.

The sound of a car skidding to a halt came from beyond the pickup and SUV. A car door opened and slammed shut.

"Joseph!" a female voice cried out.

"Here, Natalie!" Doug called.

A middle-aged woman charged forward. As if the woman's arrival had somehow summoned the fallen runner back toward consciousness, Joseph convulsed, his body shaking.

Natalie dropped to her knees at Joseph's head. Matching gold wedding bands circled her and Joseph's ring fingers.

"I'm here, Joe," she said, caressing Joseph's cheek. "I've got you."

Doug tapped at his phone, put it to his ear, and explained the situation in clipped sentences.

"They want us to meet them on the way to Lone Pine," he said when he finished the call, looking at the group gathered around Joseph. "It'll be faster."

Joseph's eyes fluttered open. His gaze darted about, then settled on the face of his wife, leaning over him.

"Natalie," he croaked, reaching for her. "What happened? What's going on?"

Natalie wiped saliva from Joseph's lips. She helped him sit up and drew him close, her arm around his shoulders.

He leaned his head against her chest, his hand resting on his belly, breathing quickly. "Oh, God, I feel so awful," he said, groaning.

Doug pointed at his phone. "I told 911 we'd get moving. They're sending an ambulance this way."

"I'll take him," Natalie said.

She and Liza lifted Joseph to a standing position. He shuffled between them to the Natalie's car. She leaned the passenger seat far back and helped Joseph settle in it. He closed his eyes and put his hands on his stomach, his chest rising and falling with his breaths.

Natalie climbed behind the wheel, spun the vehicle around, and shot back in the direction of the county road.

Doug gazed after the departing car. "Joseph Hendon is one of the kindest human beings I've ever known," he said. "Generous as all get out. He and Natalie have been friends of ours since year one of the race." He closed his eyes and shook his head. "He'll be all right," he said like an incantation. "He's gotta be."

Several runners who had come upon the scene set off once more across the lakebed.

"And…cut," Chuck heard Rosie whisper to herself as she lowered her phone, watching the runners depart.

"What just happened back there?" Chuck wondered aloud as he drove the truck back toward the check-in point with Rosie, Clarence, and Liza. "The guy was in really bad shape." He glanced at Liza, who shared the back seat with Rosie.

"It was more than just exhaustion from the race. It had to be," she said. "He keeled over so fast. He went down hard, all at once. It wasn't like he sank to the ground. Plus, he was coughing and wheezing. I wouldn't associate that with exhaustion or heat stroke."

"What *would* you associate it with?" Rosie asked.

"Dust," Liza replied. "He went down right after the dust clouds started blasting everyone out on the lakebed."

"But it didn't mess up the other runners."

"I'm betting he had an asthma attack. They're fairly common with our customers on river trips. His symptoms certainly fit—wheezing, coughing, increased heart rate and breathing, even the gray color of his lips and fingers. The dust definitely could've set him off."

Rosie shook her head. "Nope. I'm not buying it."

"What are you thinking?" Chuck asked her.

"Poison," she said, with a definitive up and down movement of her chin.

"What on earth are you talking about?"

"Just think about it," she said. "First, Doug gets run over by Margot's dad. Second, that woman, Darlene, gets cut by the fishing line. Then, this guy falls right over in the middle of the road."

Clarence tapped his lips with his finger. "Hmm."

Chuck hit the brakes, bringing the truck to an abrupt stop at the junction of the dirt road and paved county road. The pickup rocked back and forth as it settled on its leaf springs. He turned to Clarence. "You actually agree with her?"

"That guy Rick, Margot's dad, already tried to kill Doug. Maybe he slipped Joseph something that would make him sick. And tied the fishing line around the trees in the canyon, too."

"Why would he do all that?"

"I don't know. Maybe to screw with the race somehow. But you have to admit, Rosie's got a point—the bad stuff is really starting to pile up."

"Yeah, I do have a point," said Rosie. "A good one."

"Doug just said Joseph is a good friend of his and Marian's," Clarence added. "I bet Darlene is a good friend of theirs, too."

Chuck caught Liza's eye in the rearview mirror. "How about you?"

"Asthma attack," she said without hesitation. Then, after a weighted pause, she added, "But you know who else has gotten to be good friends with Doug and Marian?"

Chuck looked past the county road at the parched floor of Owens Valley stretching to the foot of Mount Whitney. An icy fist clamped itself around his midsection.

He pressed the gas and turned the truck onto the county road, gripping the steering wheel with both hands.

"Carmelita," he said grimly, earning a rigid nod from Liza.

12

Working fast, Chuck folded the chair and umbrella while Clarence, Liza, and Rosie boxed up the food and drinks and rolled up the table. They tossed everything in the back of the truck and hopped inside. Chuck sped away, rounding the south end of the lakebed and heading for the ghost town of Keeler on the eastern shore of the former lake.

"We'll meet her in Keeler, like we planned," he said.

"If she hasn't been poisoned," said Rosie.

"Don't you start."

"I'm just joking."

"You saw what happened to Joseph. This is not a joking matter."

Chuck sped along the shoreline, skirting the rectangular fields that filled the southern half of the lakebed.

Beyond the swath of cultivated plants, the compact street grid of what had once been the thriving refinery town of Keeler climbed the slope away from the east side of the dry lake. With its access to water from Owens Lake, Keeler a century ago had been home to hundreds of people and the site of a massive silver refinery. Using charcoal from the Wildrose kilns, the refinery had smelted silver ore coming out of mines in the nearby Cerro Gordo Mountains and the more distant Coso and Panamint ranges. Bars of pure silver produced in Keeler had been shipped across the lake by steamboat, then hauled south by mule train to the port of Los Angeles.

Today, a hundred years after the closing of the refinery and the emptying of Owens Lake, Keeler was home to a handful of stubborn residents willing to inhale the toxic dust that rose off the dry lakebed whenever the winds picked up.

The dirt track across the former lake ended in Keeler, making the largely deserted town a good location for crews to meet runners along the race route.

Chuck glanced back at Rosie. "Find Carm on the map, would you?"

She bent over her phone and tapped at its screen. "Got her," she said after a moment. "She's still passing people like crazy. She's getting close to the front."

Chuck exhaled with relief. Carmelita was clearly healthy. "How far across the lake is she?"

Any view of the racers on the dirt road was blocked by the plots of plants outside his window.

"More than halfway. Way more." She turned her phone to the front of the truck. "See?"

Clarence took her phone and held it up to Chuck, who glanced at it as he drove. He spotted the number thirty-two in its tiny bubble approaching the east shore of the former lake.

"You're right," he said to Rosie. "She *is* moving fast."

"Which means she doesn't have any poison in her," Rosie said.

Chuck squeezed his eyes shut for a second as he drove. "You're a conspiracy theorist through and through, you know that?" he said, looking back at her.

"Damn straight, I am," she said. "Besides, what if I'm right? What if someone really did poison that guy, Joseph?"

"We'll make sure everything's completely okay with Carm when we see her in Keeler. We're her support crew. It's up to us to make sure she's safe." He hesitated. "Maybe we should see if she wants to leave the race when we meet up with her."

"Ha," Rosie scoffed. "Like that'll ever happen."

"I'm just saying we could ask her."

"The race is barely getting started," said Liza.

He sighed and looked at the two of them in the rearview mirror. "I know you're right. Both of you."

A cultivated field of dark green plants festooned with large white flowers shaped like trumpets streamed past the truck.

"There's the jimsonweed you were telling Rosie about," Liza said to Chuck. She turned to Rosie in the back seat. "Do you remember what he said about it?"

"That it's poisonous!" Rosie exclaimed.

Liza nodded. "There's your conspiracy for you, right out in plain sight. Jimsonweed is a hallucinogen. It grows wild in the Grand Canyon. A couple of kids on one of my trips tried it once. They made a tea out of it and drank it, but instead of getting high, they got really sick. We had to helicopter them out to the hospital."

Chuck looked back at her. "What were their symptoms?"

"Now that you mention it, some were the same as what happened to Joseph—increased heart rate, convulsions."

"What about the coughing and wheezing?"

"No, not those." She raised her eyebrows at Rosie. "But still…"

They passed the field of jimsonweed and turned north toward Keeler, driving alongside a huge rectangle of sagebrush planted in straight lines. Beyond the cultivated sage, billows of dust rose off the northern half of the lakebed, driven by the gusting wind.

Chuck peered through the windshield at the dust, appalled. "I read that, along with the lower spring temperatures, Doug and Marian schedule the race for early April to beat the summer winds that kick up the worst of the dust storms on the lakebed." He groaned. "But the wind's really whipping today. It worries me, what the dust might be doing to Carm's lungs."

"She's only running through it this one time," Clarence reasoned.

"I know," Chuck said with a resigned shrug. "It's just…" He sat back in his seat. "Anyway, it's too late to do anything about it at this point. She's already out there in it."

His phone, resting in the front console, chimed with an incoming text.

Clarence picked it up and frowned at the screen. "Looks like it's from Janelle."

"What's she got to say?" Chuck asked.

She'd checked in regularly from Durango throughout the lead-up to the race and during the first hours of the competition this morning, but this was her first contact since Joseph's collapse.

He recited his passcode to Clarence, who tapped it into the phone, then studied it.

"Whoa," he exclaimed. "She says she's on her way here."

"But she has to work."

"I bet she was following the race on the map," Liza said, "and she saw Joseph's dot disappear from the racecourse and got all freaked out."

Clarence tapped at Chuck's phone some more. "You're right," he told Liza. "She says she'd already been thinking of heading out here for the end of the race. When she saw Joseph's dot show up as the first runner on the DNF list, it tipped the balance. She says she managed to talk someone into covering her last shift for her."

Rosie raised her arms. "Mamá's coming!" she cheered.

Chuck smiled as he drove, looking up the road at Keeler. Janelle's unexpected attendance was indeed good news.

His eyes rose to the dust cloud darkening the sky above the bed of Owens Lake and his smile faded.

At least, he reassured himself, Carmelita would be far from the dust-blown lakebed by the time Janelle arrived.

He slowed as they entered Keeler. No trees or grass grew around the twenty or so low-slung houses that made up what remained of the town, which stretched a handful of blocks along the county road and down the slope to the lakebed. Bleached pickup trucks and older-model sedans were parked in front of a few of the houses, providing some evidence of human habitation, but no townspeople were in sight.

His phone buzzed with an incoming call. Clarence picked it up. "It's Doug," he said, handing the phone to Chuck.

"How's Joseph?" Chuck asked as he put the phone to his ear.

"Marian got your number from Carmelita's emergency-contact information," Doug said. "Since you were there with him, we thought you should know."

"Did the ambulance meet him? Is he at the hospital?"

"No, I mean yes, I mean no." Doug drew a labored breath, its sound scratchy over the phone. "The ambulance met him. But, from what we were told, his heart took off again, beating really fast, and he had another wheezing fit. Then he stopped breathing. The paramedics tried everything, but they couldn't bring him back."

Chuck stabbed the brakes, stopping in the middle of the empty road through Keeler.

Clarence, Liza, and Rosie stared at him.

"He's…he's…?"

Doug's voice broke. "Joseph is dead."

13

"He died," Chuck said, lowering his phone to his lap. "Joseph. In the ambulance, before they could get him to the hospital."

"Dios mío," Clarence moaned. "Did they say what they think it was?"

"No. Too early to tell, I guess."

"Now that he died," said Rosie, "are you going to make Carm quit?"

"I never said anything about making her quit. I said maybe we should ask her if she wanted to leave the race." He looked back at her. "We should call your mamá, see what she thinks."

Rosie's eyes widened in alarm. "No. No way. You are *not* doing that."

"Why not?"

"She'll pull the plug on Carm. You know she will."

Clarence nodded. "It'll be tempting."

Silence filled the inside the truck.

Chuck grunted. "I'm glad she's decided to come now, even if it's because she saw Joseph's DNF. But that's the problem. Joseph died. He's *dead*."

"Yes, he died," said Liza. "Yes, he's dead. But it was an asthma attack."

"Says you," Rosie said.

"Yes, says me," Liza retorted. She smiled. "Unlike you and your crazy conspiracy theories." She grew serious and addressed everyone in the truck. "Things like asthma attacks happen. They just *do*." She waved her hand at the dust whipping through Keeler. "If Joseph really was asthmatic, then he was taking a risk—

one he obviously was willing to take—by running through that stuff out there."

"But..." Chuck said.

"But Carmelita is not asthmatic," Liza said. "None of us would want her running through dust clouds day after day, of course. As a one-time thing, though, she'll be fine. What happened to Joseph was a tragedy, a horrible thing. But Carmelita is not Joseph."

Chuck sighed heavily. "Okay."

He lifted his foot off the brake and drove slowly on into Keeler. West of the town, racers were spread along the dirt road across the lakebed, distant specks running toward them.

The wind, intensifying as the heat of the day increased, lifted more dust off the uncultivated half of the lakebed. The gritty clouds of dirt swept across the road and obscured the runners for seconds at a time.

The racers continued running through the swirling particles. Chuck tried not to think about what the toxins contained in the dust were doing to Carmelita's lungs as she ran. Like Liza had just said, her exposure was a one-time thing, afflicting her only during the crossing of the lakebed. Besides, there was no definitive proof, as yet, that the dust had played a role in Joseph's death.

He pushed himself back in his seat, his arms straight out and his palms pressed against the steering wheel. "Maybe Doug and Marian will stop the race for us."

"They didn't do it when Joseph got sick," Liza said. "I don't think his death will be enough for them to pull the plug on all the other runners, either."

"You're probably right." He relaxed his arms. "There's the financial side to consider, too. They said their slice of the betting money is what covers the race expenses—which they've already incurred for this year's race."

He pulled to a stop in front of a clapboard house with grimy windows and a listing roof over a narrow front porch. The bare sand lot around the house was outlined with rocks the size of basketballs.

A blast of wind off the lakebed surged up the street and past the house, carrying with it a dense cloud of dust. The flying particles cloaked the truck, lowering visibility to less than fifty feet. The sun disappeared overhead, as did the lakebed to the west and the Cerro Gordo Mountains to the east.

The wind let up after a moment and the dust thinned. A runner appeared, jogging up the sloping dirt street from the lakebed. A stream of wind-driven sand, flowing a few inches above the ground, snaked past the runner's ankles in streaks and runnels. It was Waitimu Mwangi, the family man who'd moved from Kenya to the US and switched from marathons to ultra racing.

Waitimu loped past the truck and across the paved county road. On the far side of the road, a two-foot length of red plastic tape, knotted by Doug and Marian around a signpost in the days leading up to the race, fluttered in the wind, marking the race route. Below the tape, a red plastic arrow affixed with twist-ties to the signpost indicated the direction of the route. The arrow pointed up a sandy track climbing away from the lakebed to the long-closed silver mines in the heart of the Cerro Gordo Mountains.

"This is so wild," Liza said as she watched Waitimu jog out of town past the flapping tape and arrow. "The sun, the heat, the wind, the dust."

Rosie raised her phone, filming the dirt flying past the truck windows. "It sure makes for great B-roll footage."

"I can't believe Carm signed up for this," Chuck said. He put his palm to the driver's side window. The dust outside whipped past his outstretched fingers.

Suddenly, a sunbeam lanced through the dust, filling the interior of the pickup with a burst of golden light.

"Nice," Rosie said, swinging her phone to capture the glow.

Still filming, she hopped out of the pickup and into the stiff breeze. When she let go of the truck door, the wind slammed it shut.

She held her phone up against the wind, filming Hannah Rinkl, the next runner to appear from the lakebed. Hannah's colorful rainbow-striped shirt shone brightly against the muted brown backdrop of the blowing dirt. She waved at Rosie as she crossed the thin strip of pavement cutting through town and headed up the two-track into the Cerro Gordos. Rosie followed Hannah's departure with her phone, her lips moving as she provided narration while the lead female racer left Keeler.

Chuck brought up the real-time map on his phone and tapped the dots of the race leaders one by one. Kelsey remained in the lead, just ahead of Matt Sharon and Domenico Lyons. The three had passed through Keeler before Waitimu reached the town. Waitimu had fallen back to fourth place, several minutes behind the leaders and a minute or two ahead of Hannah. Margot, holding onto sixth place, was still out on the lakebed.

Chuck worked his way backward dot by dot until he came to Carmelita's number, which appeared far sooner than he'd expected. She'd passed two-thirds of the runners in the race by now. Incredibly, only a dozen runners stood between her and Kelsey.

He squinted at the tiny map on his phone. The dot denoting Carmelita moved in tandem with a second dot. It appeared she was teaming with another runner, at least for the time being.

Chuck looked out at the dust-obscured lakebed, wishing Carmelita had her cell phone in one of her vest pockets.

But she didn't.

Before the race, he'd tried to convince her she should carry her phone for safety reasons, but she had steadfastly refused.

"A phone weighs eight ounces," she told him.

"That's only half a pound," he said.

"No, it's tons. Literally."

"Tons?"

"I'll be lifting everything I carry in my vest with every step I take for the whole race," she explained. "I already calculated it. At an average of 2,000 steps per mile, I'll take a total of 300,000 steps over the 150 miles of the race. That means a half-pound phone would add 150,000 pounds of lifting over the two days and nights that I'll be running. Besides, there's no cell service along most of the race route, and you'll be meeting me at most of the places along the route where there *is* service."

Which explained why Chuck could only wait anxiously with Rosie, Clarence, and Liza to check in with Carmelita about Joseph's death when she finished crossing the lakebed.

Margot materialized out of the dust minutes after Hannah, ascending the dirt lane through Keeler. A handful of crew vehicles now lined the county road through the middle of the town, the Team Chatten minivan and sedan included. Rick left the minivan when Margot appeared, joined by the three Team Chatten crew members. Carl filmed Margot's approach and the two other team members waved their hands above their heads, cheering for her. Rick, however, yelled at Margot as she drew nearer, his voice grating in the whipping wind, his words audible to Chuck inside the pickup.

"What do you think you're doing?" he berated his daughter, bringing his hands together in a single harsh clap. "You have to get a move on! Kelsey's extending his lead on you. You've got to reel him in. Do you hear me? *You've got to!*"

Margot's stride grew stilted and uneven. She eyed the ground, her head lowered, as she passed her father and climbed away from town on the old mining track.

—

Half a dozen more runners passed through Keeler before Carmelita appeared out of the roiling dust. A brawny racer—Astrid—ran at Carmelita's side.

Chuck, Clarence, and Liza climbed out of the truck and joined Rosie in the buffeting wind.

"You're doing great, Carm!" Rosie cried, her phone raised. "You, too, Astrid!"

Carmelita's gait was smooth and composed. She plucked a bottle from her vest and squeezed a shot of liquid into her mouth. Tucking the bottle away, she waved as she approached.

"She looks good," Clarence noted.

"She does," Chuck agreed.

Astrid spoke into a phone held to her ear as she and Carmelita jogged up the street. They stopped at the truck.

Despite the dust in the air, Carmelita's breaths came easily, her arms loose at her sides. "We heard you helped Joseph," she said, pointing at Astrid's phone. Astrid waved to them and turned away, still speaking into it.

"Have you heard the latest?" Chuck asked.

"That he died?" Carmelita said, her face growing pale. "Yes. Doug and Marian texted everybody carrying phones and asked them to pass the news on to everybody else. What do they think happened?"

"It was poison," Rosie said, her eyebrows raised.

Carmelita's eyes widened. "Poison?"

Astrid spun around, listening to them, her phone still pressed to her ear.

"Um, maybe," Rosie equivocated.

"Odds are it was an asthma attack," Liza said. "Very likely brought on by the dust."

Chuck caught Carmelita's eye. "We've been talking about whether you should keep going."

Carmelita gasped. "You think I should *quit*?"

Rosie jutted her chin. "I said there's no way you would do that."

"Rosie's right," Carmelita said to Chuck. "You just said it was an asthma attack."

"That's what Liza said. And it does seem to match up with his symptoms. But, honestly, we don't know what it was yet."

"I don't have time for this. I'm in the middle of the race." Carmelita glanced at Astrid. "*We're* in the middle of the race."

Astrid pointed at her phone. "Just a sec," she mouthed.

Chuck took advantage of the opportunity to say to Carmelita, "Maybe you should take your phone now, like Astrid, given what's happened."

She shook her head. "This is one of the last places along the way that has phone service. That's why Astrid is finishing up with her crew before we leave town. They're meeting her at the next check-in point."

"You could use your phone's GPS function to make sure you're on the route. You don't need cell service for that."

Carmelita pointed at the fluttering red ribbon and plastic arrow attached to the signpost. "Those are placed at every road and trail junction." She lifted the GPS tracker affixed to the hem of her shirt. "Plus, you're tracking every step I take." She looked Chuck in the eye. "Tons, remember?"

He nodded in defeat.

Astrid ended her call. "I'm all set, girl," she said to Carmelita.

"Me, too," Carmelita replied. Tears appeared, glimmering, in her eyes, as she looked around the group. "I'm sorry about Joseph."

"We all are," Chuck said.

"I can't believe what happened to him," she said, her voice trembling.

Astrid nodded, her face grave. "The vote among the racers is unanimous so far, though, from what my crew has heard. As long as Marian and Doug are willing to keep going, we all want to keep going, too."

Carmelita sighed, blinking back her tears. "We'll see you at the second check-in," she said to the group.

Chuck tipped his head to her. He was sure Janelle would agree—this was Carmelita's race, Carmelita's decision.

She and Astrid crossed the road and jogged up the old mining track out of town. In seconds, the dust swirling off the lakebed swallowed them as they headed into the mountains.

14

Rosie, Clarence, and Liza climbed back into the truck with Chuck. He angled out of Keeler toward the main highway running between Lone Pine and Death Valley National Park. The dust cloud thinned as they left the lakebed, as he knew it would for Carmelita, too.

The dust had cleared entirely and the blue sky and blazing sun returned by the time he turned east on the wide-shouldered highway leading to the national park. After the emptiness of the county road, the steady stream of traffic on the highway took him by surprise. Still, the many vehicles were a welcome sight, reminding him that, for all the talk of the wilderness aspects of the Whitney to Death 150, the race wasn't held entirely in the middle of nowhere.

"What's with all the cars?" Rosie asked from the back seat.

"This is the main road into Death Valley from the west," Chuck said.

She gestured at the desiccated landscape stretching away from both sides of the highway. "Why does anybody think this is worth driving a million miles to look at?"

He chuckled. "You're not the only one who thinks that—or who thought that when Death Valley was first declared a national monument a century ago. Back then, people said exactly the same thing."

"Yeah. Why should it be protected?"

"Death Valley was considered worth protecting precisely because of how rugged and desolate it was, and still is. For one thing, it has lots of plant species that only grow in the super-harsh environment of the Mojave Desert. Death Valley even has its own unique species of fish."

Rosie gawked at the dry rocky terrain outside the truck windows. "A *fish*?"

"The Colorado River pupfish," Chuck confirmed. "They're found in two streams in the valley and nowhere else on earth. They're a remnant population from millions of years ago, before Death Valley even existed. Which, by the way, isn't really a valley at all."

"It's a graben," said Liza.

"What's a graben?" Rosie asked her.

"Basically, a graben is a big hole in the ground. Millions of years ago, Death Valley was surrounded by a bunch of volcanoes. They sucked up lava, which made the ground collapse inward from all sides. That's why no streams run out of Death Valley, they only run into it."

"Just like Carmelita is going to do."

"Right, after she climbs up and over the old volcanoes on the west side of the park that are now the Panamint Mountains."

Chuck caught Liza's eye in the rearview mirror. "You really know your stuff, don't you?"

She tilted her head to him and smiled at Rosie. "I'm a river guide. It's my job to know that kind of stuff."

"I know lots of stuff, too," said Rosie. She yanked at the collar of her shirt. "Like, it's getting way too hot in here."

Chuck clicked the air conditioning up a notch. The outside temperature was continuing to climb as the afternoon wore on and the sun heated the ground. He looked out his side window at the sunbaked monolith of Cerro Gordo Peak, the tallest mountain in the Cerro Gordo range, rising to the north. After the flat stretch of the race across Owens Valley, the uphill stretch from Keeler into the Cerro Gordo Mountains represented the first of the race's three significant climbs, and the only ascent the racers faced during the hottest part of the day.

He peeled his gaze from the peak and focused on the road ahead, his shoulders hunched. How would Carmelita respond to the heat? Was she carrying enough liquid in her vest to remain adequately hydrated for the climb through the Cerro Gordos?

They reached the second check-in point beside the busy highway half an hour later. The runners would arrive here after descending out of the mountains on Cerro Gordo Trail, completing the first sixty miles of the race. Based on previous years' times, the race leaders would reach the highway as dusk spread across the desert at the end of the first day of the race, having averaged a four-mile-per-hour pace since the pre-dawn start in Portal Canyon.

The second check-in point was situated on a graded plot of land next to the highway. The open plot served as the trailhead parking lot for Cerro Gordo Trail to the north and Coso Trail to the south. Coso Trail ran along the flank of the Coso Mountain range, extending deep into the Coso Mountain Wilderness Area.

Doug and Marian already had the official race check-in site set up in the dirt parking lot—shade canopy erected, nourishment table loaded with food and drinks, and tech table topped with laptops and receiver box. Other crews had finished setting up their aid stations for their runners as well. The crew members bent their heads over their phones, presumably tracking the runners' progress through the Cerro Gordos on the real-time race map.

Chuck parked the truck and brought up the map on his phone, still seated behind the steering wheel.

"She's still moving up," he reported to the others, tapping dot after dot to check individual racer numbers. "She's just behind Astrid, running on her own again, in tenth place." He glanced out the window at the mountains. "She's been making her way through the pack pretty fast," he said.

"She started at the very back," Rosie said. "The only thing she can do is move up."

"But not *too* quickly. She said everybody runs at a fast pace on the first day, to provide a cushion for when things get tougher tonight and tomorrow. If she's gaining on everyone even when they're going all out today…it just worries me is all. She really needs to be ready for tonight." He pointed south into the desert from the highway. "She'll head into the Coso Mountains from here. There's not even a trail for the part that goes up and over the Coso divide—which she'll be doing in the middle of the night tonight." He shook his head. "I don't even want to think about it."

"She knows what she's doing," Rosie insisted. "She said tonight is when the race will really start for her. I'm sure that's why she's moving up now, to position herself before it gets dark." She looked up at the Cerro Gordo Mountains. "How long until she gets here?"

"Still a couple of hours."

Rosie yawned. "Good. I need a nap."

"That's not a bad idea, actually. There's still a lot of the race to go. Every bit of rest we get along the way will help us."

"And help us help Carm," Liza said.

Rosie lay across half of the back seat, while Chuck, Clarence, and Liza cracked their windows, leaned their heads back in their seats, and closed their eyes.

Chuck didn't fall fully asleep over the next hour, but the time spent with his eyes closed refreshed him nonetheless—despite the fact that his restfulness was marred by thoughts of Joseph's collapse and death.

Upon rousing himself, he checked the map on his phone. He sat bolt upright in his seat, frowning at his screen. Something about the formation of the dots denoting the lead group of racers on the map wasn't right.

In fact, something about the formation of the dots was very wrong.

15

Chuck grabbed Clarence's arm and turned the phone to him. "The dots are screwed up."

Clarence rubbed his eyes and sat up. He studied Chuck's phone, his brow furrowed. "What am I supposed to be seeing?"

"The dots of the lead runners should be lined up along the race route. But look at them."

Rosie and Liza sat up and leaned over the front seat, staring at the map on Chuck's phone along with Clarence.

"Shit," said Rosie.

"Hey!" Chuck admonished her.

"Well, you're right," she said. "Something's screwed up. The dots are stopped."

"One even looks like it's going backward," Liza noted, pointing at the map.

Chuck looked across the parking lot at the official race check-in site. As he watched, Marian stepped from beneath the shade canopy, put her hand to her forehead, and gazed up at the rocky mountainside on the far side of the highway. Then she waved for Doug to join her.

"Marian sees it, too," Chuck said. "I'm going to ask her what's going on."

He left the truck and crossed the parking lot to the race organizers.

"What's happening with the leaders?" he asked them.

"That's what we'd like to know," Marian said. "We can't figure it out."

"It's like they're lost," said Doug.

"But there's absolutely no way they could be," Marian said. "They're stopped for some reason at the junction of Cerro Gordo Trail and the road to the mines, where the trail crosses the road and drops down to the highway. We put an arrow there last week, and it's still full daylight. They couldn't possibly miss it."

She returned to the tech table and bent over her computers. "Ah," she said. "That's more like it."

Chuck checked the map on his phone. The dots of the lead runners were lined out once more on the trail leading out of the mountains. The runners were close behind one another. He tapped each of the dots in turn. His heart warmed when Carmelita's number, thirty-two, appeared at the back of the line of leaders—the snafu at the junction of the road and trail had enabled her to catch up with the lead runners, who now were just ahead of her on the course.

"They'll be here soon," Marian said, dropping into her seat. She struck a handful of keystrokes on one of the laptops and said to Doug, "I don't know what made them get all bunched up like that up there, but it sure is helping the betting numbers." She twisted in her chair to face Chuck. "The closer the leaders are to one another during the race, the more betting churn there is."

"We like churn," Doug said. "That's where we make our cut. The racers like it, too. Our payouts to the top finishers are based on the total betting amounts over the course of the race."

"We keep the maximum number of runners we accept for the race at around forty each year," said Marian. "That means the twenty percent of racers who finish before the cutoff time all have a decent shot at a podium spot and a payout."

"To keep things interesting," Doug said, "we accept a mix of new racers from the applicant pool along with returning racers. Waitimu's background as a top international marathoner sounded intriguing, so we accepted him this year. Astrid made the cut because we've never had an active member of the armed services compete with us before. Carmelita and Margot were particularly interesting because they're so young, so we accepted both of them for this year's race, too."

"As far as our payouts are concerned," Marian said, "they aren't that big. Only a few thousand bucks to the winner and even less for second and third place. There's a lot of betting on the race, but with the small cut we get, we can't offer much to the podium finishers after we account for all of our expenses."

Doug waved at the electronic equipment on the table. "Which aren't exactly cheap." He clasped his hands together. "As far as applicant numbers go, they've gone up every year, but the increase has been fairly slow. That's because the race is so tough. Some would say too tough. Only a certain kind of person wants to do it, and there aren't that many of those kinds of people in the world."

Chuck considered Carmelita's willingness to suffer to meet the goals she set for herself, whether spending hours a day on climbing walls or running miles and miles on snow-covered trails through the mountains around Durango. Just as Doug had said, there weren't many people out there like her.

"A lot of people want us to make the race easier," Doug continued. "They want us to change the route so it doesn't go so far into the backcountry. But that would defeat the whole idea of the Whitney to Death 150. We've said it before and we'll say it again: our race is about individual runners pushing themselves to the limits of human endurance in one of the harshest environments on earth. Which is to say, our race is for our runners, and not for anyone else."

"People want us to extend the cutoff time, too," Marian said. "They say it's not right that only one in five of our racers finishes in time to be counted. They say having an eighty-percent DNF rate is crazy."

"But if we extended the cutoff time," said Doug, "we wouldn't be able to stay long enough at each check-in point to meet all the racers ourselves before moving on to the next one."

"You could get others to help at the check-ins, couldn't you?" Chuck asked.

"It wouldn't be our race anymore if we did that. Our runners choose the Whitney to Death 150 because we manage all the logistics ourselves. That way, we can make sure each runner's race is their own individual competition—the chance to test their own personal limits in what we think is the toughest ultra race on the planet."

"Speaking of our runners," Marian said, looking up at the mountainside, "here they come."

Chuck hurried back to Rosie, Clarence, and Liza at the truck.

"Marian and Doug don't know what happened at the junction," he told them. He pointed across the highway at several runners descending the open slope, close behind one another on the switchbacking trail leading to the busy road. "But the leaders are on their way."

He and the others set up the aid station for Carmelita's imminent arrival. With the setup complete, he and Clarence turned to watch the approaching runners while Liza and Rosie monitored the map on their phones.

Rosie counted backward through the dots on her screen. "Carm's in eighth place!" she crowed.

"And only a few minutes out from here, looks like," Liza added.

Five lead runners—Kelsey, Matt, Waitimu, Domenico, and Hannah—reached the end of the trail on the far side of the highway in a pack. Above them on the slope, Margot bounded down the last stretch of the trail. She was followed closely by Astrid. The military runner pounded along the path, her arms pumping at her sides. A hundred feet above her, Carmelita jogged down the trail in her long-sleeved top.

"Here she comes," Chuck said, his stomach flipping. "I'll meet her at the check-in table and bring her over."

"I'll come with you and get some footage," Rosie said.

"We'll wait here," said Liza, standing at the truck with Clarence. "We don't want to overwhelm her."

Chuck spoke in Rosie's ear as they crossed the dirt lot. "Be sure to give her plenty of space, would you? She'll be tired."

"She'll be fine," Rosie said. "We talked about it before the race. She's got her job, and I've got mine."

Doug did not have cups of water filled and waiting for the lead runners at the check-in site.

"No hydration this time?" Chuck asked him.

"I only do that at the first stop," he said. "By now, they know what they want from their crews." He waved at the snacks and packets of electrolyte drink mix arrayed on the table next to the water cooler and stack of cups. "They're welcome to whatever they want, of course. I've just learned it's best not to try to force anything on them as the race goes on."

Kelsey led the pack of leaders across the parking area.

"Number one," he reported to Marian. Then he rounded on Doug. "What the hell?" he groused while the others checked in. "That was a total cluster up there."

"What happened?" Doug asked.

"At the last junction in the Cerro Gordos, the arrow was pointing up the road instead of down the trail. It looked like you changed the course this year for some reason."

"The wind must've turned it," Doug said. "We try to secure the arrows as best we can."

"Well, you did a lousy job with that one," Kelsey snapped.

Matt joined the conversation after reporting his number to Marian. "I went up the road past the trail, the way your arrow was pointing," he said in his thick Irish brogue. "I was trying suss out what was going on. Finally, I turned back and we all had a meet-up at the junction."

Hannah rubbed Matt's arm. "Foiled after taking the lead yet again."

"The story of me life," Matt moaned.

Domenico's deep voice emerged from his hood, addressing Doug. "We made the group decision to follow the old course even though your arrow was telling us not to."

"You know the rules," Doug said, addressing all the lead runners. "We put arrows and ribbons at as many intersections as we can. But route-finding ultimately is up to each one of you. It's every runner's responsibility to know the course, arrows or no arrows."

Matt pointed at Carmelita as she descended the trail on the far side of the highway, close behind Margot and Astrid. "That's what that one there said when she caught up with us."

"She knows her stuff."

"That she does."

The lead runners headed for their respective aid stations. Margot and Astrid crossed the highway and jogged to the check-in site together. Trailing them, Carmelita paused on the far side of the highway until a break in traffic appeared, then crossed the road.

"Carm!" Rosie hollered, her phone held high, as Carmelita jogged up to the check-in site. "Look here! Look here!"

Chuck braced himself for an outburst. Instead, Carmelita smiled at Rosie's phone. "Hey there, peeps," she greeted the camera, waving. "Sixty miles and we're still in this thing."

He bit his lip. Rosie was right. She and Carmelita knew what they were up to.

Margot, standing at the check-in table, added, "We sure are, peeps!"

Next to her, Astrid said, "There's still a long way to go, though."

"At least we're all in it together," Margot said.

Rick, approaching as Margot checked in, pointed at Astrid and growled to his daughter, "You're only in it with her until you punch the gas and leave her big tail behind."

The muscles at the side of Astrid's jaw tightened, but she said nothing, her lips a hard line.

Margot's face drooped. She recited her racer number to Marian in a subdued tone and departed with her father.

"Sorry about him," Doug said to Astrid after she reported her number to Marian.

Astrid lifted her broad shoulders in a shrug. "Believe me, in the Corps, I deal with guys like him every day of the week."

She left for her aid station.

Carmelita stepped up to the check-in table and stated her number to Marian. Then she turned to Rosie's phone camera. "Onward into night," she declared.

She spun her running cap around so its brim extended over her ponytail at the back of her neck, pulled her headlamp from the rear pocket of her vest, and snapped the headlamp strap around her head, centering the light, with its lavender-film cover, above her eyes.

"Purple will lead the way," Rosie announced.

The girls crossed the parking lot to Clarence and Liza at the truck, leaving Chuck alone with Doug and Marian.

"I'm really sorry about Joseph," he told them.

"Joseph was…he was…" Doug said before his voice trailed off.

"Joseph was a stellar human being, a wonderful person," Marian finished for him.

"He was a good friend to the race, and to us," said Doug.

"It's got to be hard for you to keep the race going," Chuck said, "even if the runners are okay with it."

In the evening light, tears welled in Marian's eyes. "It *is* hard," she said.

Doug swiped his hand across his mouth. "We'll get through it, though." He lifted one of Marian's hands off the computer keyboard and held it in his own. "Won't we, dear?"

She nodded, sniffling. Her eyes went to the screen of the

second computer—the one that, Chuck by now knew, tracked the race's betting activity, and withdrew her hand from Doug's. "We don't have any other choice."

Doug looked at Chuck, sadness in his eyes. "It was an accident. An unfortunate event."

"Liza thinks it most likely was an asthma attack," Chuck said.

Marian and Doug nodded together. Clearly, they'd considered the same thing.

"The dust keeps getting thicker," Doug said. "Every year is worse than the year before. We've debated rerouting the race away from the lakebed. Maybe we waited too long."

"No one has had any problems before, though," Marian said. "It could've been the direction the wind was blowing this year. Or how hard it was blowing."

"Or something changed in Joseph's immune system," said Doug.

"Whatever it was," said Marian, "we know it was only him. And we know without doubt that he would have wanted us to keep the race going. He'd have been incensed with us if we stopped because of him, and that's exactly what our runners told us when we asked them."

16

Carmelita was seated in her chair taking deep swallows from a bottle of electrolyte drink when Chuck returned from the check-in site. "Have you heard?" she asked, her voice trilling with excitement.

Rosie waved her phone at Chuck. "Mamá just texted. She's only a couple of hours away."

"That sure was fast," he said. He looked at Carmelita. "She really wants to be here for you."

"Rosie told me she's coming. I'm sooo glad," Carmelita said. "It'll be great to see her on the other side of the Cosos."

Chuck eyed the uplift of the Coso Mountains rising to the south. Though the range was thousands of feet lower than the Panamint range farther east, the Cosos were isolated and craggy, broken by deep canyons and sheer ramparts. In the hours ahead, Carmelita would follow Coso Trail south along the face of the range. Then she would leave the trail and cross the range via a pair of unnamed drainages, one up the west side of the mountain divide, the other down the east side.

"First comes tonight, though," Chuck said. "In the dark, off-trail." A shiver passed through him. "I wasn't too worried about tonight's section before the race. But I am now, after everyone got confused at the junction up in the Cerro Gordos in broad daylight."

"Actually," Carmelita said, "the junction was pretty obvious, even with the twisted arrow. Matt must've been going too fast and missed it. By the time I got there, he had come back on the road and he and the others were just ahead of me. It was a stroke of luck, really, for me to catch up with them."

"Tonight, after dark, will be different."

"I'll be fine. I've studied the map, like, a zillion times. I've pretty much got it memorized." She took a bite of peanut-butter-and-jelly sandwich, chewed, and washed it down with a slug of electrolyte drink.

"How are your legs?" Liza asked her.

"Good."

"Your feet?"

"No hot spots yet. Fingers crossed. I'll do fresh socks in the morning like we planned." She extended her legs and wiggled her feet back and forth. "The shoes are doing great."

"Hard to believe you've already run more than two whole marathons," Liza said.

"Jogged," Carmelita clarified.

"Slow and steady wins the race," said Rosie.

"Except the goal isn't to win," said Chuck. "It's just to finish."

"Winning wouldn't be bad, though," Rosie said. She turned to Carmelita. "Would it?"

Carmelita looked at her feet, stretched out before her. "No," she admitted, "it wouldn't."

"See?" Rosie said to Chuck.

He rested a hand on Carmelita's shoulder. "Rosie's right about the slow-and-steady part. You're doing great so far. More than great."

Carmelita shoved the last of the PB&J into her mouth. Liza handed her another. Across the parking lot, Kelsey and Matt jogged away from their respective aid stations, the first of the racers to return to the course.

Chuck's phone buzzed in his pocket. The call was from Tabitha. He turned away and put the phone to his ear.

"I met with the board and filled them in," she said when he answered. "I'm all set to head your way tomorrow. What time were you thinking?"

Caught up in the race, he'd forgotten all about their plan to meet at the kilns.

He gave his head a brisk shake, reorienting himself.

Based on previous years' times, the race leaders—Carmelita included, assuming she continued to do well—would pass the kilns tomorrow evening, after passing through the race's fourth and final check-in point at the mouth of Wildrose Canyon late in the day.

He glanced at Carmelita as she chewed a bite of her sandwich. He hadn't realized how all-consuming the race would be. He should have waited until the competition was over to meet Tabitha and show her the human remains—though her excitement was gratifying, reminding him of his own exhilaration upon discovering the tooth and bone fragment two days ago.

Janelle would be on hand tomorrow to provide added support for Carmelita, along with Rosie, Clarence, and Liza. That would give him the opportunity to slip away long enough to meet Tabitha at the kilns.

"How about tomorrow afternoon at four?" he suggested.

"Perfect. I'll head out in the morning and meet you there," she said, signing off.

Over the next ten minutes, while Carmelita continued to eat and drink, Waitimu, Domenico, and Hannah left their aid stations one after another, and more runners arrived at the highway and checked in with Marian and Doug.

Margot set out, followed closely by Astrid. Carmelita remained seated, sipping and chewing. After a full fifteen minutes, she stood and strapped on her replenished running vest. She turned on her headlamp and aimed it at Rosie. "Is it working?"

Rosie gave her a thumbs-up. "It looks like a glowing purple diamond in the middle of your forehead."

"The purple worked great last night," she said, clicking the light off. "Bright enough to see, but not too bright."

Liza pointed at her vest. "I put an extra set of batteries in your back pocket."

"Thanks."

"Hydration?" Chuck asked her.

Carmelita patted the vest's front pockets, bulging with soft bottles of glucose water. "Check."

"Calories?"

She patted the rear pocket, resting against the small of her back. Foil snack wrappers and gel packets crackled beneath her touch. "Check."

She drew a breath through her flared nostrils, her eyes on the trail leading south into the desert from the highway. "Time for the Long First Night."

The ruggedness of the Coso Mountains would reduce the racers' pace to half the speed they'd maintained through the first two segments of the race, making the crossing of the Cosos the second slowest stretch of the race, behind only the precipitous climb up and over the Panamint divide on the final night of the competition, and earning the first night of the race its own moniker.

There was no opportunity for crews to meet their runners at any point over the next thirty-five miles through the mountainous wilderness area. Instead, from dusk tonight until dawn tomorrow, racers would run the lengthiest stage of the race entirely on their own.

"Tonight may be long, but it won't be endless," Chuck told her. "We'll see you first thing in the morning on the other side of the mountains."

Clarence wrapped Carmelita in a bear hug. "You got this," he declared, stepping back.

Carmelita waved at Rosie's upraised phone. "See you tomorrow, peeps."

Pivoting, she crossed the parking lot and loped down the trail, the low evening sun throwing her shadow far across the sparse bunches of ricegrass sprouting on either side of the rocky path.

17

Chuck gnawed his lip, his eyes on Carmelita as she jogged away. "I'm not sure how I'm going to make it through tonight."

"Don't say that," Rosie said as she filmed Carmelita's departure. "It sounds bad."

"I'm just being honest."

"Carm's doing great. She'll do great tonight, too."

When Carmelita disappeared in the deepening dusk, Rosie tucked her phone away. "I can't wait for Mamá to get here," she said.

"Me, either," Chuck agreed.

He looked down the trail after Carmelita. Janelle's impending arrival would do all of them good—Carmelita especially. Seeing her mother on the far side of the Coso Mountains was sure to give her a welcome boost tomorrow morning, after more than twenty-four hours and nearly a hundred miles of nonstop running.

He texted Janelle, directing her to the third check-in point on the outskirts of the tiny community of Darwin, in the middle of the desert plain between the Coso Mountains and the Panamint range. After breaking down the aid station, he hopped behind the wheel of the truck and drove east with Rosie, Clarence, and Liza, the setting sun behind them, Death Valley National Park ahead.

A few miles before the highway crossed into the park, he turned south on the deserted county road leading to Darwin, population fifty. It was nearly dark when they arrived at the remote outpost, the dusky purple sky broken by pinpricks of stars. As in Keeler, no one stirred outside Darwin's handful of houses and mobile homes lining half a dozen gravel lanes on either side of the county road.

He pulled onto an open patch of ground on the far side of Darwin. The bladed expanse of sand was designated as the race's third check-in point. Support crews of the other lead racers had already arrived at the site. The Team Chatten minivan was parked on the far side of the bulldozed plot. Chuck braked the truck to a stop on the near side of the plot, as far from Rick as possible.

There was just enough cell service in Darwin for him to check Carmelita's progress on the real-time map. She continued to hold her own, not far behind the leaders.

He unfolded cots beside the truck, set up an extra camp table and opened a propane stove on it, and placed a lantern beside the stove. He emptied canned stew into a cook pot and set the pot on the stove burner.

The warm glow of the lantern enveloped the cots and table as evening gave way to night. Rosie eyed the map on her phone while Chuck stirred the stew. Its meaty aroma filled the air, reminding him how hungry he was.

"Carm's still in eighth place," Rosie reported. "Really close behind the first seven."

"Is Kelsey still in the lead?" he asked.

"Yep. Matt, Waitimu, Domenico, and Hannah are right behind him. Then Margot. Then, after a gap, Carm is right behind Astrid."

"How far is she from the turnoff to the drainage?"

Rosie brought her phone to her eyes. "I'm not sure. Can you tell, Uncle Clarence?"

Clarence studied his phone. "A few miles. Three, maybe four."

"That's where she's going to make her move," Chuck said. "The section where the race leaves the trail is her big chance, and she knows it."

"Why's that?" Liza asked.

"She said the off-trail part should play to her footwork strengths, like Smelter Mountain," he explained, referring to a rocky peak rising at the edge of downtown Durango.

In preparation for the trail-less portion of the Whitney to Death 150, Carmelita had run the rugged route that led from downtown to the top of the peak numerous times, leaping from rock to rock on her repeated climbs and descents of the mountain.

"Carm studied the split times of the other racers over the last few years," Chuck continued. "Everyone slows way down during the off-trail segment up and over the Cosos. With all her practice runs on Smelter, she's hoping the Coso crossing will be difference-maker for her. But one slip in the dark, one twisted ankle…"

Rosie's phone chimed, signaling an incoming message. She checked its screen. "Mamá just turned off the highway!" she cried. "She's almost here!"

Headlights of an approaching car lit the paved road through Darwin a few minutes later. Rosie ran to the side of the road, waved the car down, and jogged alongside it back to the truck. Janelle climbed out of her mini-SUV and entered the glow of the lantern. She embraced Chuck, then pulled Rosie to her.

"The gang's all here!" Clarence cheered.

"Except for Carm," Rosie said, stepping back from her mother.

Clarence plucked his phone from his pocket and waggled it at his sister. "Eighth place. Your daughter is doing fantastico."

"I checked on her every time I stopped on the way here. She's crushing it," Janelle agreed.

"Dad thinks she's about to *really* crush it," said Rosie.

"That's what Carm thinks," Chuck clarified. "Or hopes, anyway."

"I hope so, too," said Janelle.

She pulled on an insulated flannel shirt as an extra layer against the encroaching chill of the desert night and tossed her long, straight, black hair over her shoulder. She was slender and petite, her almond eyes aglow in the light of the camp lantern.

Smiling, Chuck again drew her to him, surprised by the weight that had instantly lifted from his shoulders upon her arrival. He hadn't realized how singularly responsible he'd been feeling for Carmelita as the race played out.

"It's good to have you with us," he told her.

"I'm glad I could get out here," she said.

Chuck pulled her tight against his side. "You're gonna love seeing her in the morning. She's doing great—strong, controlled, staying within herself, but pushing herself, too."

"Plus," said Rosie, "she's with Astrid, which really helps for tonight."

"Astrid?" Janelle asked.

Rosie nodded emphatically. "She's the best."

"Well, then, I'm glad for both of them." Janelle sniffed the night air. "Something smells good."

Chuck let go of her and filled and handed out bowls of stew. As they ate, Chuck, Rosie, Clarence, and Liza brought Janelle up to speed on the race—the harrowing start, when Rick's minivan had struck Doug; the encounter at the mouth of Portal Canyon, when Carmelita had slowed to help Darlene; and Carmelita's advance through the pack to reach the lead runners, aided in part by the confusion among Matt and the other leaders at the junction in the Cerro Gordo Mountains. Chuck concluded with the news of Joseph's collapse on the bed of Owens Lake and his subsequent death on the way to the hospital.

Janelle's mouth fell open. "He *died*?"

"Dad was going to make Carm quit the race," Rosie said.

"I barely mentioned it," Chuck said. "I…we…decided it was Carm's decision to make."

"All of the racers took a vote on their phones while they were running," said Rosie. "They agreed with Doug and Marian to keep going."

Janelle looked at Clarence and Liza. "The two of you are okay with this?"

"Sí," said Clarence.

Liza nodded, resting a hand on Clarence's beefy forearm. "Everything points to Joseph's death being the result of an asthma attack, a one-off. It's a tragedy, but…"

Janelle looked up at the night sky. Chuck followed her eyes. Thousands of stars dotted the black inverted bowl above them, the Milky Way a curtain-like swath directly over their heads.

Janelle groaned. "I don't know how I'm going to make it through tonight."

Rosie smiled. "Dad already said the same thing. I guess that's why tonight is called the Long First Night."

"It'll be shorter for Carm," said Chuck, "if she does what she's hoping to do."

Rosie tapped at her phone. "She just moved ahead of Astrid!" she exclaimed. "And she hasn't even left the trail yet."

"Seventh place!" Clarence said, clenching his fist.

Chuck eyed his phone. "Kelsey's less than a mile from the drainage. Carm and the others are right behind him."

He closed his eyes, picturing Carmelita running through the dark desert, step after step after step. He groaned, just as Janelle had a moment ago. Tonight truly was going to be long.

18

Carmelita felt good. She couldn't believe how good she felt, in fact.

Everyone she'd questioned before the Whitney to Death 150 had said her body would let her know at the halfway point in the race—right about now—if it was prepared for the brutal second half of the competition to come.

Sometimes, she'd learned, racers who had trained well and were fully conditioned would bonk in the middle of the competition for no apparent reason, while less prepared runners, who had battled illnesses or injuries in the lead-up to the race, would sail through the latter half of the competition, light on their feet to the very end.

Fortunately, she had suffered neither illness nor injury during her training—though she'd come perilously close to hurting herself a few weeks ago, when she'd slipped and fallen while descending a muddy trail outside Durango in the middle of a sleet storm. She'd tucked her shoulder and rolled through the fall, an instinctive act aimed at self-preservation. Surprisingly, her tactic had worked. She'd performed a complete head-over-heels tumble in the middle of the trail and wound up seated upright in the path, slathered in mud but unhurt.

She had climbed to her feet and continued down the mountain at a slower pace, inching her way through the storm, and had adopted a shorter stride on wet trails for the remainder of her training runs.

She had departed from the starting line in Portal Canyon this morning in great physical condition, and she continued to feel physically strong now, seventy-five miles into the race, holding her position a hundred feet behind Astrid as darkness fell over the Coso Mountains.

Ahead, Astrid's feet pounded the surface of the trail and her breaths came in harsh gasps. Every few dozen steps, the Marine issued a sharp curse.

"Come on, Astrid!" she urged herself, loud enough for Carmelita to hear from behind. "This is *supposed* to be hard. Failure is not an option. You hear me? It is *not* an option! We're almost halfway there. Halfway! And we're gonna slay the second half. It's mind over matter, girl, just mind over matter."

Carmelita held her place behind Astrid as night fell, taking advantage of the relative smoothness of the trail to squeeze packets of energy gel into her mouth and wash the cloyingly sweet syrup down her throat with swigs of TrailFire.

She tucked her bottle and empty gel packets into her vest, clicked on her headlamp, and checked her total distance on her GPS watch. Before the race, she'd memorized the mileage points of every junction along the race route. The intersection of Coso Trail with the unnamed drainage was at mile 75.4, less than a mile from here according to her watch.

She lengthened her stride and came up on Astrid. The Marine stepped aside, allowing her to pass.

"You go, girl," Astrid said, returning to the trail behind her.

Several hundred yards ahead, the lead runners wound through the desert scrub, their headlamps flickering in the darkness.

"We're close to them," Astrid said.

"Not for long," said Carmelita.

"What's the matter? Are you hurting?"

"Just the opposite. I'm feeling goooood," Carmelita said, drawing out the word. "How about you?"

Astrid grunted. "I ain't gonna lie. I'm feelin' it. But *feelin'* it and *failin'* it are two different things."

"Because failure is not an option."

"You got that right, girl."

Carmelita descended Coso Trail into the drainage a few minutes later. At the bottom of the wash, where the trail crossed the dry stream bed and ascended the slope on the other side, she turned up the rocky ravine, leaving the established path behind. Astrid followed, still close on her heels.

A quarter mile up the stream bed, the lights of the lead runners bounced off the walls of the gorge as the leaders ascended the drainage toward the Coso divide.

Carmelita swallowed, tasting the last of the syrupy goo at the back of her throat. This was the point in the race she'd been looking forward to for months.

She dug her toes into the loose gravel blanketing the bottom of the wash, launching herself forward. Where the gravel gave way to jumbled boulders, she leapt from rock to rock like a mountain goat, speeding up the ravine, just as she'd told Clarence she would.

That had been on a gray afternoon in March, when her uncle had joined her for her cool-down session after one of her training runs. She had jogged slowly on the paved riverside path through Durango, allowing her muscles to loosen after her lengthy run on dirt trails in the mountains above town, while Clarence slogged alongside her, huffing and puffing.

She told Clarence about her plan to increase her pace in the drainages leading up and down the Coso divide, just as she'd already described her idea to Chuck and her mother.

"When you leave the trail and speed up, are you gonna go as fast as you are now?" Clarence asked.

She laughed.

"I mean it," he said. "This is my top speed, sobrina."

Before Liza had entered his life, Clarence had joined Carmelita for weekly jogs, dropping a few pounds in the process.

Since he'd begun spending all his free time with his girlfriend, however, his runs with Carmelita had fallen by the wayside.

Carmelita laughed harder. "It's been a while since we jogged together, hasn't it?"

"Sí," he admitted. "Liza works her tail off, twenty-four seven, when she's on the river, so she's ready to take it easy when she's home." His face cracked open in a grin. "And if she wants to take it easy with me, who am I to deny her the opportunity?"

"Lucky you."

"Lucky me is right." He drew a breath. "So when, exactly, do you plan to hit the afterburners?"

She'd described the race route to him segment by segment as they'd jogged together along the path, nodding to passing walkers and bicyclists.

"When I start up the drainage to cross the Coso Mountains," she said. "That'll be my chance."

"To do what?"

"To win."

Clarence snorted.

"I'm serious, Uncle Clarence."

"The Whitney to Death 150 will be your first ultra race *ever*."

"I know how to win. I've done it lots of times."

"Verdad. But those were rock climbing competitions, not ultra races."

"I'm better at ultra running than I am at climbing."

Carmelita had been ten years old when her mother had married Chuck after meeting him through Clarence only a few weeks previously. After the wedding, Janelle had moved with the girls from urban Albuquerque, New Mexico, to mountain-town Durango, where the four of them had begun their new life together in Chuck's small Victorian home.

Though just a kid, Carmelita had recognized what a big deal it had been for her mother to leap into the unknown with Chuck, determined as she was to create a better life for her daughters and herself in Colorado. Carmelita, in turn, had made herself into a miniature version of her mother, determined and serious-minded, a goal-setter who pushed herself in everything she did.

When Chuck introduced Carmelita to competitive rock climbing, she threw herself into the sport, spending long hours at the indoor rock gym after school, and winning competition after competition on weekends. When she took up trail running to cross-train for climbing, she quickly came to love the new sport more—its extreme demands matching those she expected of herself in all other facets of her life. She pushed herself hard on every training run, and her per-mile times steadily dropped. She turned to apps that compared times posted by runners on various trail segments, with the best splits deemed the "fastest known times," or FKTs, for the segments. As she improved, her times on a number of trail segments around Durango surpassed the FKTs posted by nationally ranked runners.

Clarence tapped Carmelita on the arm as they jogged on the path.

"If you're better at trail running than climbing, you must be pretty good," he said. "But I'm still surprised your mamá and Chuck are letting you sign up for one of the toughest trail races on earth for your very first one."

"That's because they get it," Carmelita said.

"You mean, they get *you*."

"Exactamente."

Janelle and Chuck had offered their support to Carmelita when she'd shared with them her desire to apply for and, if accepted, compete in the Whitney to Death 150. They told her they knew the sport of trail running aligned perfectly with her natural athleticism, her competitive drive, and her willingness to work hard over long periods to achieve goals she set for herself.

But when it came to the Whitney to Death 150 in particular, the one thing they did not know about was the money.

19

After dinner in Darwin, Rosie lay down on one of the cots and pulled a sleeping bag up around her shoulders. Clarence kept his eyes glued to his phone, and Liza showed Janelle how she'd arranged the food, drinks, and gear Carmelita would need when she arrived in the morning, at the end of the Long First Night.

When Doug and Marian pulled into the check-in point, Chuck helped them set up their site. After everything was in place, Marian pulled herself up to the tech table in her folding chair and eyed the dual laptops. The light from the screens cast a blue sheen across her face. Chuck looked over her shoulder as she brought up the real-time race map on one of the computers and clicked the dots of various racers glowing on the screen.

"The leaders have left the trail," she reported, eyeing the computer. "They're starting up the drainage."

The dots of the race leaders glowed in a line on the screen, close behind one another, superimposed over topo lines indicating the ravine leading to the top of the Coso divide. Marian clicked each dot, working her way backward, first revealing Kelsey's number, then Matt's, then those of the other lead runners in the same order as when they'd left the second check-in point beside the highway: Waitimu, Domenico, Hannah, and Margot.

"They're staying together," Chuck noted.

"There's no need for anyone to try to take off on their own yet," Doug said. "Crossing the Cosos tonight is all about survival. The real push will come tomorrow. That's when the leaders will start to duke it out."

Rick strode up to the check-in site. "What the hell's going on?" he snarled at Marian, the camp light on the table capturing his angry glare.

Doug stepped between Rick and Marian. "What are you talking about?"

"The betting. It's off the charts."

"How do you know that?"

"It's my job to know it."

"We don't make any of our numbers public."

"The betting sites do. On every site I've checked, Margot's numbers are through the roof, and they keep going higher the longer she hangs with Kelsey."

"She's popular, I'll grant you that."

"Her popularity means dollars in your pocket. Lots of them."

"We don't make as much money off the betting as you might think."

"Don't snowball me," Rick snapped. "You've got to be rolling in it—thanks to my daughter."

"Actually, Kelsey is the real betting engine," Doug said. "His second win two years ago attracted a lot of big-money bettors. They love repeat winners. They make most of their money by betting big when there's a solid favorite. His numbers took off when he went for his third win last year."

"He came through. He won."

"Which explains why his numbers are even higher this year. The big spenders are pulling for him to four-peat. Meanwhile, the little guys are betting against him, figuring he can't keep winning forever."

"The second bunch is right. Margot's going to take him out this year, I promise."

"You can bet all the money you want on her to do just that."

"No, no, no," Rick said, shaking his head. "What I'm saying is, Margot deserves a cut of what *you're* making. All the runners deserve a cut, based on their individual betting numbers, on top of the little bit you give the podium finishers. You're making a fortune off the race, but the runners are the ones doing all the work."

"No one's forcing them to run. They sign up for the race. They commit to it. That's what they're in it for—the commitment, the competition."

"More money certainly wouldn't hurt."

Doug huffed at Rick. "Marian and I spend the whole year preparing for the race. It takes every spare minute we have over the entire twelve months to pull it off. Other than our payouts to podium finishers, we use all the betting money we make to buy equipment and pay for improvements like this year's real-time map."

"That map has got to be making you tons more money this year by letting people bet all along the way."

"That's what we're hoping. If it turns out to be true, we should be able to share more of the proceeds next year."

"While your runners remain poor and unfunded this year," Rick snapped.

Chuck addressed Doug and Marian. "I'm fine with the two of you keeping the betting money for yourselves. The race is yours. You provide the ultimate competition for runners like my daughter, and you deserve to be paid for it."

"The runners deserve to be paid, too," Rick griped.

Chuck turned to him. "Like Doug said, you can place all the bets you want on all the runners you want."

"I already did. I bet on Margot to win."

"If she does," said Doug, "you'll make plenty of money."

"Oh, she'll win, all right." Rick directed a smirk at Chuck. "Something tells me you don't have the same faith in your daughter."

"I have plenty of faith in her. But she's not in it for the money."

"Ha," said Rick. "It's always about the money. For *everybody*."

20

Carmelita accelerated up the drainage in the night, her thoughts on the financial opportunity she'd identified upon reading about the huge betting amounts the sport of trail running attracted.

The opportunity, she realized, would be available to her only once, only if she competed in the correct race—and only if she won.

After studying the various ultra races held around the country each year, she zeroed in on the Whitney to Death 150 for two reasons: the race's off-trail sections matched up well with her climbing and scrambling abilities, and the race was small, with only a few dozen competitors, giving her a reasonable shot at winning.

Having identified the best race to compete in, she faced a key problem she hoped her Uncle Clarence would be willing to solve for her.

"There's something Mamá and Chuck don't know about the Whitney to Death 150," she confided to him during their jog on the paved path in Durango. "They don't know why I picked it as my first ultra."

He stopped in the middle of the path and turned to her. "What are you saying?"

She halted and faced him. "I chose it as my first race for a particular reason."

His brows drew together between his dark eyes. "Talk to me, sobrina."

She told him that the race was popular among bettors, and that it was small, with only forty or so competitors. She explained to him how well suited she felt she was for the race's off-trail segments. "Which means," she said, "that even though it'll be my first race ever, I think I'll have a decent chance of winning."

Clarence scratched his forehead. "I'm afraid I'm not following you."

She held her uncle's gaze. "I've never posted any of my training times online. Not once. But compared to the times posted by others, mine are solid. Like, *really* solid."

"Knowing you, I'm sure they are."

"For my first race, because I haven't posted any of my times, no one will know who I am."

"So?"

"So, in a small race like the Whitney to Death 150, with only forty or so runners, the odds for a podium finish will never be very high, meaning the payoff on a bet for me to finish in the top three wouldn't be very high, either. But to win…"

"*Ohhh,*" Clarence said, his eyes widening. "Now I get it. It's about the betting." His face broke open in a broad grin, his teeth gleaming. "Hell, I'll bet on you myself."

"I appreciate that. But, no. I don't want to be worried about having to win for you or anybody else. Whereas for me, it's a different story."

His smile disappeared. "Let me get this straight. You want to bet on yourself, but you want to be the only one to do it, and you want to bet on yourself only to win?"

"You got it," she said. "A guy named Kelsey McCloud has won the race the last three years in a row. He's the heavy favorite to win again this year, which makes for even better—which is to say, longer—odds for all the other runners. That's especially true for an unknown like me." Carmelita felt the corners of her mouth lifting into a smile of her own. "In past years, bets on unknown, first-time racers to win the Whitney to Death 150 would have paid off at close to hundred-to-one odds."

Clarence's eyes bulged. "A hundred to one?"

"No one has ever done it, though."

"But if they did, that would mean a $1 bet to win would pay $100."

"And a $3,000 bet would pay $300,000—the cost of four years of college. *Private* college."

"Wait, wait, wait," Clarence said, waving his hands. "Un momento. Am I hearing you right?" He looked up and down the path, as if assuring no one was listening. "You honestly want to bet on yourself as a way to pay for college?"

"Bet *and* win." She allowed her smile to spread across her face. "My own self-funded scholarship." Then her smile faltered. "But Mamá and Chuck won't do it for me. I know they won't. They'd say I was putting too much pressure on myself."

"And they'd be right," Clarence said. "But Dios mío, that's a lot of dinero." He shrugged and his grin returned. "I'm in. Liza will be, too, I'm sure of it. What do you need from us?"

Early in Clarence's relationship with Liza, Carmelita had maintained her distance from her uncle's girlfriend. Over time, however, Liza had proven herself a true soulmate to Clarence, and Carmelita had learned to share with Liza the time she'd previously enjoyed with her only uncle. These days, Carmelita and Liza were tight, with Liza offering a welcome ear to Carmelita in addition to that of her mother.

"I've got $1,500 to put up," Carmelita said. "But I'd like to bet $3,000, if you'd be willing to front me the other half."

"I'd love to. I'm sure Liza would love to, too."

"I'll pay you back if I don't win."

"Are you sure you'd be okay losing that much money?"

"Sure, I'm sure." She scrunched her nose, looking her uncle in the eye. "The thing is, I'm as happy about the bet for the fun of it as I am for the possible payoff. If—as is almost certain—I don't win the race, then fine, I'll survive. But it'll be great to be thinking, during the race, about the *potential* the bet gives me. I mean, $300,000. What's not fun to be thinking about that?" She smiled. "I know how hard the race will be. The bet will lighten my load a little bit, so I can run just a little bit faster."

Clarence grinned back at her. "And maybe even win."

Carmelita extended her hand, which disappeared in Clarence's big paw as they shook.

Now, she whispered to herself in the darkness at the foot of the drainage leading to the Coso divide. *Now, now, now.*

She rocketed up the gorge ahead of Astrid, trusting her feet to find the right landing places in the stream bed with lightning quickness.

"Take it to 'em, girl!" Astrid cried, falling back.

Carmelita increased her speed where the ravine steepened near the top of the ridge. Maintaining her blistering pace, she closed in on five of the six lead runners, whose headlamps were tightly grouped as they climbed the final few hundred feet of the gorge close behind one another. A single runner had broken away from the others and, headlamp aglow, was running solo, out front, to the top of the divide.

The walls of the ravine closed in on Carmelita and the second-through-sixth-place runners, who now were just ahead of her. Above, the ridge line marking the divide cut a straight line across the star-filled sky. She raced toward the head of the gorge, head down, intent on catching the runners before they topped the ridge.

She glanced up. She was only a few feet behind the five racers grouped behind the leader. The steady breaths of the runners and the crunch of their shoes in the rocky earth were the only sounds in the otherwise still night.

Suddenly, the quiet was broken by a loud buzzing noise that filled the gorge, reverberating off the walls of the ravine.

One of the racers in front of Carmelita screeched in terror.

PART THREE

“Since the day settlers first came to our area, we’ve been pushed off our lands, we’ve been robbed of our water.”

—Dean Tonenna, Kootzaduka’a botanist

21

The runner's cry and the buzzing sound resonated in the night.

"Snakes!" another of the racers ahead of Carmelita screamed.

"They're...they're everywhere!" a third runner cried out.

Amid the yells, the buzzing noise continued, filling Carmelita's ears.

For an instant, her headlamp illuminated Margot scampering past her and back down the drainage.

A racer in front of Carmelita crumpled to the ground. Carmelita saw in the light of her headlamp that the fallen runner was Hannah Rinkl.

"Get back!" Hannah cried. She leaned forward, moaning and grasping her lower leg.

Carmelita ran to Hannah's side, trembling, her breath caught in her throat.

"Look out!" Hannah cried, swinging her headlamp in an arc and lighting the ground around them.

A blur of movement shot toward them from the darkness. The fully outstretched body of a snake entered the light of Hannah's headlamp. A pair of fangs extended from the upper jaw of the reptile's wide-open mouth, glinting in the light.

The snake flew toward Carmelita's lower leg. Before she could so much as twitch a muscle, it sank its fangs into the bare skin of her calf above her sock.

"Ahhhh!" she screeched. She shook her foot, but the snake remained attached to her leg, its fangs impaling her skin. She grabbed the reptile behind its head and yanked, freeing herself.

She hurled the snake away from her and tracked its departure with her headlamp as it slithered away. It was several feet long, its body as big around as her forearm.

"That's the one that bit me, too," Hannah said, still huddled over her leg. "I never lost sight of it."

Carmelita crouched beside her. A pair of red puncture wounds, half an inch apart, showed on the skin of Hannah's lower leg, just above her ankle sock. Globules of venom, each the size of a pea, showed beneath the twin wounds, indicating she'd received a large dose of the snake's poison.

Carmelita looked down at her own leg, her breaths coming in quick gasps. Puncture wounds marked the skin of her lower calf, but no venom showed beneath the site of the punctures.

Tumbling rocks struck one another higher in the ravine. She looked up. The lights of the four remaining lead runners gyrated wildly as they ran away in different directions, sending stones rolling from the sides of the gorge. Two runners ascended the south side of the drainage. Another climbed the north side. The race leader, who'd been gaining ground on the others, raced straight up the last of the incline. All four runners disappeared over the top of the ridge, their headlamps winking out one by one as they began the descent on the far side of the divide.

Carmelita remained at Hannah's side. Though the snake that had bitten both of them had slithered away into the darkness, the buzzing of other snakes continued around them, loud in the night air.

"Don't move," Astrid said from several feet behind them.

Carmelita bit down so hard on her lower lip that she tasted blood. "I'm so glad you're here," she whispered, her voice quivering.

"Well, I'm not so sure *I* am," Astrid drawled.

Carmelita swiveled her head, sweeping her headlamp in a circle. Her light illuminated a dozen rattlesnakes surrounding her and Hannah on three sides. She gulped, her mouth going dry, and dug her fingers into Hannah's shoulders. The snakes were less than a dozen feet away. The distinctive squares on their backs were dark green, marking them as Mojave green rattlesnakes native to the Mojave Desert. The Mojave greens around Carmelita and Hannah were coiled and ready to strike, their rattles buzzing on the ends of their tails.

"One of the snakes bit Hannah," Carmelita told Astrid. "We have to get her out of here."

"It bit you, too," Hannah reminded her.

"I know, I know, I know," Carmelita acknowledged in a quick burst. She again checked her wound. No pain emanated from the site of the bite, and no globules of venom showed beneath the fang marks.

Hannah moaned, massaging her leg.

Carmelita checked Hannah's wound. The area around the bite was beginning to swell.

"I think Hannah got all the snake's venom," Carmelita said to Astrid. "It looks like I got a dry bite. I'm all right, but Hannah's bite is getting worse."

"Stay where you are until I distract them," Astrid said. "As soon as I draw enemy fire, the two of you will need to *move, move, move*. Got it?"

Carmelita nodded, stifling her breathing. Hannah leaned her head back against Carmelita, grimacing, her face pale.

Astrid's light went out. Rocks knocked against one another as she climbed the side of the ravine in the darkness, bypassing the snakes gathered in the bottom of the gorge.

"Okay, kill your lights," she called from above.

Carmelita clicked off her headlamp, then Hannah's. Inky blackness filled the drainage.

"Now!" Astrid yelled. "Go, go, go!"

Her headlamp came on and its light flashed across the bottom of the ravine. "Here snakes, snakes, snakes!" she cried out to the coiled reptiles. "Here snakies!"

The reptiles stopped rattling in mid-buzz, as if startled into silence by Astrid's cry. In the sudden quiet, Carmelita dragged Hannah backward down the wash.

Astrid's headlamp lit the silent snakes, their snouts turned toward her and their tails raised and motionless. She dashed toward them, continuing to command their attention. The buzzing of the snakes' rattles recommenced as they focused on her threatening approach.

Carmelita covered twenty feet with Hannah, halting when they were well away from the rattlesnakes.

Astrid sprinted past the rattlers, which did not strike out at her, and continued down the drainage to Carmelita and Hannah. She skidded to a halt and stood over them.

"Why'd you stop?" she demanded. "We've got to keep moving. We've got to get away from them."

"We're far enough," Carmelita said, turning her headlamp back on. The buzzing of the snakes' rattles died away and the night grew quiet once more. "They're Mojave green rattlesnakes. They're like the western diamondbacks that rattle at me when I'm on my training runs back home. They just want us to stay away from them. They won't come after us."

"You sure about that, girl?" Astrid asked.

"It's Hannah I'm worried about."

Hannah lay on the ground before Carmelita, her head back and her eyes closed.

Footfalls approached from lower in the drainage. A headlamp clicked on and Margot spoke from beneath the light as she returned up the ravine. "Are you all right?"

"A rattlesnake bit Hannah," Carmelita said. She aimed her headlamp at her calf. Still no swelling showed around the fang punctures. "I got bitten, too, but it looks like I got a dry bite."

"What's a dry bite?" Margot asked.

"The same snake that bit Hannah bit me. Luckily for me—

but not for Hannah—it looks like it injected all its venom into Hannah's leg. When it bit me, it didn't have any poison left."

Astrid aimed her headlamp at Carmelita's lower leg. "Are you sure about that?"

"Rattlesnake poison acts fast. We'll know for sure in just a few minutes. But, yeah, so far so good. I think I'm fine."

"But Hannah's *not* fine," Astrid said to Margot, turning her headlamp to the fallen runner.

"Well, that's not good," Margot squeaked.

Astrid grunted. "You almost knocked me over when you ran away."

"One injured runner is enough." Margot crouched next to Hannah and looked at Carmelita. "Will she die?"

"I'm right here," Hannah said through clenched teeth. "And no, I'm not planning on it."

"What about your phone, Astrid?" Carmelita asked. "We can use its 911 emergency satellite function."

"Sorry, no can do," Astrid replied. "I knew there wasn't any cell service in the Cosos, so I left it with my crew at the last stop."

"I'm phone-free, too," Margot said.

"Me, too," said Hannah, grimacing.

"Do we need to suck out the poison or put on a tourniquet or something?" Margot asked.

"They covered snakebites in my field first-aid class with the Corps," said Astrid. "There's no more of that tourniquet stuff or cutting the skin and sucking out the venom. You're supposed to just keep the victim calm and get them to a hospital ASAP." She looked up the drainage, where the rattlesnakes waited silently in the darkness. "I can buddy-carry Hannah down the gully a ways to get farther away from the snakes. We'll wait there and warn the other runners as they come up from below."

"We'll help," Carmelita said.

"You two are so teeny you couldn't buddy-carry a fly. The

best way for you to help is to get to the check-in point at Darwin as fast as you can. That'll be quicker than going back to the highway. You know the whole story. The sooner you get there, the sooner you'll be able to make sure help is headed this way." She hesitated. "But…"

"But what?" Margot asked.

Astrid looked at Carmelita. "Your bite."

"I'm okay," Carmelita insisted. "It's not swelling."

"It's not swelling *yet*."

"The venom starts acting right away."

"What if you're wrong?"

"There are plenty of rattlesnakes along the trails I train on at home. People get bitten every now and then. Dry bites are pretty common."

Astrid looked down at Hannah. "You're sure it was the same snake?"

Hannah nodded, her eyes slitted open. "I couldn't keep my eyes off it. It only crawled off a little ways after it bit me. When Carmelita came, it got her, too."

Astrid aimed her headlamp out at the night. "It's just us. The four guys took off and left us here on our own." She looked back at Carmelita and Margot, her voice taking on a hard edge as she continued. "They don't deserve to win the race. It's up to the two of you to beat them for Hannah and me."

"What about the snakes?" Margot asked, shining her headlamp up the drainage.

The rattlesnakes remained quiet in the ravine.

"You can go around them, like I did before," Astrid said. She bent down, lifted Hannah in her arms, and addressed Carmelita. "I don't want you and Margot out there on your own if your bite starts to swell." She swung her headlamp beam between Carmelita and Margot. "You have to promise me, both of you, that you'll turn around and come back here if it does."

"I promise," Carmelita said.

"Me, too," said Margot.

"Okay," Astrid growled, holding Hannah against her chest.

Carmelita leaned forward, aiming her headlamp at Hannah's ankle. The swelling beneath the puncture wounds was worse than it had been just minutes ago.

"Astrid's right," Margot said to Carmelita. "We have to get help. Besides, Dad will see on the map that I've stopped. He'll be worried."

"He won't be worried," Astrid said. "He'll be pissed."

"That, too," Margot said. She faced Carmelita. "I don't have any choice." Turning away, she angled up the side of the wash. "We're getting help, remember?" she called back as she hurried away.

Carmelita rested a hand on Hannah's arm. "Astrid's got you," she told her.

"I'm in good hands," she murmured, her head against Astrid's shoulder.

"You're in the *best* of hands," Astrid said. She faced Carmelita, clutching Hannah. "You have to catch up with Margot. I don't like the idea of either of you running alone tonight, not with all these snakes around."

"All right," Carmelita conceded. "You win."

"No," said Astrid. "*You* win."

Carmelita angled to the top of the divide behind Margot, bypassing the snakes.

"Do it, girls! Get your butts to Darwin for us!" Astrid shouted as Carmelita dropped off the ridge after Margot. "You hear me? Beat those guys and win this thing for me and Hannah!"

22

Carmelita ran steadily down the drainage on the east side of the divide. The wash was wide and sandy-bottomed, with few rocks. She caught up with Margot after a couple of minutes and they ran together through the darkness, their headlamps casting twin circles of light on the ground in front of them.

No more snakes rattled at them as they descended the broad ravine, but they still were far from the third check-in point. Previous runners had reported mental letdowns after topping out on the Coso divide, when the knowledge struck them that, though the climb was over, much of the Long First Night remained—five trail-less miles down the east drainage, followed by ten trail miles to Darwin.

"I'm scared there'll be more snakes," Margot said, jogging down the wash a step ahead of Carmelita. "Aren't you?"

"That was an anomaly back there," Carmelita replied. "An aberration."

"Oh."

"There won't be any more snakes."

"How can you be so sure?"

"Because they're reptiles. Rattlesnakes are nocturnal in the summertime. They come out at night, when it's not as hot as in the daytime, and when the mice and kangaroo rats they eat are out and about, too. Snakes are ectothermic—they're cold-blooded—which means they have no way of heating themselves. They use their natural surroundings to regulate their body temperature, so in cooler months like now, they come out during the day to warm up."

"Then why were they out at night back there? And why were there so many of them?"

"I think it had to do with brumation."

"Bru-*what*?"

"The snake version of hibernation."

"You sure use a lot of big words."

Carmelita let Margot's comment pass. It wasn't the first time she'd heard it.

"Bears hibernate," she explained. "They sleep through the winter. Rattlesnakes do the same kind of thing, but different, so it has its own name."

"Brumation."

"Now *you're* the one using big words."

Margot laughed.

"Mojave green rattlesnakes are mostly inactive during the winter," Carmelita said. "But they don't entirely go to sleep. And they den up in groups when it's cold. As many as ten or twenty Mojave greens will spend the winter all coiled up together underground for warmth."

"Ewww."

"Well, yeah, I guess. But they don't stay clumped up the whole time. They leave their dens to find water every now and then."

"Ah-ha!" Margot exclaimed as she ran in front of Carmelita. "The ones back there were out because they were thirsty."

"That would explain why they were gathered in the drainage, where there would likely be seeps of water. There's one thing I can't figure out, though. Assuming the snakes wanted water, they still should have come out during the daytime. It's cool at night in the desert in April. That's why Marian and Doug hold the race now instead of July, so all of us racers don't die of heat stroke. But the rattlers were out in the middle of the night back there."

"They came out at night because they were thirsty at night," Margot reasoned. "I wake up at night to get a drink all the time, especially after a long run the day before." She ran a few steps. "It gets lonely on all the training runs we do, don't you think?"

"I guess," Carmelita replied. "I kind of like it, though, being out in the mountains on my own. Before I started running, I trained indoors at a rock gym for climbing competitions. That got old real fast—all the crowds after school, everybody jockeying to climb the best routes. Compared to that, it was a relief to get out on the trails and away from everybody in the gym."

"And away from the smells, I bet."

Carmelita chuckled. "That, too. All the guys smelled like water buffaloes. Or what I would guess water buffaloes smell like, anyway."

Margot laughed. "I'm going to appreciate my training runs on my own a lot more now." She paused. "You live in the Rocky Mountains, right? I didn't know there were rattlesnakes there."

"I live in the southern Rockies, close to the desert, at the northern edge of their range."

"Have you ever been bitten? Before tonight, I mean."

"Nah. They just shake their rattles to warn me they're there, and I get out of the way."

"That's not what happened to Hannah—or you, either—back there."

"Of all the different rattlesnake species, Mojave greens are the most aggressive. When they feel threatened, they go ballistic defending themselves."

"As you and Hannah found out."

"Even so, none of the other runners ahead of her got bitten. When she came along, the snake that bit her had finally had enough."

"You can't really blame it, I guess."

"Snakes don't necessarily want to bite. That's why their bodies are camouflaged, and why they have rattles. The camouflage is their first line of defense, to remain invisible. Their rattles are their second line of defense, to warn anything they think is threatening them. Biting is their last line of defense, which explains why none of them struck Astrid when she ran back through them. Their primary instinct was to stay coiled and not bite her."

"They didn't bite me, either. They let me go."

"You were lucky."

"Not Hannah. Her bite looked really bad."

"It *was* bad," Carmelita agreed. "In addition to being the most aggressive rattlesnake species, Mojave greens are the most poisonous species of rattlesnake in the world, too. Luckily, though, rattlesnake bites are hardly ever fatal, including bites from Mojave greens—as long as the person gets to a hospital in time."

"That's our job."

They increased their pace, racing through the night.

Carmelita glanced around at the darkness pressing in from all sides. Behind her, as the Long First Night wore on, Hannah was involved in a very different kind of race—against the deadly poison circulating through her body.

23

Once again, Chuck stared in disbelief at the race map on his phone. It was later in the evening in Darwin, and for the second time in the competition, the dots denoting the leaders were not following the route in their usual lined-up formation. This time, though, rather than grouping up as they had at the junction in the Cerro Gordo Mountains, the leaders were scattering away from one another in all directions.

"Are you seeing what I'm seeing?" he asked Janelle, his eyes on his screen.

She nodded, staring at her phone. "I can't figure it out."

They sat beside the truck with Clarence and Liza. Rosie was curled in her sleeping bag on her cot. The camp table was lined with their washed stew bowls, and a pot of water steamed on the stove, ready for hot drinks.

Rosie sat up, gathered her sleeping bag around her waist, and checked her phone. "Two are going one way," she said. "Another is going the other way. And someone else is going straight ahead, still on the race route." She tapped at her screen, her fingers flashing in the lantern light. "Those are the four leaders—Kelsey, Matt, Domenico, and Waitimu." She kept tapping. "Hannah is stopped. Margot is going backward."

"And—?" Chuck asked.

"Carm is stopped, too," Rosie said.

"It's kind of like what happened before," he said.

"They straightened that out just fine," Liza reasoned. She held up her phone. "Just like they're doing now."

Chuck checked the map on his screen. Having topped the Coso divide, the four lead runners had returned to the race route and were now heading down the drainage on the east side of the mountains. Behind them, however, four dots remained halted near the top of the west side of the divide.

"Not quite," he said.

"Margot came back," Rosie reported. "Her, Carm, Astrid, and Hannah are all stopped together."

Chuck eyed the unmoving dots on his phone, the muscles at the back of his neck tight as steel bands. The others stared at their phones, too.

Seconds passed. A minute.

"Move," Chuck beseeched the runners. "Please."

As if in answer to his plea, one of the four dots began to ascend the side of the wash to the divide. Before he could even begin to imagine what was going on, a second runner side-hilled to the top of the divide and returned to the route. The first runner to depart from the group moved down the east-side drainage, and the second runner followed the first.

"That's Carmelita!" Rosie cried out. "She's in sixth place now. She's right behind Margot."

After a minute, Carmelita caught up with Margot and the two continued down the drainage together.

"They've teamed up!" Rosie exclaimed.

The other two dots retraced their steps back down the drainage, then halted.

"Astrid and Hannah are stopped again, after they went backward a ways," Rosie said.

Farther back on the race route, a number of trailing runners neared Astrid and Hannah. Additional racers were spread along Coso Trail at the foot of the mountains, approaching the turnoff to the west-side drainage. Chuck clicked on the dot of the last-place runner, who was a few miles out of the second check-in point. Darlene's number appeared above the dot. Just as she'd vowed, she was still in the race.

"Carm and Margot are flying down the divide," Liza reported.

"Something must be wrong with Hannah and Astrid, though," said Rosie. "They're still stopped."

"Something *is* wrong with them," Clarence said. "They've been running for, like, eighty miles. They need a break and they're taking it."

"It's weird, though," said Rosie, "both of them going backward and then stopping at the same time."

"Carm stayed with Darlene when she cut her leg," Chuck said. "Maybe one of them is doing the same for the other."

Rosie tilted her head sideways, studying her screen. "Maybe."

"I don't like it," Janelle said. "Something must've happened up on the divide, when the four lead guys scattered. We have to figure out what it was."

Chuck worked his jaw. "What do you suggest?"

"Maybe Marian and Doug will know."

He glanced around at crew members at the other aid stations. In the light of their camp lanterns, they relaxed in folding chairs, glancing nonchalantly at their phones. It appeared none of them had either picked up on or were concerned about the odd movements of the race leaders over the last few minutes.

"Good idea."

But when Chuck introduced Janelle to Doug and Marian at the race check-in site and she expressed her concerns to them, they politely shrugged her off.

"That's how this thing goes," Doug explained to her. "Every year, we have runners who bonk at the top of the Coso divide. The same thing will happen on the Panamint divide tomorrow night."

"But Hannah was looking so strong," Chuck said.

"I was pulling for her. I thought maybe this would be her year."

"Astrid was doing great, too."

"Frankly," Marian said, "I'm surprised she hung with the frontrunners as long as she did. This is her first year with us, the same as Waitimu, Carmelita, and Margot. To have four newbies in the top ten so deep into the race was a real surprise." She pointed at the map glowing on her computer screen. "And to have the other three of those four still at the front of the pack is truly amazing."

"But there was confusion up on the divide," said Janelle. "The leaders went every which way."

"And then they got back on the race route," Doug said, a hint of annoyance entering his voice. "We're glad to have you joining us for the rest of the race, but there's lots you may not understand yet. For one thing, the racers don't have to stay on the exact race route. They're allowed to leave it, as long as they don't shorten the overall distance. That's in the rules. Sometimes they have no choice—if there's been a trail washout or a collapsed section on one of the old mining roads."

"So you're not going to do anything?"

"What could we possibly do? We're tracking every racer in real time. Everyone is on the course. It's all good."

"But it's *not* all good," Janelle insisted.

"I think we're just going to have to agree to disagree on that."

Back at the truck, Janelle turned to Chuck. "We have to go out there."

"We?"

"You and me. Clarence and Liza and Rosie can stay here." She held Chuck's gaze. "You know as well as I do, we won't be able to sleep while we wait for Carm tonight. We might as well go meet her instead."

"But she's cruising down the drainage. She's in sixth place, right behind Margot. She's doing great. Whatever happened up there on the divide didn't hurt her. If anything, it helped her."

"It's the 'whatever happened up there' part I can't let go of. I know everything's probably all right. I'm sure Astrid and Hannah are just resting, and Carm and Margot are feeding off each other's energy. But there's no harm in heading out on the trail a ways to find out for sure."

Minutes later, Chuck stood beside Janelle, slipping his arms through the shoulder straps of his daypack.

"I can't believe you're going out there," Clarence said.

"Me, either," said Chuck, summoning a weary smile as he turned on his headlamp.

Janelle punched his arm and addressed her brother. "If you'd seen all the stuff I've seen at work, you'd understand. I just want to make sure everyone's okay."

"Spoken like a true paramedic," said Liza.

The trail out of Darwin crossed the plain to the foot of the Coso Mountains. Chuck brought up the real-time map on his phone as he started out on the path with Janelle, checking the positions of the lead runners before he lost cell service beyond the town limits. Janelle strode down the trail ahead of him.

"Astrid and Hannah still aren't moving," he told her. "They're in the same place on the far side of the divide. Carm and Margot are still coming this way, and the lead guys are ahead of them."

The four lead runners were more than fifteen miles from Darwin, moving steadily toward the check-in point. Carm and Margot were half a mile behind them. Chuck worked out the timing in his head.

"We should meet the leaders two or three hours from now," he said. "And Carm and Margot not long after that."

He tucked his phone in his pocket and strode into the night behind Janelle, the lights of Darwin growing dim in the distance behind them. He checked his watch every few minutes, pressing the button to light its face.

An hour passed. Another. The stars glowed more brightly the farther they ventured into the desert. The only sounds were the quiet thumps of their shoes on the trail and their steady breaths as they hiked.

He sucked water from the drink hose extending from the reservoir in his pack and forged onward, mile after mile, behind Janelle.

Nearly three hours after they'd left camp, four headlamps appeared in the distance, headed their way.

"Hey, there!" Janelle called when the lights drew near. "Are you all good?"

"Yep," Kelsey's voice came from beneath the lead headlamp. Controlled breaths from Matt, Domenico, and Waitimu sounded behind him.

"What happened back there? It looked like everyone scattered up on the divide."

"Snakes," said Matt in his Irish accent from a step behind Kelsey. "Rattlers."

"Rattlesnakes? More than one?"

The four male runners halted on the trail in front of Janelle and Chuck.

"Aye, several," Matt said. He spoke between breaths. "You're right, everyone went every which way up there. We're back on track now, though."

"Not everybody."

"What d'you mean?"

"Hannah and Astrid have stopped moving."

"Not good," Matt said. "We'll let them know about the snakes when we get to Darwin. Speaking of which, the sooner we get there…"

The four runners aimed their headlamps down the trail in the direction of the desert outpost. Chuck and Janelle stepped aside and the four race leaders commenced running, sweeping by in a tight group.

"They didn't sound too worried about Hannah and Astrid," Janelle observed.

"They're in a race that has an eighty percent DNF rate," Chuck reasoned. "Plus one death already this year."

"And they're still racing."

"So's Carm."

They returned to the trail and continued south. Chuck fought the desire to pull out his phone and bring up the race map on it, knowing the effort would be futile here, deep in the desert and outside of cell range. He looked past Janelle, willing Carmelita and Margot to appear ahead.

Finally, a pair of headlamps materialized out of the darkness, one close behind the other, approaching from the south. One of the headlamps glowed white, the other purple.

"Carm!" Janelle cried out.

"Mamá?" Carmelita called back. "Is that you? What are you doing here?"

"We've…we're…"

"You brought your phones, right?"

"Of course."

"Use the SOS button to text 911. *Now.*"

Chuck grunted, his gut constricting. Janelle halted in front of him and tapped at her phone. Its face glowed red as the phone's emergency function engaged with an orbiting satellite overhead.

"Are these your *parents*?" Margot, in the lead, asked Carmelita as they stopped before Janelle and Chuck. "Both of them?"

Carmelita's headlamp bobbed as she nodded.

"Did someone get bit?" Chuck asked them.

"Hannah," Margot confirmed.

"It's locked onto our location," Janelle said, looking up from her phone. "It's asking me to text more information. There's a limit of a hundred characters."

"Let me have it," Carmelita said, extending her hand to take the phone. Her thumbs flew across its screen. "There."

She returned the device to Janelle. “I dropped a pin where the responders need to go, up on the ridge where Hannah and Astrid will be.”

She outlined the events on the divide—the threatening Mojave green rattlesnakes, Hannah’s snakebite, and the decision, at Astrid’s urging, for Carmelita and Margot to go for help while Astrid stayed behind with Hannah.

“I ran away at first,” Margot confessed. “Carmelita pulled Hannah back from the snakes before any others could bite her.” Her voice shook as she continued. “There were so many of them. One of them bit Carmelita, too.”

“*What?*” Chuck exclaimed.

“It was a dry bite,” Carmelita said, turning her ankle to them. “See?”

“You’re sure?” Janelle asked, crouching and training her headlamp on the wound.

“It’d be swelling by now. Way before now. And it doesn’t hurt at all.”

“Agreed,” Janelle said, rising. “Whew. You were lucky.”

“Lucky is right,” said Chuck. He glanced back in the direction he and Janelle had just come. “The trail from Darwin to here was clear of snakes.”

Margot ran a few steps in place, her elbows swinging. “Ready?” she asked Carmelita.

“You know it.” She faced Chuck and Janelle. “We’re racing for Astrid now, and Hannah.”

Chuck and Janelle stepped aside and raised their hands. Carmelita and Margot slapped each of their palms as they passed, continuing toward Darwin together.

24

The knowledge that help for Hannah was on the way put a spring in Carmelita's stride as she ran toward Darwin with Margot, leaving her parents behind. She focused on the task before her, speeding along smooth stretches of sand behind Margot and placing her steps with care on stony sections. After Hannah's snakebite and Joseph's death, she was glad she wasn't running through the night alone.

The trail curved eastward, away from the mountains and toward Darwin. From the top of a low hill, she spied four lights winking on the otherwise black desert plain, one behind the other, roughly half a mile ahead.

"We're closer to them than I thought," she said.

"We might be able to catch them before Darwin," said Margot.

Carmelita checked the mileage on her watch. "Eight miles to go."

"Let's rocket."

"Let's."

Margot surged down the trail. Carmelita ran behind her, taking the cool night air into her lungs and enjoying the challenge of matching Margot stride for stride. Margot pulled a bottle from her vest and squeezed liquid into her mouth, her head tilted back. Carmelita did the same, swallowing between breaths.

"Your turn to lead," Margot said, stepping off the trail.

Carmelita tucked her bottle away and accelerated down the trail in front of Margot, her competitive juices rising like a warm tide inside her. The combined power that came from running with Margot was intoxicating, feeding energy into her legs despite the eighty-plus miles she'd already logged.

"How are you doing?" she asked Margot over her shoulder.

"My body feels good. I'm scared, though. First Joseph, now Hannah. This race is cursed."

"Are you thinking of quitting when we get to Darwin?"

"Oh, no. Dad would totally lose it if I did."

"I'm sorry to hear that."

"He means well," Margot said. "It's just, I don't know, I think he's sad." She spoke in short bursts between deep breaths as they ran. "He's a lot meaner than he used to be. He wasn't so bad before. But my mom left us and he lost his job, and now it's all about me and my races. It's a great opportunity for us. I mean, me. But it's getting harder."

"What is?"

"More and more, for him, it's about the odds. But after every race I win, my odds are worse for the next one."

Carmelita hooked a toe on a rock in the trail and stumbled, regaining her balance after a couple of off-kilter steps. She wasn't the only one aware of the financial opportunity the Whitney to Death 150 represented. "You mean your betting odds?"

Margot nodded, the beam of her headlamp tracing the back of Carmelita's body down and up. "I have a whole bunch of sponsors, but all I get from them is free stuff. He says the betting is the important thing. He gets a cut, too. But he says it's getting to the point where it's hardly worth betting on me anymore. That's why he said he had to go all in on this race, before my odds get so bad it's not worth it."

"What do you mean, 'all in'?"

"He put everything I've won, in all my other races, on me to win this race. He said it was now or never."

Carmelita curled her hands into fists and stabbed the ground with her shoes as she ran. She and Margot were pursuing the same goal.

Then again, other runners no doubt were betting on themselves to win the race, too.

How much money was Kelsey, for example, likely to have riding on himself to win the Whitney to Death 150 for the fourth time in a row this year? Plenty, Carmelita imagined.

Waitimu, as an internationally ranked marathoner, must have wagered a good amount on himself to displace Kelsey atop the podium.

Surely, Matt and his many supporters were betting that this year, finally, he would arrive at the finish line first.

Then there was Domenico, the hooded runner who'd come to Doug's aid at the start of the race and was quietly sticking with the leaders. Maybe he had big money riding on himself as well.

"Did your dad put anything on a podium finish for you?" Carmelita asked.

"No," Margot said. "After all my other top finishes, he said betting on me to win was the only thing that made sense."

Carmelita looked up the trail, her headlamp creating a tunnel of light in the night. She'd been wise to keep her training times to herself, resulting in her bet on herself with the help of Clarence and Liza at such great odds—though still, like Margot, only if she won.

And there could be only one winning payout for the Whitney to Death 150.

Ahead, the four lead runners forged their way across the dark desert plain, their headlamps glowing. Carmelita put her head down, intent on the stretch of trail directly ahead of her—and on catching the leaders.

She and Margot arrived at the check-in point in Darwin a couple of minutes after the four men, as the first hint of dawn splashed gray in the eastern sky.

"Vamos!" Clarence cheered from the truck as Carmelita and Margot jogged up to the check-in site.

The leaders already had checked in and were seated at their individual aid stations, lit by camp lanterns.

"You got past the snakes all right?" Doug asked Carmelita and Margot as they recited their racer numbers to Marian. "Sounds like that was some scary stuff up there on the divide."

"We did," Margot said. "But one of them bit Hannah. Astrid stayed behind with her."

"That's what we heard from the sheriff's department." Doug waved his cell phone at them. "Did you see your parents?" he asked Carmelita. "They're the ones who got help on the way."

"They met us on the trail," Carmelita said. "We used the SOS function on their phone."

Margot pointed at Carmelita's lower leg. "Carmelita got bitten, too."

"Whoa!" Doug exclaimed.

Carmelita displayed her lower leg to Doug and Marian while she described the dry bite she'd received. The two fang marks were barely visible as tiny red dots on her unswollen calf, and she remained free of any pain from the bite. "It was the same snake that had already bitten Hannah. It gave her all its poison," she concluded. "I'd know by now if it had given me any."

"Hannah's bite is real bad, though," said Margot. "When we left, her ankle was, like, humongous."

"We had a snakebite a few years ago," Doug said. "The runner did okay. I'm sure Hannah will be all right, too." He turned to Carmelita. "Thanks to your folks, that is."

She dipped her head to him and bumped fists with Marian, seated at the tech table, then headed for the truck.

Handing her vest to Liza, she sank into her chair and stretched her legs out in front of her. "Ohhh," she moaned, accepting a bottle of electrolyte drink from Clarence and taking a deep swallow. She leaned back, suddenly overwhelmed with fatigue.

"How're you doing?" Liza asked as she removed empty drink bottles and gel packets from the vest.

"I'm sooo tired," she said, her head resting on the back of the chair.

"You should be," said Clarence. "You've run ninety miles so far."

"And you still have sixty to go," said Rosie.

"Don't remind me," Carmelita said, managing a small smile.

"Do you want to lie down?" Clarence asked, pointing at the cots lined beside the truck.

"Do I *want* to? Yes. But I don't think I'd be able to get up again if I did." She straightened in her seat. "I've got fifteen minutes before my muscles really start to tighten up." She held out a hand. "PB&J, por favor."

"Por supuesto," Clarence said, grabbing a peanut butter and jelly sandwich from the table and handing it to her.

"I told them that's what you'd want," Rosie said proudly. "We made them in advance."

Carmelita took a bite. "Mmmm," she said. "I hadn't planned on eating anything at this stop, but this is perfect."

Clarence's phone buzzed in his pocket. "Hermana!" he exclaimed, answering. He put his hand over the receiver and reported to Carmelita, Rosie, and Liza, "They're in cell range, on their way back."

He put the phone to his ear and offered affirmative responses: "She's here." "Yes." "She says she's tired, but she looks good." "Yeah, she's working on a PB&J." He ended the call and caught Carmelita's eye. "Your mamá says to knock 'em dead."

Liza looked up from restocking Carmelita's vest. "Wasn't this when you were going to put on new socks and maybe new shoes?"

"New socks would be good," Carmelita said, her mouth full.

"The shoes are doing fine. I don't want to risk changing them out."

Rosie pulled a clean pair of socks from Carmelita's duffle bag and waved them in the air. "These?"

Carmelita nodded. Rosie crouched at her feet and slipped off her sweat-dampened running shoes and socks.

"Oh, my God, that feels incredible," Carmelita said, wiggling her toes. She waved Rosie off from putting the fresh socks on her feet. "Let's let my toes dry out a little first."

Energy flowed into her as she ate and drank, driving away the tidal wave of exhaustion that had washed over her when she'd first sat down.

As Carmelita looked on, chewing and swallowing, Rosie picked up the damp running shoes and windmilled her arms, swinging the shoes through the air in an attempt to dry them.

"No jokes about how bad they smell?" Carmelita asked.

Rosie stopped swinging the shoes. "Nope." She resumed spinning her arms.

"You're nice to do that for me, you know that?"

"Yep."

Carmelita slid lower in her chair and took another bite of sandwich, her thoughts turning inward. She was where she'd hoped to be at this point in the race, the first three segments completed in a little over twenty-four hours, leaving more than half the allotted race time to complete the final two segments before the fifty-hour cutoff. Better yet, she was hanging with the race leaders. And best of all, she was suffering from neither nausea nor muscle cramps. She was as primed and ready as could be for the second day of the race—the freakishness of Joseph's death and Hannah's snakebite notwithstanding.

Today's upcoming segment covered the remainder of the desert plain that separated the Coso Mountains from the Panamints, crossing into Death Valley National Park in the process. Though the segment was flat, like yesterday morning's stretch across Owens Valley, racers would move much more slowly across the plain than across the valley floor, using a combination of slow jogging and fast walking to survive the hot, sunny, second day of the race.

Carmelita knew from her research that in past years, a number of runners had stumbled into the fourth and final check-in point on the far side of the plain in severe distress, after running out of liquid too early in the segment, and had been forced to abandon the race. To avoid becoming one of those casualties, she planned to do as racers in past years had successfully done before her—greatly reduce her pace across the plain beneath the soon-to-be pounding sun, and dole out the food and liquid from her vest with meticulous care over the miles to come.

She took slugs of electrolyte drink and bites of PB&J, her stomach expanding beneath her running top as she consumed as much food and liquid as possible before leaving Darwin. While she ate and drank, Kelsey departed from his aid station and set out on the cross-plain trail. Seconds later, Matt, Waitimu, and Domenico jogged away from Darwin as a trio, less than a hundred yards behind Kelsey.

At the Team Chatten aid station, Margot waved off the woman crew member massaging her legs, stood up from her lounge chair, and accepted her running vest from Rick.

Carmelita checked her watch. She'd been seated for fourteen minutes. It was time to get moving again. She tugged on her fresh socks. Rosie placed her shoes on the ground before her and she pulled them on and cinched them tight. She stood and shook out her legs, pleased to find that her thighs and hamstrings were showing no signs of seizing up on her.

She shrugged on her vest, restocked by Liza, and strapped it in place. It was heavy, its pockets packed with refilled drink bottles, packets of energy gel, and snack food for the thirty roadless miles ahead.

She caught Margot's eye at the Team Chatten aid station. Margot beckoned her with a subtle tilt of her head and set out on the trail away from Darwin at a slow pace.

A rush of gratitude flowed through Carmelita as she followed, anticipating teaming with Margot for the challenging day ahead.

Buoyed by cheers from Rosie, Clarence, and Liza behind her, she rejoined Margot on the path, the eastern sky blazing pink above the Panamint Mountains on the far side of the plain.

25

Chuck neared Darwin with Janelle shortly after sunrise, returning to the third check-in point. Over the preceding hour, they had stepped aside for several runners who'd jogged past them on the way to the town at the end of the Long First Night.

A distant thumping filled the air. Seconds later, a helicopter appeared, a tiny dot flying south from the direction of Lone Pine. The chopper flew above the main highway between Lone Pine and Death Valley, then turned south, tracking the county road to Darwin. It passed over the town and followed the trail across the plain toward Chuck and Janelle.

The helicopter zoomed close over their heads, the roar of its engine loud in Chuck's ears. He spun and watched as it chuffed along the base of the Cosos. After a moment, the chopper turned and disappeared into the mountains, following the race route up the east-side drainage toward the top of the divide.

"They're sticking right with the route," Chuck observed.

"No way they'll miss her," Janelle said.

They walked straight up to the race check-in site in Darwin.

"Good work out there," Doug complimented them, gripping his phone. "They picked up Hannah and are on the way to the hospital in Bakersfield. It has a good supply of antivenom."

"She's awake and alert," Marian added.

"They offered Astrid a ride," Doug said, "but she stayed behind so she could warn the other runners to go around the snakes."

Marian, seated, pointed at her computer on the tech table.

"The last runner just reached her and she's on the move again. We told her crew what's going on. Hannah's crew already left for Bakersfield."

A runner arrived at the check-in site, and Chuck and Janelle returned to the truck. They shared the news of Hannah's rescue with Clarence, Liza, and Rosie, who, in turn, recounted the details of Carmelita's fifteen-minute rest stop in Darwin.

"She changed socks but kept her same shoes," Rosie said. "No blisters yet."

"How'd she look?" Janelle asked.

"Good. Really good."

"Ninety miles and still going strong," said Liza. "She took in a lot of calories while she was here." She displayed her phone, the map glowing on its screen. "She and Margot are still together. They're holding onto fifth and sixth place."

Janelle looked out across the desert plain stretching to the Panamint Mountains. Chuck shielded his eyes from the morning sun, gazing east alongside her. Like the crossing of the Coso Mountains last night, no roads intersected the race route until the trail reached Wildrose Canyon at the foot of the Panamints.

"One more check-in to go," he said. "But not until this evening."

Janelle shook her head. "I don't know how I'm going to make it through the day today."

Rosie chortled. "Not again."

Rick's voice sounded from the far side of the sandy plot, where he and the other Team Chatten crew members were dismantling Margot's aid station.

"No, it is *not* okay!" he barked at Carl, who stood stiff and unmoving before him. "She's never teamed with another runner before. I don't care what you say, it's not good for her. It can't possibly be. That girl from Colorado has no idea what she's doing. Margot is helping her by running with her, and if she keeps it up, it's going to bite her in the ass." He waved his arm, taking in Carl and the other two crew members standing at attention beside him, their faces rigid. "It's going to bite *all* of us in the ass."

Chuck pressed his arms to his sides. Before he could stomp over and confront Rick, Janelle rested a hand on his shoulder. At her touch, his anger ebbed and he turned away from the Team Chatten aid station, his back to Margot's father.

"The leaders are running together, too, ahead of Carm and Margot," Chuck said. "Everyone will get back to competing against one another when the time comes."

A couple of hours later, he arrived at the fourth and final check-in point with Janelle, Rosie, Clarence, and Liza in their two vehicles. The last check-in was situated on the shoulder of Wildrose Canyon Road at the foot of the Panamint Mountains, several miles inside the western boundary of Death Valley National Park. Just beyond, the road made a sharp turn and entered the mouth of the canyon, climbing into the mountains.

Chuck parked the truck beside the road. Janelle braked her mini-SUV to a stop behind him. He climbed out and checked Carmelita's progress on the race map.

Rosie tapped at her phone screen beside him. "Carm's still with Margot," she reported. "They're doing great. They're right behind the first four."

Chuck stared out across the desert plain, looking back in the direction of Darwin, the morning sun now behind him. He was glad to know Carmelita was on the move with Margot. But with the sun well up in the eastern sky and the day already growing hot, he was anxious for her as well.

Liza opened a camp chair and sat down in it, shaded by the truck. She peered up at the clear morning sky. "A few clouds sure would help."

"Carm will be okay," said Rosie. "She's got her hat and long sleeves."

"Unlike Margot," Liza said. "I've been wondering what effect her outfit might have on her today. I mean, all that skin she's showing."

Chuck pooched his lips. "That's got to be Rick's doing, to try to boost her follower numbers."

Clarence faced the Panamint Mountains, rising on the far side of the road. "Caramba!" he exclaimed. "Carm has to go up and over those?"

"Tonight," Chuck confirmed. "The same as the Cosos last night."

"Except those ones are way higher," he said, pointing at the Panamints.

"And they come at the very end of the race."

"This isn't anything like what I was expecting. I saw a picture of the Death Valley racetrack before we came here. It's not mountainous, it's flat."

Chuck smiled. "The racetrack would only come into play if Carm was racing against rocks instead of people."

"Rocks?"

"Those are what race across the Death Valley racetrack."

"Racing rocks? You've gotta be kidding me."

"For a long time, it was one of the greatest mysteries on earth. Gouges showed where dozens of rocks weighing hundreds of pounds each had moved across the surface of a flat dry lakebed in the middle of the park. But no one knew how or why they moved. Various theories were proposed over the years. The most widely accepted one was that winds pushed the rocks across the bed of the lake after rainstorms, when the surface was slick and muddy. But studies proved the wind could never blow hard enough to move the rocks."

"Maybe aliens did it," Clarence said.

"Some people actually thought so. Others figured it was pranksters who pushed the rocks across the lakebed when it was muddy. But there were no telltale footprints. And the lakebed is at the end of a long, one-way, four-wheel-drive road—not an easy place to pull off a stunt like that in secret."

"What about tornados?" asked Rosie.

"The theory of super-powerful dust devils was also proposed, but the physics didn't add up, just like with the wind."

"You said it *was* one of the biggest mysteries on earth," Clarence said.

"Right," Chuck said. "Until a group of scientists got approval from the park service to attach motion sensors to the rocks on the lakebed. A year passed. Nothing. Another year passed. Still nothing. Then, the scientists just happened to be at the lakebed, changing out the batteries on their equipment, when the rocks began to move, right there in front of them."

"So it wasn't just plain old aliens, it was *invisible* aliens," said Rosie.

"Not quite. There were two hints. First, the scientists were visiting after a big rainstorm in Death Valley. Second, the rainstorm happened in January, in the middle of winter."

"So mud had something to do with it after all," said Clarence.

"Mud, yes. Aliens, no. Rainwater from the storm covered the surface of the lakebed a few inches deep. The surface of the water froze overnight in the winter cold, creating a thin layer of ice. The next day, the sun warmed the ice, which broke into massive sheets. A light wind was blowing, just enough to push the sheets of ice floating on the water. The ice sheets were gripping the rocks, so even though the rocks were heavy, they moved right along with the ice, gouging the mud in the process. The sheets of ice moved only an inch or two per hour, which was so slow the movement couldn't be seen with the naked eye. But over the next few days, between the freezing of the surface water at night and the wind pushing the ice sheets during the day, the rocks moved hundreds of feet across the lakebed."

"Mystery solved," said Rosie.

"That's what scientists do," Chuck said. "Speaking of which, I'm meeting Tabitha, the head of the foundation that hired me, at the kilns this afternoon to show her what Carm and I found."

Clarence cocked one of his dark eyebrows at Chuck. "I thought you were here for Carm's race."

"I am. But if I can help solve another Death Valley mystery out here at the same time, so much the better."

26

Using his jacket as a pillow, Chuck stretched out across the back seat of the truck and took a nap before the growing heat of the day made sleep impossible. He sat up after an hour and peered out at the sunbaked desert plain. He felt surprisingly refreshed, as he had after the short period of shut-eye he'd managed the day before. The same couldn't be said for Carmelita, however. She was out there somewhere, running across the plain on zero hours of sleep, well over twenty-four hours and a hundred-plus miles into the race.

He checked the real-time map and found she and Margot were still running together, holding their place a few minutes behind the leaders.

"If Carm holds her pace throughout the day today, she should get here somewhere around five o'clock," Chuck said to the others.

"Dinner hour," said Clarence.

He sat with Liza, facing out at the vast expanse.

"Not that the time will matter to her," said Liza. "She'll be fueling all along the way today."

"She's rock-steady with Margot right now," Chuck noted. "If she gets here at five, she'll have fourteen hours left to cross the Panamints and meet the fifty-hour cutoff in Badwater Basin."

Clarence scrutinized the race map throughout the morning, cheering when Carmelita and Margot tightened the distance to the leaders a little, and moaning when they fell back by a similar amount. When Doug and Marian arrived at the mouth of Wildrose Canyon early in the afternoon, he wandered over and chatted with them while helping assemble the race check-in site.

"Doug and Marian agree," he exulted when he returned to the truck. "They said Carm's still a long shot, but that she has a chance of actually winning the whole thing!"

"Who is it they agree with?" Chuck asked.

"Well, me, for one."

Chuck narrowed his eyes at Clarence. "It's not good for you to be pulling so hard for her to stay up with the leaders."

"But it's a race, jefe."

"It isn't for Carmelita."

"Right," said Janelle, at Chuck's side. "For her, it's a test, an internal competition."

Clarence waggled his phone at them. "Well, it's a lot more than that for everybody else. The betting sites are tracking the amounts wagered on the different racers. I've been following all the money that's being placed on Carm as the race goes on. It's not just me. There are a lot of other people out there who are starting to believe in her, too."

Chuck shook his head. "Winning doesn't matter to her."

"She's told us all along that she just wants to meet the cutoff time," said Janelle.

Clarence's eyes skittered away. "If you two say so."

Chuck departed in the truck for the kilns two hours later. He glanced at his watch as he entered Wildrose Canyon, anxious to get back to the kiln site ahead of Tabitha and make sure everything was as he and Carmelita had left it.

Carmelita remained on track to reach the final check-in point at around 5 p.m., giving him the couple of hours he needed to complete the show-and-tell with Tabitha and return to the mouth of the canyon in time for her arrival.

He twisted his hand on the steering wheel. Had he and Carmelita really uncovered the tooth and bone fragment three days ago? With all that had happened since, the discovery seemed almost surreal now.

The sides of the gorge tightened on both sides of the road, which wound its way up the dry Wildrose Creek drainage. The road was deserted. Today, as on most days, no national park visitors were venturing up the canyon to visit the kilns.

Reaching the historical site, he parked at the first conical structure, killed the truck's noisy diesel engine, and climbed out. The engine ticked as it cooled. A steady afternoon breeze coursed up the canyon, humming as it swept along the rough stone walls of the defile.

He retrieved his flashlight from the truck, crouched in the low doorway of the first kiln, and shone the light inside. The mound of ash was steepled in the center of the structure, just as he and Carmelita had left it. He crawled forward and swept away the ash with his fingers, drawing a quick breath of renewed exhilaration when the molar and finger bone reappeared.

Returning to the truck, he snugged his headlamp around his forehead and settled his mask over his nose and mouth. Back inside the kiln, he lifted fresh bladefuls of ash on his trowel blade and sifted through the ash with his fingers, taking advantage of the time before Tabitha arrived to search for more remains.

As he worked, he pictured Russell Raining Bird's body burning away to nearly nothing in the kiln. The young Paiute man from Lone Pine had died for his commitment to Owens Lake. But his long-ago death had made no difference. No one had even bothered to report his disappearance. And in the years that followed, the lake had been emptied, its bed turned to toxic dust.

Chuck shuffled sideways on his knees, lifted a fresh bladeful of ash, and sifted through it with his fingers. Nothing. He deposited the ash on the floor, lifted another bladeful, and searched it. Still nothing.

The sound of an approaching vehicle came from down the canyon, the rumble of the car's engine echoing through the kiln doorway. Chuck checked his watch. 3:50. Tabitha was a few minutes early.

The vehicle stopped outside and its engine died.

Chuck clicked off his headlamp and crawled out of the kiln, taking off his mask as he stood up outside the entryway. In front of him, Rick Chatten leaned against the Team Chatten minivan, his arms folded over his chest and his legs crossed at the ankles.

Chuck held the trowel out of sight behind his back. "What are you doing here?" he asked.

"I could ask you the same thing," Rick said.

"That's none of your business, I'm afraid."

Rick sneered. "You're wrong about that, *I'm afraid*. What you're doing here is entirely my business."

"Look, Rick, I don't know why you're here. But what I'm doing here has nothing to do with you or Margot or the race."

"I know," said Rick. "I'm here for the same reason you are—I'm here for Tabitha."

27

Chuck took a backward step, coming up against the brick wall of the kiln. "Tabitha? How do you—? What are you—?"

Rick's sneer grew more pronounced, the corner of his mouth twisting into a tight curl. "What's the matter? Cat got your tongue?"

"What do you know about Tabitha?" Chuck demanded. He pushed himself away from the kiln and strode up to Rick, stopping in front of him.

"I know she called me," Rick said. "I know she told me you found something for her."

"She called *you*?"

"What makes you think you're the only one she would call?"

"Because I'm working for her."

"I'm working for her, too."

Chuck kept his mouth shut, waiting.

"She called all of us, actually," Rick admitted. "Or, as many of the support crews as she could get hold of, I suppose."

"What'd she want?"

"Publicity."

"The same thing you're after for Margot?"

"That's it exactly." Rick puffed out his chest. "Tabitha said she saw Margot's pictures and stories everywhere online as soon as she started looking into the race. She said I was one of the very first people she contacted after you told her about your find."

Chuck felt his face heating up as blood rushed to it. "What are you talking about?"

"She wouldn't tell me what you found or where you found it. But I put two and two together. It was easy since I ran into you out here the other day. When you headed up the canyon a little while ago, I figured what the hell, and followed you up here."

"I still don't understand why she called you."

"She told me to be ready. She swore me to secrecy. She said you'd found something really amazing and that she'd love it if I would share the news on Margot's social media when the time came."

Chuck ground his teeth together, his jaw clenched. What was Tabitha thinking?

From down the canyon came the sound of another car engine. A small sedan rounded the final bend below the kilns, drove up the road, and pulled to a stop behind Rick's minivan. Tabitha Eddy stepped out.

Now, Chuck would learn from Tabitha herself what she was up to.

The executive director of the Native Peoples Foundation and professor of Native American Studies wore hiking boots, jeans, and a plaid shirt. A bandanna was knotted around her neck, and her close-set eyes twinkled in her cheery round face. Tabitha's black hair was cropped in a chin-length bob, and colorful beaded earrings dangled from her earlobes. She gave Chuck and Rick a friendly wave. As she walked toward them, she glanced at Margot's scantily-clad likeness plastered on the side of the minivan.

"You must be Margot Chatten's father," she said, halting before Rick.

They shook. She turned to Chuck and rubbed her hands together. "I can't wait for you to show me what you found."

"You told the race crews?" he asked incredulously, his voice rising despite his effort to control it.

"Of course. I wanted everyone to be ready. The more we can get the news out there, as fast as we can, the better."

"But there isn't any news yet to get out. It's all conjecture at this point."

Her lips flattened. "I think I can be the judge of that, Chuck."

He tipped his head to her, acquiescing. She had contracted with him to survey the kilns, and he had found what she'd hoped he would find. From here, it was up to her and the Native Peoples Foundation board to determine how to proceed. "What I'm saying is, I don't see the need to rush things."

"We have a chance right now that we simply cannot pass up," Tabitha said. "I'd never heard of the Whitney to Death 150 until you told me you were coming out here for it. But now that I know about it, I see it for the opportunity it offers us." She grew increasingly animated as she continued. "Nothing I can do will bring back Owens Lake or return Owens Valley to the Paiute people in its original condition, when it was under their care. But the find at least gives us the chance to do something for Mono Lake before we lose it, too."

She looked from Chuck to Rick. "Have either of you heard of the Indian Ditches? They were shallow trenches the Paiute people dug and maintained in Owens Valley to flood-irrigate the wild ricegrass they harvested each year. The ditches divided the creek water from the mountains into smaller and smaller waterways, like a giant spider web that stretched all the way across the valley floor. The water saturated the soil and maintained the water table at ground level, which made the entire valley a lush green oasis of plant and animal life, all of it nurtured over centuries by the Paiutes. The Indian Ditches name came from US government cartographers back in the 1800s. They mapped how the Paiutes perfectly contoured the trenches across the valley, following the lay of the land to deliver water to the entire valley floor. The cartographers were so impressed by the trenches that they took their maps back east to show everyone how irrigation should be done out here in the arid West. But, of course, no one listened to them. When the farmers and ranchers showed up and drove the Paiute people out of the valley, they channeled the water onto smaller and smaller plots of the land and let the rest of the valley turn into desert."

The corners of Tabitha's eyes tightened.

"Then the Los Angeles Department of Water and Power bought up most of the valley floor and finished the job of desertification the farmers and ranchers had started. The water company still owns more land in Owens Valley than the entire landmass of the city of Los Angeles. Can you imagine? And the company has decimated the land it owns. It wasn't content with just stealing every drop of water flowing into Owens Lake. It wanted the underground aquifer, too. It drilled well after well to suck up all the groundwater the Paiute people had so carefully tended over the years. The company is still sucking up the last of the aquifer to this day, deep underground. The result is the bone-dry desert that Owens Valley has become, with ricegrass that barely grows a few inches out of the parched earth left behind by the water suckers."

Tabitha's mouth formed a straight line.

"Russell Raining Bird was murdered, his body incinerated right here in this canyon, so Owens Lake could be drained down to *nothing*. Now, north of here, the push is on to finish draining Mono Lake, too. Rumor has it some big players are trying to suck Mono Lake dry. From what we're hearing, they've been emboldened by the failure to keep Great Salt Lake from being drained down to nothing in Utah."

"You're right about Great Salt Lake," Chuck said. "It's disappearing before everyone's eyes, and nobody's doing anything about it."

"We've heard Los Angeles has quietly put the water rights to Mono Lake back up for grabs," Tabitha said. She addressed Rick. "If LA sells the rights to a different jurisdiction, that jurisdiction could empty the lake while a new court case plays out." She turned to Chuck. "Thanks to your find, we have the chance to make a preemptive strike to protect Mono Lake before any changes to the lake's water rights are announced, and before someone else gets hold of Russell Raining Bird's story and twists and distorts it to their own ends."

"And that preemptive strike would be…?" Chuck asked.

"Everybody loves a good mystery. Better yet, a murder mystery. The news of the discovery of Russell Raining Bird's incinerated body is certain to go viral, especially if we can piggyback on all the social media coming from the race this weekend."

"But we're a long way from having any definitive proof yet."

"I can't be worried about definitive proof right now. I just want to get pictures of the find and the story of Russell Raining Bird posted online, anywhere and everywhere, by sharing them with Rick and the other race crews while the race is happening and lots of people are tuning in."

"I'm happy to oblige," Rick said, a vision of politeness, his hands clasped. "Everyone else will be, too."

Chuck scowled at Margot's father. Then he turned to the kiln. Its dark doorway was an accusing eye staring back at him.

Tabitha's plan to prematurely publicize the find went against everything he stood for as an archaeologist. The basis of archaeology was the methodical accumulation of evidence leading over time to widely accepted proofs. In Chuck's world—and in the world of Death Valley National Park officialdom, because the Wildrose kilns and Russell Raining Bird's remains were located within the park—the discovery of the tooth and bone fragment represented the very beginning of a lengthy process involving voluminous amounts of paperwork and, undoubtedly, heated jurisdictional disputes between national park and local law enforcement officials.

Everyone would be angling for a piece of what was sure to be a fascinating story—which meant that the instant Tabitha informed park and law enforcement officials of the find, she and the Native Peoples Foundation would undoubtedly be sidelined.

He turned back to Tabitha. She had a point. Owens Lake and the verdant Owens Valley oasis nurtured by the Paiutes were gone, destroyed, never to return. But Mono Lake still existed. Why shouldn't the Native Peoples Foundation do everything it could to protect the remaining water in the sacred lake of the Kootzaduka'a people by publicizing the discovery of Russell Raining Bird's burned remains in the kiln right away, before officialdom took over?

"I can see where you're coming from," he said.

"This is our chance—now, today," she said. "Releasing the news of the find during the race will help us make the biggest splash possible." She eyed the kiln. "But first, I have to see it for myself."

"Me, too," said Rick.

Chuck wheeled on him. "You're not going inside. Not a chance." He faced Tabitha. "It's a survey site, still being processed. We have to keep disturbance in there to an absolute minimum. In fact, I've already sent you all the pictures you could possibly need."

"You're the one who said I have to be able to tell everyone I saw it firsthand."

Chuck grunted. "Okay."

She turned to Rick. "Just us. Sorry."

"You scientists, with all your rules," he muttered, his politeness gone. "But that's okay by me—on one condition."

"What's that?"

"I get a timed exclusive on the pictures and story. Er, *Margot* gets the exclusive, for release on all her feeds. That'll be great for her brand."

"How long were you thinking?"

"Twenty-four hours."

"I'll give you one hour. Sixty minutes. Not a second longer."

"Deal."

While Rick waited at the cars, Chuck crouched over the tooth and bone fragment inside the kiln with Tabitha.

"This is truly astonishing," she said, her voice hushed and reverent.

"It's sad and astounding and mind-blowing all at once," he agreed. "Although, when you think about the amount of money involved even back then, what happened to Russell Raining Bird unfortunately was all too predictable."

She sank back on her heels. "I often think about the St. Francis four hundred—how little their lives were worth, and how little they're remembered today, just like Russell Raining Bird."

"The 1928 St. Francis Dam collapse?" Chuck asked, recalling his preliminary research into the creation of LA's water system.

She nodded. "It led to the downfall of William Mulholland." She peered at the remains resting in the ash before her. "Not in time for Russell Raining Bird, though."

"You think William Mulholland had him killed?"

"Not directly. But I have no doubt Mulholland's schemes to grab water for the city of Los Angeles led to his execution."

"The St. Francis Dam collapse killed more people than any other manmade disaster in California history, didn't it?"

"Yes, it did," she said. "Four hundred and thirty-one souls died when the dam burst that night. Some of their bodies were washed all the way into the Pacific Ocean. Almost all of them were dam workers, employees of Los Angeles Department of Water and Power, which made it easy for the company to downplay what happened."

"But you said the disaster took out Mulholland, at least?"

"As the head engineer in charge of the Los Angeles Aqueduct and all the storage reservoirs between Owens Valley and LA, he knew the dam was being built on unstable soil. But the city was booming and everyone was in a hurry for the water, so he signed off on its construction."

"Money," Chuck said simply.

"He was a servant to the forces of growth, doing their bidding. To his credit, though, he took responsibility for the collapse and retired after it happened."

"But he wasn't charged with anything?"

"No one was ever charged with any crime connected to the collapse. Back then, it was pretty easy for powerful people to get away with total disregard for human life—even four hundred human lives." She peered down at Russell Raining Bird's remains, lit by Chuck's headlamp. "They could get away with cold-blooded murder, too."

She took pictures of the tooth and fragment from several angles, then crawled out of the kiln. Chuck followed her, retreating on his hands and knees while smoothing the ash covering the floor of the kiln with his palm.

Outside, he warned Rick, "We'll know if you go in there."

Rick raised his hands. "Don't you worry about me—as long as Margot gets her exclusive." He turned to Tabitha. "When will it be?"

She held up her phone. The last photo she'd taken, of the molar and finger bone nestled in the ash, filled the screen. "Right this second, as far as I'm concerned. I want to get the pictures and story whipping around the internet as far and fast as possible this weekend, before Los Angeles Water and Power starts trying to put their own spin on it."

"No," Chuck said. "Not yet."

"Why not?"

"I agree with you that the pictures will go viral as soon as you release them, which means the park service will get wind of the story pretty quickly. They're sure to shut down Wildrose Canyon Road—which will shut down the race—to keep people from heading up here and poking around until they can protect the kiln somehow. If you want to boost the story through all the social media coming from the race, then you'll have to make sure the race continues and the racers get past the kilns before the park closes the road."

"He's right," Rick said grudgingly.

"How much time are we talking about?" Tabitha asked.

"The leaders will pass by the kilns around nightfall," said

Chuck. "The last of the runners should be past here a few hours after that."

"Fine." Tabitha eyed her phone. "It's 4:15. If I wait until eight to release the photos, that should be enough time for the last runners to get by here. I've talked with Josie, the park superintendent, about Mono Lake before. She knows the danger it faces. I'll give her a call right after I release the photos. That'll give her the chance to send people to guard the kiln while they figure out what to do next."

"She won't be happy when the pictures start showing up online."

"Everything the Native Peoples Foundation is doing is for my people—the Kootzaduka'a, the Mono Lake people—and for the legacy of Russell Raining Bird and the Paiute people, too. She'll understand. She'll have to."

28

Chuck drove down Wildrose Canyon behind Rick and Tabitha. Outside the canyon mouth, Rick pulled to stop at the Team Chatten aid station, while Tabitha continued past the check-in point, a plume of dust rising behind her sedan as she headed back toward the highway.

Chuck parked behind Janelle's car and summoned the race map on his phone as he left the truck.

"She'll be here in an hour, maybe less," Rosie told him before the map appeared on his phone, her voice quivering with excitement. "She and Margot are gaining on the leaders. Kelsey has been slowing some, and Matt, Domenico, and Waitimu are hanging right behind him. Carm and Margot have slowed down, too, but not as much. They're barely off their pace from when you left for the kilns."

"Three-and-a-half miles per hour," Chuck recalled. "Barely more than a fast walk. Carm said it's the best pace for a long, flat, hot segment like today, especially this deep into the race. How far back from the leaders are they?"

Rosie studied her phone. "Between a quarter and half mile, I'd say."

"That's close enough for Carm to have them in her sights," said Chuck. "She'll know she's gaining on them."

"She *and* Margot," Rosie reminded him. "The top six, tight and getting tighter."

Chuck described to Rosie and the others Tabitha's plan to wait and release the pictures to Rick and the other support crews later in the evening, precluding any chance for the park service to close Wildrose Canyon Road and shut down the race.

"Are you sure Carm will be past the kilns in time?" Clarence asked.

"Assuming Tabitha keeps her word. And Rick." He aimed a thumb at the Team Chatten aid station. "As long as he stays quiet over there, we should be all right."

"Good luck with that," Rosie said, rolling her eyes.

Minutes later, four figures appeared out on the plain, jogging toward the check-in point: Kelsey in his black and white running outfit, followed by Matt in his shamrock-green top and shorts, and, close behind them in third and fourth place, Domenico shrouded in his sun hoodie, and thin-legged Waitimu, the black, red, and green Kenyan flag silkscreened on the front of his shirt.

Chuck checked the real-time map on his phone. The leaders had increased their pace toward the end of the segment. Carm and Margot were now half a mile behind the four frontrunners and would arrive ten minutes or so after them.

"Carm is falling back," he couldn't help noting. "She and Margot."

"They're sticking to their pace," Janelle said.

"Three-point-five was Carm's plan, like you said," Rosie added. "Slow and easy all the way across the plain." She aimed her phone at the four race leaders, their bodies lit from behind by the late-day sun. "Carm will take those guys out tonight," she said confidently. "She'll take out Margot, too."

"You got that right," Liza said, slapping hands with her.

Chuck walked over to Doug and Marian at the check-in site as the leaders drew near.

"Can't stay away, eh?" Doug teased him.

"I want to get a good look at Carm's competition," he said.

Kelsey and the other three lead runners arrived, reported their numbers to Marian in subdued voices, and immediately departed for their aid stations, shuffling down the dirt road to their waiting crews with their heads down and their feet dragging.

Chuck watched as the race leaders slumped in their seats at their aid stations, their support crews hovering around them. How could it possibly have taken this long for the leaders to finally begin showing signs of fatigue? He scanned the plain, searching for Carmelita. If the top runners in the Whitney to Death 150—some of the best distance runners in the world—were feeling the strain of the competition at this point, she had to be feeling it by now as well.

Carmelita and Margot appeared after several minutes. Their bodies were canted forward, their fingers crimped into their palms, their feet barely clearing the ground with each stride. The smile Carmelita had displayed when she'd departed in the morning was gone, and her cheeks were pale and sunken.

"You got this, Carm!" Rosie called to Carmelita as she drew near.

She kept her gaze fixed on the ground in front of her as she and Margot plodded the last few steps to Marian and Doug beneath the shade canopy.

"Good work, you two," Doug told them, his voice calm and steady.

Margot recited her racer number to Marian dully and left for her aid station. Carmelita stepped forward and stated her number.

Marian tapped at her computer and looked up. "You're doing great, Carmelita. You and Margot are having a phenomenal race."

"It doesn't feel like it right now," Carmelita said, her voice dry and coarse.

"Go have a seat," Doug urged her. "Eat. Drink. You'll be amazed where your body will be in just a few minutes."

Chuck took her by the elbow and guided her away from the check-in site. She leaned against him, shivering.

"I've got you," he told her. "We've got you."

Rosie filmed their approach from a distance, then lowered her phone when they drew near. "Everything's ready for you, Carm," she said softly.

Carmelita sank into her seat beneath the umbrella without taking off her vest.

Perspiration stains circled her running cap and grit matted her ponytail, which hung down the back of her chair.

She looked out at the broad desert plain she'd just crossed, her face blank. The plain glowed golden in the late-day sun.

"You did it," Rosie said to her. "You made it across."

"I still have the hardest part to go," Carmelita said, her voice barely above a whisper.

"But it's the last part. The very last."

Carmelita accepted a bottle of TrailFire from Janelle and drank deeply, her head back and her throat working with each swallow.

She lowered the bottle and wiped her mouth with the back of her hand. "I ran out of fluids an hour ago," she said absently.

Liza unfastened Carmelita's vest and eased it from her shoulders, then teamed with Janelle to refill the empty bottles stowed in its pockets.

"Do you want a PB&J?" Rosie asked, offering Carmelita a quartered peanut butter and jelly sandwich on a plate.

"Ugh," Carmelita said. "That's all I've eaten for the last thirty-six hours."

Clarence crouched next to her. "What can we get you, sobrina?" he asked gently, looking up into her face.

Her chin fell to her chest. "Quesadilla?" she whispered.

"Por supuesto."

Rising, he fired up the cookstove on the camp table next to the truck. He tossed a flour tortilla on a skillet centered over the burner, topped it with shredded cheese, and placed another tortilla on top.

Within seconds, the aroma of the heating tortillas and melting cheese filled the air.

"Two minutes," he told Carmelita.

"That smells good," she said, straightening in her chair and taking another swallow of electrolyte drink.

Liza and Janelle finished restocking Carmelita's vest. Liza looked toward the Team Chatten aid station. As at every other check-in point during the race, the Team Chatten masseuse kneaded Margot's calves and thighs while Margot reclined in the lounge chair.

Liza knelt at Carmelita's feet and drew her legs out from her chair until they were fully extended, her heels resting on the ground. "May I?" she asked, massaging Carmelita's dust-coated calves with her fingers.

"Oh...my...God," Carmelita moaned. "That feels so great. I need it sooooo bad."

She lay her head back and closed her eyes as Liza kneaded each of her calves, then moved to her thighs. Clarence handed her a plateful of quesadilla slices, browned on both sides and cut into triangles, cheese oozing from between the top and bottom tortillas.

She ate the slices between swallows of TrailFire. Clarence prepared another quesadilla while Liza continued to massage her legs.

Kelsey, Matt, Waitimu, and Domenico left their aid stations and jogged toward the mouth of Wildrose Canyon, cheered by their crews. They disappeared into the canyon, beginning the final ascent into the Panamint Mountains.

Margot rose from her lounge chair and shook out her legs while pulling on her restocked running vest.

Eyeing her, Carmelita chewed a bite of quesadilla, swallowed, and stood up. Janelle held the refilled vest out to her. She strapped it across her chest and pulled her headlamp over her head and clicked it on. Its lens glowed purple in the slanted end-of-day sunlight.

"The batteries are fresh," Janelle told her. "We just changed them. All the bottles are as full as we could get them. We doubled the TrailFire mix in each bottle for the last leg, like you wanted. And we stuffed in as many gel packets as we could." She frowned at Carmelita's vest, which hung low on her shoulders, its pockets packed for the final night of the race. "Is it too heavy?"

Carmelita rolled her shoulders. "It's fine."

"Your shoes and socks?"

"They'll get me through the night."

Janelle stared at the welter of fresh scratches and bruises covering Carmelita's shins, inflicted over the preceding thirty-six hours. She opened her mouth to speak, but Carmelita spoke first.

"I'm fine, Mamá. Really."

They put their foreheads together, facing each other.

"I'm glad you came," Carmelita said to her.

"I'm glad I came, too," said Janelle.

Rosie filmed them as they looked into each other's eyes.

Janelle stepped back, grasped Carmelita's arms, and said, "You got this. Badwater Basin is just over the hill. *You got this.*"

Carmelita slapped hands with Liza, Clarence, and Rosie, and turned to faced Chuck.

He glanced up at the mountains, bathed in the light of the evening sun, then gazed deep into Carmelita's eyes. "Up the cliffs on this side and down the Golden Staircase on the other, that's all there is to it."

She nodded, her jaw set, and looked at her watch. "Doug knew what he was talking about. Fifteen minutes was all it took."

She swung her arms and twisted her hips. Up the road, cheers sounded from the Team Chatten aid station as Margot headed toward the mouth of the canyon.

"You can win, Carm," Rosie said. "I know you can."

"I know I can, too," Carmelita said.

She jogged away. Tiny clouds of dust lifted from her heels and floated above the ground behind each step.

29

Chuck unscrewed the gas line from the cookstove, breaking down Carmelita's aid station after her departure from the final check-in point. A car approached on Wildrose Canyon Road from the direction of the highway. He leaned around the truck for a look and slapped his hand to his mouth in surprise. It was Tabitha's sedan, returning on the dirt road.

She drove by without slowing and rounded the curve into the canyon, heading back up the gorge in the direction of the kilns.

"What's she up to?" he wondered aloud to the others. "That was Tabitha, from the Native Peoples Foundation."

"You said she took pictures," Rosie said. "Maybe she needs more. Or maybe she's going to do some filming. I could help her with that if she wants."

"Maybe," Chuck said uncertainly. He checked his watch. Still plenty of time for Tabitha to accomplish whatever she was doing in the canyon and drive back out of the mountains, returning to cell phone range, to release the pictures and news of the find to Rick, then to the other support crews an hour later.

Minutes after Tabitha passed by in her sedan, Chuck turned at the sound of a car engine starting up. The Team Chatten minivan peeled away from the check-in point, the setting sun lighting Rick, visible behind the wheel, as he sped up the dirt road and around the curve into the canyon.

Chuck stared after the minivan. "Rick, too?"

"I bet he's going up the road to cheer for Margot," said Rosie. "He hasn't done that before. Not that we know of, anyway."

"Maybe she's having trouble."

Chuck turned to Clarence, whose head was bowed over his phone. "How far back is Margot from the leaders? Is she slowing down?"

"Oh," Clarence said. "I'll check." He tapped at his phone screen. "Ten minutes or so," he reported after a few seconds. "She's holding steady up the canyon. Carmelita is a minute or two behind her."

"You weren't looking at the race map before?"

He glanced away. "Uh, no."

"What were you looking at?"

"Um." He looked at Chuck. "One of the betting sites, Worldwide Wagers."

Chuck had seen the name of the site on Marian's computer. "You're still fixated on Carmelita's betting numbers?"

"No," he said. He licked his lips. "I mean, not really."

Clarence looked at Liza, who paused from folding one of the camp chairs.

"Liza," Chuck urged her.

She locked eyes with Clarence. "Tell him," she said. When Clarence remained silent, she set the chair aside and faced Chuck. "We've been wanting to tell you, but she made us promise not to."

Chuck stiffened. "She?"

"Carm," Clarence said.

Chuck spun to face Janelle. "Do you know anything about this?"

"Not a thing." She rounded on her brother. "Spit it out, Clarence."

Blood drained from Clarence's face. "It was Carm's idea. You know how she is. She has a way of getting what she wants."

"What did she want?" Chuck demanded.

Clarence's shoulders slumped. "She wanted to bet on herself to win the race, but she couldn't."

"Well, of course, she couldn't. She's in the race."

"That's allowed, actually. It's okay for racers to bet on themselves. Carm said that's one of the ways the top runners make money. She said some of them actually pick which races they compete in based on their betting odds. But in her case, she couldn't bet on herself because of her age. You have to be eighteen."

Chuck's mind raced. "As a first-time racer, unknown to anybody, her odds would've been astronomical. And the amount she could make on just a small bet would be just as astronomical."

Clarence nodded. "That's exactly how she explained it to me."

"But the pressure that would put on her…"

Clarence turned his palms up. "That's why she said she couldn't ask you. She knew you'd say no. And even if you said yes, she knew you'd worry too much."

Janelle glowered at her brother. "So she asked you to bet for her instead. And you did."

Liza stepped to Clarence's side. "She was very persuasive, Janelle. But I admit, we saw her logic. She said it was a once-in-a-lifetime opportunity. She said if we wouldn't help her, she'd find someone else. It's for college, for her tuition. Besides, she's good. She's really good. I know how worried you've been for her, and I get it. But if she wins, she'll have paid for college all by herself. Just think what an accomplishment that would be."

Chuck groaned. Why had he waited to tell Carmelita about the scholarship program for children of Stanford contractors? "How much did you bet for her?" he asked.

Liza hesitated. "Three grand," she said finally. "Three thousand dollars."

"She doesn't have anywhere near that kind of money."

"She has half. Fifteen hundred. We put up the other half for her. She said she'd pay us back if she doesn't win—not that we'd let her."

Clarence grabbed Liza's hand. "She can win. We know she can."

Chuck stared at them, his eyes wide. "Wait. Did you bet on her *only* to win?"

"That was the only way the numbers worked," Clarence said. "There are less than forty runners in the race. With such a small field, the odds aren't very good for a podium finish, even for an unknown like Carm. But to win? Her odds were fantástico. I mean, you've got the Kelsey guy returning, who has won the last three years in a row. Plus, you've got the guy from Kenya, one of the top marathoners in the world. And you've got the Irish guy, who has almost beaten Kelsey the last three years. With all of them in the field, the odds for Carm to win were unbelievable. We locked in the three grand before the race at ninety-six to one."

"Does Carm know?"

"I texted her after we placed it," Clarence said, his eyes downcast.

Chuck multiplied the number in his head. "That'd be a $288,000 payout."

Clarence's gaze lifted. "Right."

"But only if she wins." Chuck shook his head in dismay.

Janelle glared at Clarence. "What were you thinking, hermano?"

Clarence tightened his grip on Liza's hand. "I…I've never seen anything like this." He glanced at the check-in site, where a newly arrived runner struggled to remain upright while reciting his racer number to Marian. The runner wavered on his feet, his legs jerking spasmodically. "I had no idea how insane this thing is."

Chuck spun to Janelle. "We should drive up the canyon and talk to her. We can reassure her, make sure she knows the money doesn't matter to us."

He looked up the road. Plus, they could find out what Tabitha and Rick were up to in the canyon.

Janelle nodded. "We'll have to hurry. It'll be dark soon."

—

Less than a minute later, Chuck drove the truck up Wildrose Canyon. Janelle sat in the passenger seat. Clarence, Liza, and Rosie remained at the check-in point, breaking down the last of the gear and stacking it next to Janelle's SUV.

The canyon was deep in evening shadows, the rock walls purple and gray in the fading light.

"Do you think talking to her will make any difference?" Janelle asked.

"Honestly? Not really," Chuck replied.

"She's gotten to be so independent."

He attempted a smile. "Which is all your fault."

They passed a handful of runners making their way up the canyon. After a few minutes, the kilns appeared in the fading light, lining the straight stretch of road ahead. Tabitha's car was parked in front of the first kiln.

As he drove nearer, Chuck saw that Tabitha was seated in her sedan. He braked to a stop behind her car. It would only take a moment to find out what she was up to.

He and Janelle left the truck. Tabitha climbed out of her car and faced them.

"The more I thought about it, the more I agreed with what you were thinking," she said before Chuck could speak. "The story of Russell Raining Bird definitely will be big, which means the remains will need to be protected, sooner rather than later. I changed our plans and called Josie when I got out of the canyon. I made her promise not to shut down the race. She's sending a couple of rangers to guard the site until all the runners go by, then they'll close the road at the mouth of the canyon. I decided to drive back up here and wait, just to make sure nobody messes with anything until the rangers get here."

Chuck looked up at the Panamint Mountains, lit by the evening sun. Carmelita was somewhere up the road past the kilns, heading for the finish line.

He lowered his gaze to the first kiln. Russell Raining Bird's remains rested inside. "I can't say I blame you."

She inclined her head to him.

"Did Rick come by here in his minivan?"

"He blasted right by me," she confirmed. "When the rangers get here, I'm going to head out of the canyon and back into cell range. If he's not back in time, I'll release the photos to all the crews."

"We're heading on up the canyon. When we see him, we'll let him know."

Chuck returned with Janelle to the truck. He pulled around Tabitha's sedan and pressed hard on the gas, intent on catching Carmelita before she left the road and started up the cliffs to the Panamint divide—and on finding out what Rick was up to as well.

They left the first kiln behind. The other kilns flashed by one after another, their low doorways dark and yawning. Beyond the kilns, the road disappeared around a tight bend in the canyon.

Chuck glanced out the side window at the final kiln as the truck drew even with it. The kiln was identical to the ones before it, twenty feet high, its igloo shape formed by row upon row of brick and mortar from the ground to its top. The doorway of the kiln gazed back at him, inky black except for two spots of lighter color at its base.

He stabbed the brakes. The truck careened to a halt in the middle of the deserted road, a cloud of dust boiling around it. He stared at the doorway.

"What is it?" Janelle asked, her eyes large. "What's wrong?"

He pointed past her at the kiln.

A pair of running shoes rested on the ground at the base of the kiln doorway, toes up and heels down, the light green soles facing the road.

30

Chuck leapt out of the truck and raced with Janelle to the kiln. Just inside the doorway, Waitimu Mwangi lay on his back on the ash-covered floor of the structure, his face to the ceiling. In the gloom of the kiln's interior, Waitimu's mouth hung open, the tip of his tongue showing at the side of his lips. His eyes were closed, his arms lying slack on the ground.

Chuck's stomach convulsed. He and Janelle dragged Waitimu out of the kiln and into the evening light. The runner's body was loose and yielding in Chuck's grip. A stream of blood trailed behind Waitimu's head as they moved him.

Chuck dropped to his knees beside the runner. Janelle knelt and pressed her fingers to Waitimu's neck. She eyed the runner's thin chest beneath his vest and Kenyan-flag-bearing singlet. After several seconds, she leaned her ear close to his mouth and waited.

She raised her head after a moment. "Nothing. No pulse, no breath."

"He's…he's *dead*?" Chuck's thoughts careened from Waitimu, before him, to Carmelita, somewhere farther up the road. What danger was she facing right now?

Janelle leaned low to the ground and peered at the back of Waitimu's head. She felt beneath his skull with her fingers. When she removed them, they were covered with blood, dark in the evening shadows, like that left on the ground.

Chuck sat back, stunned.

Janelle rose and hurried toward the truck. She stopped and pointed at a softball-sized rock lying at the side of the road. It was coated with shiny liquid—also blood. "I saw this when I got out," she said. "But I didn't think…"

Chuck spun on his knees, looking all directions. Other than Tabitha, who stared up the canyon at them from her car, the canyon was deserted.

He scanned the line of kilns. If the rock had been used to attack Waitimu, was his killer hiding in one of the structures? No. The killer would have fled after the attack, and presumably would have arrived at and departed from the scene by vehicle. But no cars had passed Chuck and Janelle heading down the canyon as they had driven up it. And the only vehicle farther up the canyon, as far as Chuck knew, was the Team Chatten minivan—and Rick.

Chuck looked down the row of brick structures at Tabitha, standing beside her parked car.

"Carm," Janelle said, choking on the word. "Carmelita."

Chuck rose from Waitimu's side. "No one drove by us when we were on the way up here," he said. "Which means…"

"…Rick," Janelle concluded. "But Tabitha said he drove by the kilns when she was here."

They sprinted to the truck. Chuck swung a hard U-turn, raced down the road, and skidded to a stop when he reached Tabitha. She met him at his open window. Her hands were empty at her sides, clean of any blood, and her eyes were filled with honest questioning.

She had not killed Waitimu.

"It's one of the racers," Chuck told her, pointing at Waitimu's body lying outside the last kiln. "You have to get out of the canyon and call 911."

Her mouth fell open. She stared up the road at Waitimu. "He's…he's…?"

"Someone killed him."

She pivoted, eyeing the canyon around them.

"Make sure they send everything they've got this way," Chuck told her.

She spun back to him. "What about you?"

"We're heading on up the road. Our daughter is up there."

He turned the truck around and roared past Waitimu's body and around the first bend in the road beyond the kilns. It was nearly full dark in the shadowed bottom of the gorge. He turned on the headlights. The truck rocked violently as he sped up the rutted road, blasting over stones littering the unmaintained two-track leading to the long-abandoned mine.

"Nothing," Janelle said, peering up the empty track as far as the headlights reached. "Nobody."

"We'll find her," Chuck vowed. He clung to the steering wheel as the truck bucked, its tires caroming. "She can't be far."

He rounded a curve. The old mine appeared in the failing light at the end of the road, its broken stone walls extending from the base of the mountainside. Metal flashed in the truck headlights—the Team Chatten minivan, stopped just ahead, halfway up the final straightaway to the mine. The minivan tilted crazily on the edge of the road, its headlights shining down into the dry creek bed, its rear wheels a foot in the air.

Chuck skidded to a stop at the minivan and killed the truck engine. He and Janelle hopped out. Janelle snugged her headlamp around her forehead and turned it on. Chuck tugged his headlamp over his head as he approached the minivan with her. He leaned forward, shining his light into the car's interior. It was empty. He turned a wary circle.

A handful of stars speckled the sky above the walls of the gorge as night came on. The jagged peaks of the Panamint range serrated the eastern horizon, gray against the black sky.

He held his breath, listening. Beside him, Janelle did not move or speak.

No sound. Nothing. The canyon was silent.

Suddenly, Rick rose into view from behind the minivan.

31

Carmelita jogged away from the final check-in point toward the mouth of Wildrose Canyon, bolstered by the cheers ringing out behind her from her mother and Chuck, her Uncle Clarence and Liza, and—by far the loudest—Rosie.

Other runners' support crews cheered for her as well, and Doug and Marian raised their thumbs to her as she passed the race check-in site.

Not until the last of the cheers died away behind her did the enormity of the challenge she faced over the coming night fully register with her.

Her body had begun expressing its discontentment with the pounding she was giving it during the thirty-mile stretch across the desert plain. Her arches had begun to ache when she was still far out on the plain. A mile later, her ankles had started to hurt, too, followed by insistent throbbing in her knees and hips.

The pain clouded her thoughts and merged with her sleep-deprived state to turn the last miles of the crossing into a haze of pain and suffering. She'd clung like a lifeline to the soothing back-and-forth conversation she and Margot had shared while they jogged across the plain together. Margot had told Carmelita the mile-by-mile tale of her most recent race win. In return, without revealing the actual discovery of Russell Raining Bird's remains, Carmelita had described to Margot the work she'd performed in the kiln in Wildrose Canyon with Chuck, in support of the Native Peoples Foundation's goal of saving Mono Lake.

Finally, mercifully, the last miles had ticked off and they had reached the final check-in point at the foot of the Panamints.

The aches in Carmelita's lower joints disappeared the instant she sank into her seat. But they returned shortly after she entered Wildrose Canyon.

Rather than attempt the impossible by trying to ignore them, she applied what she'd learned when faced with seemingly insurmountable routes in the finals of climbing competitions. In those cases, she had reminded herself that the routes were as difficult for her fellow competitors as they were for her, and that she did not have to complete the climbs to the top of the walls in order to win the competitions. Rather, she only had to climb higher than anyone else.

Now, trailing Margot and the other four racers up the canyon, she reminded herself that all the runners in the Whitney to Death 150 undoubtedly were in pain at this point in the race, those ahead of her included. The assaults on her body were part of the competition, and her task was to keep forging her way to the front in spite of them.

She sought to relax her body and mind, running smoothly and steadily up the road as evening gave way to night, and accepting the pains emanating from her feet and knees and hips as part of the race. Each stride up the canyon was what she was here for, she told herself—this stride, and the next, and the next.

She thought only glancingly of her bet to win the Whitney to Death 150. The bet had occupied nearly all her thoughts in the early stages of the race, propelling her forward through the pack of runners. Now, however, she was focused simply on remaining upright and powering forward, battling the nearly overwhelming desire to lie down in the middle of the road and go to sleep.

She ascended the canyon until the kilns appeared around a bend in the road in the murky evening light. She caught sight of Margot a quarter mile ahead, in the middle of the road, jogging past the last of the kilns. There was a slight hitch in Margot's step and she swayed to one side.

Carmelita fixed her gaze on Margot and accelerated up the

graded road. Margot disappeared around the bend in the road beyond the brick structures. Carmelita concentrated on the ground in front of her, intent on maintaining her form as she passed the kilns one by one, focusing on catching Margot higher in the canyon.

She drew even with Margot half a mile beyond the kilns.

"Hey," she said between breaths, matching Margot's stride in the rutted two-track leading to the abandoned mine at the foot of the high peaks.

"Hey, yourself," Margot replied, a catch in her voice.

"How're you doing?"

"Not so great," Margot admitted. "I'm seeing things. It's scary. Nothing like this has ever happened to me before."

"What sort of things?"

"There were people ahead of me at the kilns. I swear it. But then, all of a sudden, they were gone."

"It must've been Kelsey and the others."

"But they weren't on the road. They were over by the kilns. And they weren't running. They were stopped."

"It's pretty shadowy in the canyon."

"I know. I could barely see them. I heard a yell, but it ended real fast. It was too dark to see anything else. I just put my head down and kept going."

"Good for you."

"But if I'm seeing things…"

"What else have you seen?"

"Nothing."

"You're okay, then."

"How do you know that?"

"It was a one-off. If you really were losing it, you'd be seeing more weird stuff by now."

Margot ran in silence beside Carmelita for a moment. "Maybe you're right."

"How are you doing otherwise?"

"Everything hurts, like, everywhere."

"Same with me. Feet, ankles, knees."

Margot put her hand on her hipbone, jutting through her bikini running shorts. "Hips, too. Don't forget about them."

"This is how it's supposed to be, though."

"Doesn't make it fun."

"Define 'fun.'"

A brief honk of laughter left Margot's lips. "We're nuts, aren't we, to be doing this?"

Carmelita warmed inside. Margot was experiencing the same pain, the same exhaustion as she was. And by pressing on, Margot was sharing the same thrill of the competition and the same opportunity for triumph at the end of the race.

But Kelsey was still ahead of them, as were Matt, Waitimu, and Domenico—and Rick, Carmelita realized.

"Your dad drove by me on the road," she said, "but we haven't passed him yet."

"He's up ahead. He passed me, too. He yelled that he was heading to the end of the road, but he'll probably just get stuck again."

Carmelita glanced over her shoulder at the empty road behind her. Would anyone from her crew drive up the canyon?

She looked ahead. She had entered the race for herself—though, she had to admit, it was nice to be running with Margot again.

"Kelsey and the others can't be too far ahead," she said. "What say we do what Astrid told us to do?"

"You mean, reel them in?"

"That's exactly what I mean."

"Excellent plan."

Margot sped up the rough road. Carmelita leaned forward, staying with her.

Night fell as they ran up the last stretch of the road together.

While they ran, they pulled their headlamps from their vest pockets, centered the lights on their foreheads, and clicked them on.

They rounded the final bend in the road, coming to the straight stretch of canyon before the mine. Halfway up the straightaway, the Team Chatten minivan sat sideways at the edge of the track. The vehicle was cocked at a sharp angle, its headlights shining down into the dry creek bed beside the road, its rear end in the air.

"Ugh," Margot said. "I was right."

Drawing nearer, Carmelita saw that the minivan was perched on the edge of the road, just shy of where it had been impaled by the boulder three days ago. The car's rear wheels were well above the ground, its front wheels clinging to the steep slope dropping from the road into the drainage. Rick stood next to the tilted vehicle, his hands on his hips.

"Dad!" Margot cried as she and Carmelita approached. "What happened?"

"I should ask you the same thing," Rick snapped. "I drove up here to check on you. And I'm seeing exactly what I suspected. You're supposed to be in the lead right now. What happened to passing everybody before the end of the road, like I told you?"

Margot's shoulders sagged. She wavered as she advanced, the hitch in her step returning.

"You're doing great," Carmelita said in Margot's ear, her voice low so Rick wouldn't hear. "You're solid."

Margot straightened and threw back her shoulders. "You know what? You're right," she said to Carmelita. She aimed the beam of her headlamp past her father and ran by him without slowing. "Good luck with the car, Dad," she called over her shoulder.

She and Carmelita continued running up the road, closing in on the old silver mine and the start of the cliff-to-cliff ascent to the Panamint divide.

"You'll...you'll...!" Rick sputtered behind them before finally falling silent.

A red ribbon marked the place where the race route left the end of the road at the old silver mine. The ribbon was tied to a rusted shank of rebar protruding from a chunk of concrete next to the mine. Below the ribbon, a red plastic arrow was twist-tied to the length of rebar, pointing up the steep face of the mountain.

Carmelita paused at the mine. Margot halted and peered up with her at the dark mountainside above.

The roar of a diesel engine came from lower in the canyon—Chuck's big pickup. Carmelita spun and peered back down the road. What was going on?

The truck hurtled into view, then braked hard, coming to a stop at the minivan. The truck's headlights illuminated the tipped car.

Why was the truck here? Had her parents and the rest of her crew decided to drive up the canyon and cheer for her as she climbed the cliffs above the mine? If so, they wouldn't be able to drive around the stuck Team Chatten minivan on the narrow road.

The truck's engine died and its doors clicked open and slammed shut.

Should she wait?

She looked back up at the mountainside. Pinpricks of light—the headlamps of the lead runners—flickered above.

She frowned, staring at the lights.

On the approach to the Coso Mountain divide last night, before the rattlesnakes had intervened, the lights of the lead runners had appeared in a uniform line ahead of her as the leaders made their way up the trail-less ravine one behind the other. There had been six lights then, those worn by Kelsey, Matt, Domenico, Waitimu, Hannah, and Margot.

Tonight, all four lights of the lead male runners should have been visible on the bare mountainside. But only three lights showed above. And rather than ascending the mountainside one behind the other, the trio of lights danced about, beaming in all directions.

"Nooo!" came a cry, low and echoing in the night, from directly up the slope.

32

Carmelita darted past the mine and scrambled up the face of the mountain. She turned after a moment and looked back at Margot standing motionless below.

"Come on, Margot!" she said urgently. "We have to help!"

Grunts sounded from higher on the mountainside as a struggle ensued.

"I…I…" Margot stammered.

Carmelita resumed her ascent, grasping boulders protruding from the slope to hoist herself upward. The sound of dislodged rocks knocking against one another came from below as Margot climbed up the mountain after her.

"What the—?" the same low voice that had yelled seconds ago cried out from above. "What in God's name are you doing?"

Carmelita drew a gasping breath. She recognized the bass voice as Domenico's. Why was he yelling? What did his shouted words mean?

More grunts sounded, now less than a hundred feet up the slope from Carmelita.

She reached the first vertical rock face and swept her headlamp across it. The wall of rock extended ten feet straight up, the first of the cliffs topped by ledges on the brutally steep ascent to the Panamint divide.

When Carmelita had been here with Chuck two days ago, she'd spotted the easiest routes to climb each of the short cliff faces. But there was no time to find those routes now.

She mentally absorbed the cracks in the section of the cliff in front of her. Then she flashed the face, using her rock-climbing skills to ascend the wall with blazing speed and mantle herself onto the ledge atop the short vertical face. The climb was easier than she'd expected; Margot would be able to follow her up the face without difficulty. She clambered to her feet on the rock shelf and peered upward. Thirty feet above, Domenico in his hoodie and Matt in his green top grappled with one another on the ledge atop the next cliff band, their arms extended and their hands gripping each others' shoulders.

Carmelita scrambled up the slope to the bottom of the second cliff. As with the first, she flashed the second wall, pulled herself onto the shelf atop it, and scrambled to her feet. In front of her, captured in the purple glow of her headlamp, Matt pummeled Domenico's head with his fists, his windmilling arms a blur in her light. Domenico raised his hands, deflecting the blows.

As Carmelita straightened, looking on, the Irish runner changed tactics, grasping the back of Domenico's hoodie with both hands and tugging it upward until it trapped Domenico's extended arms. Still clutching the hoodie, Matt leaned backward, drawing Domenico off balance. Using the weight of his body as leverage and the hoodie like a rope, Matt spun Domenico in a half-circle and slung him off the second cliff.

"Ahhhh!" Domenico cried as he plummeted down the short face.

He struck the gravelly slope at the foot of the cliff and tumbled downward, coming to rest on the first ledge, inches from tumbling over it as well.

"My leg!" he screamed. "Ahhh! My leg!"

Carmelita's heart pounded, her chest heaving. She peered over the ledge. Margot had climbed to the top of the first cliff. She crouched on the ledge next to Domenico, who writhed in agony, grasping his right leg.

"I'm here," Margot said to him. "I've got you."

The shattered end of Domenico's lower leg bone poked through his skin, a flash of white below his knee.

Margot rubbed his arm. "You'll be all right, Domenico," she said. "You're going to be all right."

Matt squared himself on the second ledge, facing Carmelita in his green shirt dotted with white four-leaf clovers. "You," he growled.

Carmelita turned to face him. "Me—?"

He charged at her before she could say anything more, his arms outstretched and his fingers reaching for her throat.

Time slowed. Carmelita did not move.

She remained still, holding her position.

She tracked Matt's approach millisecond by millisecond—his digging feet, the forward lean of his body, his out-flung arms.

She lifted her chin when he was two paces away from her. He stared at her exposed throat, his face contorted, his green eyes above his red beard hard dots in the light of her headlamp.

She rose on the balls of her feet.

Her plan would work. It had to.

His hands rushed through the air, four feet from her, reaching for her neck.

A tick of time passed.

Two feet.

Another tick.

Matt's fingers were so close to her throat that it felt as if an electric charge was passing between his fingertips and her skin.

She ducked her head sideways, feinting in the direction of the shelf's edge. At the same instant, she relaxed her muscles, allowing her body to collapse toward the ground.

Matt's eyes bulged. He tipped his hands downward, grasping without success at her descending neck, his fingers closing on air.

She tensed, halting her descent inches before her lower body met the ledge. In the same instant, she reached up between Matt's extended arms and struck outward with her fists, driving his hands away from her throat.

She continued the upward sweep of her arms, wrapped her hands around the back of Matt's neck, and yanked down hard. Maintaining her grip, she tucked her body and tumbled, just as she had when she'd protected herself from injury on the muddy trail back home. She landed on her backside on the rocky shelf and lifted her legs, slamming her feet into Matt's crotch.

"Oof!" he wailed, air bursting between his lips.

She pulled harder on his neck, driving his chin to his chest, and continued her backward roll, flipping Matt forward and sending him flying head-over-heels off the cliff, exactly as she had intended.

She twisted on the ledge and watched as he struck the mountainside at the bottom of the short face. His momentum propelled him past Domenico and Margot and off the first shelf as well.

He screamed as he disappeared from sight, plummeting down the face of the lower cliff. His screech sharpened when his body struck the slope below, his continuing cry joined by the rattle of rocks rolling down the mountainside with him.

33

On the far side of the minivan from Chuck and Janelle, Rick squinted and raised his hand, shielding his eyes from the glare of the truck headlights.

Before Chuck could identify himself to Rick, a yell rang out from somewhere on the mountainside rising steeply above the mine at the end of the road. A single word, deep and sonorous: "Nooo!"

Jolted into action by the cry, Chuck sprinted past Rick. Janelle joined him. They ran up the road together, their headlamps lighting the ground in front of them, leaving Margot's father behind.

More yells came from the mountainside above, the words unintelligible to Chuck as he ran. He took small comfort in the fact that the shouted words were low-pitched, coming from a man rather than from Carmelita. The yells would serve as a warning to her. She would turn off her headlamp and hide in the darkness, remaining safe.

He and Janelle halted next to the old mine at the end of the road. Headlamp beams moved about on the mountainside above. He counted four white lights and, to his horror, the lavender glow of Carmelita's headlamp.

He sprinted to the base of the mountain and began to climb. Janelle followed.

He looked up after a moment. Carmelita's light was advancing above him, nearing two white lights higher on the slope.

He suppressed the urge to cry out to her that he and Janelle were on their way and that she should conceal herself by dousing her light, fearing the attention he would call to her presence on the mountainside.

The fourth light, lowest on the slope, was close above. He resumed his ascent, climbing toward it.

He came to the first short cliff face, rising ten feet in front of him. Janelle reached the rock wall and stopped beside him. A scream came from higher on the slope. One of the three higher white lights flashed in the night and plunged downward. The light disappeared, cut off by the edge of the cliff above Chuck's head.

A deep-throated cry came from the ledge above: "My leg! Ahhh! My leg!"

"I'm here. I've got you," Margot said, her voice also coming from out of sight atop the cliff. "You'll be all right, Domenico. You're going to be all right."

Before Chuck could climb the rock face to Margot and Domenico, another cry came from higher on the mountainside. A second later, a body rolled over the edge of the ledge above and fell down the cliff face past him and Janelle. The body struck the mountainside and tumbled downward, arms and legs flailing, finally coming to rest on the slope below.

Chuck hurried down the mountain and aimed his light in the victim's face: Matt Sharon.

Matt lay sprawled on his back. He moaned, his face contorted.

"Matt threw Domenico off the cliff!" Carmelita hollered from higher on the mountain. "Then he came after me!"

"Are you all right?" Janelle called to her from the foot of the first cliff.

"I'm fine. But Domenico…" Her voice trailed off.

"His leg is broken," Margot called from the ledge above. "It's, like, totally trashed."

Chuck glared down at Matt. "Talk," he demanded.

Matt's eyes widened. "I…I…" He raised a hand toward Chuck, his fingers outstretched, beseeching.

Chuck pressed Matt's hand to the ground and knelt on it, trapping it in place.

Matt grimaced.

"Tell me," Chuck spat.

Matt sucked a breath between his parted lips. "I had to stop him. I had to stop everybody after the snakes didn't do their job."

Chuck stared at him, aghast. "What are you talking about?"

"The snakes," Matt repeated. "They only stopped the rainbow girl, Hannah."

"You tried to kill her with the rattlesnakes?" Chuck snarled. He leaned harder on Matt's hand. "You tried to kill my daughter, too?"

Matt's lips twisted upward in a cruel smile. "I ran ahead and opened the door to the cage," he recounted. "The snakes came out in a hurry, going every which way."

"One of them bit Hannah. And my daughter."

"They'll survive. That's what Doug and Marian said." Matt's eyes narrowed to slits, his smile disappearing. "I studied up, bought the tongs, found one of their dens. I knew what I was about. It was a long hike up there for me with all them slithery things on me back, weren't it? Then I ran ahead in the Cerro Gordos and pointed the arrow up the road at the turnoff. I pretended I was lost, just so's I could bunch everybody up. The snakes was supposed to put the whole lot of them off the race later in the night. But the damn things didn't do their job, not by a long shot."

Chuck's stomach contracted, forming a hard knot. "So you killed Waitimu."

"That wasn't part of the plan. It wasn't part of anything. But it was getting so late. I had to do something. When he stopped to take a leak, I fell back and conked him on the head with a rock. Then I caught back up with Kelsey and Domenico."

"You *killed* him," Chuck repeated. "He's dead."

"I knocked him out is all," Matt insisted. "I left him there at the kilns and kept going. I caught up with Domenico. I had to stop him, too. Then I'd have my go at Kelsey."

"But why? You were in good position to win. Surely you wouldn't have gotten lost again."

"They call me The Flake. Can you imagine that? I have to pretend I like it. But, oooo, it drives me batty."

"All you had to do was prove them wrong."

"I couldn't take that chance, could I? Not with all the money I had riding on me-self."

Chuck blinked. Matt had bet on himself to win the race. Of course.

"We all of us put money on ourselves," Matt continued. "It's the way of the world, in't it? We runners have to make do somehow, haven't we?"

Chuck stared down at Matt in disgust, then raised his head, looking up at the mountainside. Russell Raining Bird had been executed, his body burned. Joseph Hendon had died, too, likely the result of the toxic dust rising off the bed of drained Owens Lake. Hannah Rinkl, bitten by a rattlesnake. Carmelita bitten as well. And Waitimu Mwangi, bludgeoned to death.

All for money. Only for money.

But Carmelita, thank God, somehow alive above.

He gritted his teeth, barely believing the thought taking shape in his brain.

He would have been happy if Carmelita had chosen to quit the race right after Joseph's death. But now, in the wake of everything that had happened since, he realized to his utter amazement that the very last thing he wanted was for her to abandon the competition.

Matt's greed-driven actions should not, would not, put an end to her dream of completing the Whitney to Death 150.

The improvised assaults by Matt, first on Waitimu at the

kilns, then on Domenico on the cliff above, meant the Irish runner had no more rattlesnake-like boobytraps set farther along the course. Moreover, the primary reason Chuck and Janelle had driven up the canyon—to reassure Carmelita about her bet on herself—was, at this point, wholly irrelevant.

"Carm! Margot!" he shouted up the mountain. "We've got it from here. We'll get help for Domenico. And we'll take care of Matt, too."

"You want us to keep going?" Carmelita hollered down, disbelief in her voice.

"Janelle?" Chuck said, aiming his light up the slope at her.

Janelle called up to Carmelita, her voice firm, "If you have it in you."

"I do," Margot cried from the ledge above Janelle and Chuck.

"Well, then, I guess I do, too," Carmelita called down. "But there's something I can't figure out. There's only one light above us. There should be two."

Chuck froze, weighing his response. There was no need for Carmelita and Margot to know about Waitimu's death right now.

"DNF," he called up the mountain. "Waitimu." He held his breath, hoping his truncated explanation would be adequate.

A beat of silence filled the night. Matt remained quiet, no doubt recognizing that Chuck would throttle him if he attempted to speak so much as a single word.

"Do you want to make Astrid proud of us?" Margot hollered up to Carmelita.

"Let's," Carmelita called back.

Chuck exhaled.

Rick shouted from the foot of the mountainside, within earshot below. "Beat that girl's ass, Margot!" he yelled. "You know what to do. Run her into the goddamn ground!"

34

Carmelita climbed the mountainside ahead of Margot to the next cliff band. A headlamp winked above, nearing the notch next to Telescope Peak—Kelsey's lead over the two of them was now significant.

Carmelita ascended the rock wall, the concentration required to ascend the cliff serving to dampen her thoughts of Matt's assault. He had attacked her, but she had prevailed. For now, that was all that mattered.

Margot imitated the hand grabs and footholds Carmelita used on the wall, surmounting the face behind her.

Carmelita led the way up the next wall, and the next, with Margot following.

At the top of the divide, Margot darted past her.

"My turn to lead!" she cried, running through the notch and plunging off the far side of the Panamint range on Golden Staircase Trail. "Down we go!"

The little-used path, a faint trace clinging to the side of the mountain, descended nearly two vertical miles in a seemingly unending series of switchbacks to Badwater Basin, a smudge of tan in the darkness far below.

Carmelita paused atop the divide and drew a bracing breath. The soaring summit block of Telescope Peak blotted a portion of the stars above her head. She faced back the way she and Margot had just come. In the distance, the snow-covered peaks of the High Sierra formed a thin white line on the horizon, the chalky prow of Mt. Whitney highest among them. No lights shone at the bottom of the mountainside below. By now, presumably, Chuck and her mother had secured Matt and departed down the canyon in the truck with Domenico, transporting him to medical help.

Carmelita turned to face east. Death Valley yawned before her, a dark cavernous depression surrounded by mountains, with Badwater Basin at its center.

She took a deep slug of electrolyte drink and began the long descent into the valley, tucking the bottle into her vest pocket as she dropped off the divide. She focused on the stretch of trail immediately in front of her, finding her stride as her aching joints adjusted to the steep downward pitch of the trail.

Two lights shone on the slope below her, the headlamps of Kelsey and Margot as they wended their way back and forth down the mountainside, Kelsey several switchbacks ahead, Margot a single switchback below.

Carmelita lengthened her stride, gaining a step or two on Margot with each turn in the trail. Eventually, she drew close enough to hear Margot's labored breaths ahead of her in the darkness.

Margot was in trouble.

Carmelita shuddered, unnerved. Would she be next? Her legs wobbled beneath her and she tripped over a rock in the path, catching herself before she fell headlong in the trail.

Having run so hard and so fast for so long, would both she and Margot collapse short of the finish line, leaving Kelsey to run onward to yet another victory? Would they be seated next to the path, unable to take another step, when dawn came and trailing runners began passing them one by one?

Margot spoke from the darkness ahead. "I'm not sure I can keep going."

The air left Carmelita's lungs in a whoosh.

Margot slowed to a walk. Carmelita came up behind her.

Margot's head drooped, her headlamp shining on her shoes. "I'm done," she whispered.

"Not until you can't take another step," Carmelita said, finding strength for herself in her words even as she spoke them to Margot.

"I drank all my TrailFire. I'm so thirsty. I'm dying."

Carmelita withdrew a bottle of electrolyte drink from her vest. "Here," she said, handing the bottle to Margot. "It's double-dosed for the last stretch."

Margot squeezed the supercharged liquid into her mouth. "Oh, my God," she murmured. "Thank you."

"You got this, Margot."

"I don't think I can."

"*We* can."

Margot resumed walking. After a few minutes, enough time for the shot of liquid energy to take effect, she resumed jogging. Carmelita followed her down the trail, reveling once again in the added power that came from running through the night with a fellow racer—and friend.

They reached the base of the divide and set out on the dirt road sloping gently downward to the lowest point in Badwater Basin. Rocks lined the sides of the road, shoved aside by graders, leaving the surface of the road smooth and sandy.

"Ten more miles," Margot said.

"Time to take out Kelsey."

"Kelsey? Are you serious?"

"Damn straight I am."

Kelsey's light shone as a distant beacon half a mile down the road.

"We can't catch him."

"We'll see about that. We've got ten miles, and we'll have him in our sights every step of the way."

Carmelita handed Margot one of her soft bottles of double-charged electrolyte drink.

"We'll split what I have left and push our pace to five miles an hour. The TrailFire should hold us for the last two hours."

Margot squeezed the liquid into her mouth. "Ahh," she said, wiping her chin with the back of her hand. "Okay. Ready when you are."

Carmelita emptied her remaining bottle into her mouth, relishing the syrupy sweetness on her tongue.

"Now," she said aloud. *And now, and now, and now,* she said to herself.

She set out down the road with Margot, her gaze fixed on Kelsey's light still far ahead.

She no longer was capable of bounding lightly down the road. Instead, her feet struck the ground with the force of a sledgehammer as she ran, one jarring step after another. She forced herself to maintain her speed despite the pains emanating from every joint in her lower body. There would be no in-between tonight—she would either catch Kelsey before the finish line or she would collapse from the effort.

She flared her nostrils, drawing the dry night air deep into her lungs with long inhalations and exhaling in equally sustained fashion.

After several minutes, she checked the mileage indicator on her watch: 142.

Two miles down, eight to go.

Kelsey's light flared backward every few minutes as he checked the progress of Carmelita and Margot, revealed by their headlamps behind him. In response to their increased pace, he sped up as well.

Beside Carmelita, Margot's breaths grew labored.

"How are you doing?" Carmelita asked.

"I'm…hanging…in…there," she said between gasps.

"We're pushing him. We've got to be."

"Good."

Margot said nothing more.

—

Another mile passed. Carmelita and Margot stuck to their five-mile-per-hour pace. Kelsey's headlamp continued to flash back at them each time he glanced their direction, still holding his lead over them.

Right about now, Carmelita imagined, with only a few miles to go, Kelsey would find another gear and motor ahead of her and Margot. He was the three-time race champion, after all. The favorite.

Another mile passed. Kelsey maintained the torrid pace in front of them. But his headlamp flared their way with greater frequency as he checked their position over and over again.

Carmelita summoned a grim smile. Kelsey's increased looks over his shoulder were a good sign. He was growing nervous. And the only possible reason for him to be growing nervous was because he was growing tired.

"Hang tough," Carmelita told Margot. "We're close to breaking him."

Kelsey slowed. Carmelita and Margot maintained their speed. The distance between them and Kelsey rapidly diminished.

"We're doing it," Carmelita said.

Kelsey's lead over them dwindled steadily over the next mile until they came upon the race leader.

Lit from behind by their headlamps, Kelsey wandered from one side of the road to the other, his head lolling.

Carmelita and Margot drew alongside him.

"Are you okay?" Carmelita asked him.

"I'm…I'm…" he said, his voice low and defeated. "I'm beat. I'm all in."

"Do you need help?"

"No," he said. "I'm upright. I'm still moving. I'll make it."

Margot nodded at Carmelita. They left Kelsey and continued down the road, taking over the lead.

35

"We did it," Carmelita told Margot when they were out of earshot of Kelsey. "We broke him."

"Yay," Margot said.

Carmelita's throat was raw now, her lips dry and splitting. According to her watch, the finish line was still two miles away.

Two brutal miles.

Yet near enough, she saw, peering ahead, that lights now glowed beckoningly from the lowest point in Badwater Basin. She stared longingly at the lights. Everyone was surely there by now, waiting at the finish line—her mother and Chuck and Rosie, and her Uncle Clarence and Liza—all of them in Death Valley to welcome her if she could just make it to the end of the race.

She gritted her teeth. She would finish what she'd set out to accomplish. Because that was who she was and that was what she did. Always.

She jogged down the road, focused on maintaining her pace, and drew ahead of Margot, who whimpered behind her. She looked over her shoulder. "We're almost there. We just have to keep moving."

"I'm…trying."

Margot took lurching steps, her upper body leaning sideways, her arms limp at her sides and her mouth hinged open. Dried saliva formed a streak of white from the corner of her mouth to her chin.

"Dad," she croaked. "Daddy."

Carmelita looked ahead at the lights marking the end of the

race, now only a few hundred yards away. She was in the lead, the finish line tantalizingly close.

She stopped in the middle of the road.

Rick had bet everything on Margot to win the Whitney to Death 150. If Carmelita won instead, Margot would face her father's punishing wrath.

Carmelita drew her lower lip between her teeth. How could she possibly do that to Margot? But how could she allow Margot to win the race in her place?

Suddenly, the answer came to her.

She walked back to Margot.

"'Unforeseen circumstances,'" she quoted.

"Huh?"

Carmelita explained.

"You're sure?" Margot said when she finished.

"One hundred percent."

"But—"

"No buts."

She turned and again peered at the lights. This close, she saw that they were the headlights of cars parked in a circle, facing one another and illuminating a patch of dirt marked in the middle by a white stripe. As she watched, several of the vehicles' headlights flashed brighter, then dimmer, then brighter again, pulsating between low and high beams.

"They've spotted us," she said. "They can see our headlamps. They're welcoming us home."

She resumed jogging. Margot jogged beside her for a moment. Then she slowed to a walk, again falling behind, her toes hooking the ground.

"I...I can't," she said, her voice low and defeated.

Carmelita slowed and allowed Margot to draw even with her.

"You don't have to wait for me," Margot said.

"I'm waiting for you because I want to," said Carmelita. "For both of us."

She put an arm around Margot's waist, pulling her close, and walked down the road with her.

They entered the circle of lights together and halted after crossing the white line chalked in the center of the circle. Margot slumped against Carmelita, her head down.

Cheers erupted around them, loud and boisterous. Carmelita smiled, tears rolling down her cheeks. At her side, Margot lifted her head.

Together, they turned a slow revolution, their arms around one another, waving as the cheering continued.

Carmelita picked out individual cries.

"You did it, Carm!" Rosie cheered.

"Magnifico, sobrina mía!" came Clarence's rich baritone.

"Carmelita Ortega has *arrived*!" Liza hollered. "She is *in*... *the*...*house*!"

Chuck and her mother strode across the circle to Carmelita and Margot, followed closely by her Uncle Clarence and Liza. They lifted their arms, and Carmelita and Margot leaned into their group embrace.

Looking past her mother's shoulder as they hugged, Carmelita spotted Rosie entering the circle of lights.

Rosie held her phone aloft in one hand, filming, her eyes tight with concentration. She jiggled the camera slightly as she approached. Then she stopped and squared her feet and held the phone motionless, filming the celebratory end-of-race hug with focused stillness.

Rosie's eyes widened as she spied Carmelita watching her as she worked. They grinned at each other. Still holding the camera steady, Rosie raised her free hand above her head and curled her fingers into a triumphant fist for Carmelita.

EPILOGUE

The day after the race, Chuck sat at a large circular table in the shade beneath the stone-walled portico that surrounded three sides of the outdoor veranda at the luxurious Death Valley Inn.

The five-star resort, built in the 1920s by the Pacific Coast Borax mining company in a bid to attract tourists to the valley, sat high on a sandy bench on the east side of Death Valley. Seeking greater profits through tourism than through the continued low-yield excavation of borax in the remote desert basin, the company had followed up its construction of the resort with a years-long campaign to secure the federal declaration of Death Valley as a national treasure.

Chuck looked out at the undeveloped valley from the veranda. The primary aim of the mining company's campaign had been to limit the construction of competing hotels in the valley, but a beneficial side effect was the valley's ultimate protection, through the creation of Death Valley National Monument by Congress in 1933, from the ravages of borax mining that otherwise would have been wrought by Pacific Coast Borax and other extraction companies.

The veranda overlooked the hotel's impossibly blue swimming pool and impossibly green lawn. Flanked by towering palm trees, the lawn ran downhill to the sunbaked valley floor. In the distance, Badwater Basin was a beige oval beneath the clear blue sky, backed by the Panamint Mountains. Chuck couldn't see Golden Staircase Trail from where he sat, but he could imagine the switchbacking path down which Carmelita and Margot had run in the predawn hours yesterday, on the way to their shared first-place finish.

The entire crew—Janelle, Rosie, Clarence, and Liza—sat around the table on the patio with him, along with Carmelita and Margot, all of them enjoying milkshakes from the hotel snack bar. Though little more than twenty-four hours had passed since the end of the race, Carmelita and Margot appeared well on their way to recovery from the demands of the competition. They'd limped across the veranda to their seats on stiff legs, but their cheeks were ruddy pink and their smiles wide as they sipped their tall frosty shakes.

"Domenico posted a thumbs-up selfie from his hospital bed this morning," Carmelita reported between sips. "And Hannah posted a picture of herself on crutches in front of the hospital in Bakersfield. She's already saying she'll be back for next year's race."

Chuck sighed. "I just wish Waitimu could've been as lucky."

Carmelita's smile faded and tears leapt to her eyes. "There's already an online funding campaign for his family. He had two little kids. They look so sweet in the pictures." She pressed her tears away from the corners of her eyes with her fingertips. "Before the race, he posted his training routine on his website. He recommended some really great stretches. I tried some of them. They really worked."

Margot, sitting next to Carmelita, blinked back tears of her own. "I used some of his stretches, too. They were, like, bomber."

Clarence turned to Chuck, his brows drawn together in a deep frown. "Matt The Flake barely had a scratch on him, didn't he?"

"He walked down to the truck under his own power," Chuck confirmed. "There was no fight left in him at that point."

Rosie punched the air. "That's because Carm took all the fight out of him."

"What'll happen to him?" Margot asked.

"We turned him over to the park rangers at the kilns," said

Chuck. "I'm sure he'll be charged for Waitimu's murder and Domenico's assault."

"Plus," said Rosie, "the attempted murder of Hannah and Carm and everybody else by rattlesnake."

Margot looked across the table at Chuck and Janelle. "That was nice of you to drive my dad out of the canyon last night in the middle of everything. I told him I'm done with him. No more of him yelling at me. No more betting. And for sure no more bikini running shorts."

"After the way he behaved at the end of the race, I'd say you're making a smart decision," Chuck said.

Margot nodded. "That was, like, the last straw."

After the group hug at the finish line, Carmelita had walked to the truck and dropped into her folding chair, while Margot had hobbled over to Rick and the rest of the Team Chatten support crew at the Team Chatten sedan.

Liza had handed Carmelita a bottle of TrailFire and she had lifted her chin just enough to take a swallow. The liquid soothed her parched throat. She tilted back her head and gulped the drink down.

Minutes later, as she looked on, reclining in her chair with a second bottle of TrailFire balanced in her lap, Rick accosted Doug and Marian in the center of the circle of car headlights illuminating the race finish line.

"You will pay me every goddamn penny you owe me!" he screamed at the race organizers, his chin thrust out and his arms pressed to his sides.

"It's not up to us," Doug responded, facing Rick. "It's up to the betting sites."

"If I don't get my money for winning," he growled, "I'll sue you for everything you're worth."

"But Margot *didn't* win."

"She only tied for first place," Marian said, facing Rick alongside Doug, "and the betting sites will act accordingly."

"'Unforeseen circumstances,'" Carmelita said from her chair beside the truck, clutching her bottle.

Marian nodded to her. "Still the smart one." She addressed the support crew members seated around the circle next to their vehicles. "Bets placed on the race come with a long list of so-called unforeseen circumstances, all of which release the betting companies from making payouts if they come to pass—things like weather delays or cancellations due to wildfire." Her gaze came to rest on Rick. "Or in the event of a tie."

"What are you talking about?" he demanded.

Carmelita sat forward in her seat. "The betting sites don't make payouts for ties. In this case, they'll be more than happy to deny the big returns they'd have been required to shell out if either Margot or I had won outright."

Rick's face darkened. "But…but…but…" he sputtered, droplets of spit flying from his mouth. "I put everything on Margot to win. Everything. And she *won*!"

"She did no such thing," Marian said. "Carmelita hauled her across the finish line. You saw it. We all saw it."

"I filmed it!" Rosie exclaimed.

"Margot got to the finish line first," Rick declared. "Her foot did."

"Even if that's true, it doesn't matter," said Marian. "The betting companies require definitive GPS proof of finishing position for every payout they make. No matter where Margot's foot was positioned at the finish line in comparison to Carmelita's foot, the GPS trackers on her and Carmelita's shirts will show that they finished together." She set her hands on her hips. "Besides, the only reason Margot even made it across the finish line at all is because Carmelita helped her."

"She's right, Dad," Margot said from where she sat slumped

in the shadows beside the Team Chatten sedan, surrounded by Carl and the two female support crew members. "I bonked, big time. Carmelita saved me."

"Don't say that!" Rick snarled. He glanced around the circle of lights, then glared at her. "People are filming this right now. Not another word, do you hear me?"

"Oh, yeah, I hear you," Margot said. "I hear you loud and clear."

Rick scowled at her a moment longer, then turned back to Marian and Doug. "What about all the money I put up?"

"The sites will refund it to you," Doug said. "There just won't be any winning payout on top of it." He looked at Carmelita. "The same goes for you, I'm afraid."

"Oh, she knows," Rosie said before Carmelita could respond. "She's my sister. She knows everything."

At the big round table on the patio of the Death Valley Inn, Rosie asked Margot, "Are you going to quit running?"

"Oh, no," Margot said. "That's been all me, from the very beginning. I mean, ultra running is who I am."

"That's who Carm is now, too."

Carmelita tilted her head. "Partly."

"That's totally who you are," Rosie insisted. "Now that you can't go to college, that is."

"Whoa, not true," Chuck said.

Before he could say anything more, Margot pressed her shoulder against Carmelita in the seat beside her. "There's lots of scholarships out there for runners, especially at private colleges," she said.

Carmelita turned to face her. "For *trail* runners?"

"Well," Margot hedged, "partial ones, maybe."

"I'd take one if I could get one."

"Me, too."

They smiled at each other. Chuck pressed his lips together, saying nothing. When he'd spoken with Tabitha earlier in the day, she had assured him that, with his Stanford contract fulfilled, Carmelita would qualify for the university's scholarship program, and with her perfect grades, she would be a strong candidate for one of the scholarships as well.

But that news could wait.

For now, he sat back, beaming, as Carmelita and Margot bumped fists over their milkshake glasses.

Clarence raised a hand. "Can someone help me understand what was fact and what was fiction during the race, por favor?"

"Joseph, you mean?" Liza asked.

"He's question number one in my mind."

"Asthma attack," she said. "Had to be. Which means the water company killed him, back when they first drained Owens Lake."

"Just like they killed Russell Raining Bird," said Rosie.

"I doubt we'll ever know the answer to that for sure," said Chuck.

"Just like they *maybe, probably* killed him," she said with a toss of her curls.

"What I can't figure out," Janelle said, "is what would make Matt plant the rattlesnakes. I mean, sticking a bunch of poisonous snakes way out in the middle of nowhere? It just seems crazy to me."

"Not to me," said Liza. "Tourists on our river trips have no idea rattlesnakes just want to keep to themselves. When they see one on a day hike, they about have a heart attack. They think rattlers are the deadliest creatures on earth. I'm sure Matt was the same way. He's from Ireland, so everything he knew about rattlesnakes was from what he'd read or seen in movies." She shrugged. "He'd been failing and failing with the race, year after year. He was The Flake, after all. He probably liked the idea of being in command with the snakes. He figured he could slow everybody down with them and finally take first place and cash in on the bets he placed on himself."

Janelle put a finger to her chin, nodding. "I'll buy that."

"Darlene finished in time despite her fishing-line cut," Carmelita reported. "She came in with Hester Baldwin in just under fifty hours. Astrid finished, too, half an hour ahead of them."

"Sweet!" Rosie cheered.

Clarence looked around the table. "Last one: Doug, in the parking lot, before the start."

Rosie screwed up her nose at Margot. "Was your dad trying to hit Carm to get her out of the race?"

"Uh, no," said Margot. "He's not all bad. But, I mean, he's not all good, either." She looked at Chuck. "Carmelita told me about the work she was doing with you in the kiln to save Mono Lake. My dad would never do that kind of thing—unless it helped *him*, of course. Like how he figures posting the pictures of the tooth and bone on my feeds is good for my quote-unquote 'brand.'" She ticked the air with her fingers. "All the other racers have posted the pictures on their feeds, too."

Chuck dipped his head to her and addressed everyone at the table. "Russell Raining Bird's story is going everywhere online, just like Tabitha hoped. She told me the whole world wants to interview her right now. She said she keeps saying the words 'Mono Lake' over and over, as many times as she can, to everybody who calls her."

"Last year," Margot said, "I put the picture of me standing under the big 'Save the Lake' arch at the finish line of the Great Salt Lake 100 on all my feeds. I have no idea if it did any good, though."

"It had to," said Carmelita. "Just like the pictures of Russell Raining Bird's tooth and finger bone will help save Mono Lake. How could they not?"

A vision invaded Chuck's mind: Russell Raining Bird lying in the center of the kiln, dead, his sunken eyes and slack face lit by flickering flames.

The young Paiute man had been killed to assure the complete emptying of Owens Lake. Would Great Salt Lake ultimately be drained dry, too, resulting in the same toxic dust storms sweeping through Salt Lake City as those that lifted off the bed of former Owens Lake? Would Mono Lake be drained as well? Chuck couldn't say. But a big part of him believed Carmelita was right—that today, a century after Russell Raining Bird's killing, the revelations surrounding his death really would help.

He raised his milkshake glass. "Here's to Great Salt Lake. May it forever have water in it."

"And here's to Mono Lake," Carmelita said, tilting her glass at him. "May it forever have water in it, too."

ACKNOWLEDGMENTS

As always, my early readers offered advice and suggestions that immeasurably improved the final version of *Death Valley Duel.* My sincere thanks go to Margaret Mizushima, Mark Stevens, Chuck Greaves, Pat Downs, John Peel, and C. Matthew Smith, as well as the Graham crew—Sue, Kevin, Taylor, and Logan.

The good people at Torrey House Press are as dedicated and giving and tireless and friendly as any group of folks I've ever had the privilege to work with. Thank you to publisher-editors Will Neville-Rehbehn and Kirsten Johanna Allen, and to Scout Invie, Gray Buck-Cockayne, Alexis Powell, and Kathleen Metcalf.

I'm fortunate beyond words to have the artistry of David Jonason gracing the cover of *Death Valley Duel* and my past National Park Mysteries.

My sincere appreciation goes to all the booksellers at independent bookstores who have placed my mysteries in the hands of book buyers, putting my National Park Mystery Series on the map in the process. Thank you.

ABOUT SCOTT GRAHAM

Scott Graham is the National Outdoor Book Award-winning author of fourteen books, including the National Park Mystery Series from Torrey House Press. Graham is an avid outdoorsman who enjoys whitewater rafting, skiing, backpacking, and mountain climbing with his wife, an emergency physician. He lives in southwestern Colorado.

ABOUT THE COVER

"For me, the appeal of the park has always been as much about its quiet serenity as scenic wonders. After a few days of wandering and exploring, my mind begins to settle and I'm more receptive to the magnificent patterns and textures of nature."

—David Jonason

Acclaimed Southwest landscape artist David Jonason painted *Mountain Cloud*, a portion of which appears on the cover of *Death Valley Duel*. Combining a keenly observant eye and inspiration drawn from a number of twentieth-century art movements, including cubism, futurism, precisionism, and art deco, Jonason achieves a uniquely personal vision through his vividly dreamlike oil paintings of the American Southwest. Jonason connects on canvas the traditional arts and crafts of the Southwest's Native tribes with the intricate patterns in nature known as fractals. "For me as a painter," he says, "it's a reductive and simplifying process of finding the natural geometries in nature, just as Navajo weavers and Pueblo potters portray the natural world through geometric series of zigzags, curves, and other patterns."

Mountain Cloud is used by permission of The Jonason Studio, davidjonason.com.

FURTHER READING (AND VIEWING)

Released in 1986, Marc Reisner's *Cadillac Desert: The American West and Its Disappearing Water* remains the preeminent resource for anyone seeking to learn about, and begin to understand, the long and troubled history behind the unending thirst for water that to this day lies at the heart of virtually every land-use and environmental squabble in California and across the arid West.

Death Valley National Park: A History, by Hal Rothman and Char Miller, offers a concise overview of the park and its creation, including "the reconceptualization of what a national park consists of" required a century ago to win over hearts and minds to the cause of preserving the harsh desert landscape of Death Valley.

Fictionally, the 1974 Oscar Award-winning film *Chinatown* offers an entertaining account of the murderous machinations behind the scheme to bring water from Owens Valley to early Los Angeles.

TORREY HOUSE PRESS

Torrey House Press publishes books at the intersection of the literary arts and environmental advocacy. THP authors explore the diversity of human experiences and relationships with place. THP books create conversations about issues that concern the American West, landscape, literature, and the future of our ever-changing planet, inspiring action toward a more just world.

We believe that lively, contemporary literature is at the cutting edge of social change. We seek to inform, expand, and reshape the dialogue on environmental justice and stewardship for the natural world by elevating literary excellence from diverse voices.

Visit www.torreyhouse.org for reading group discussion guides, author interviews, and more.

As a 501(c)(3) nonprofit publisher, our work is made possible by generous donations from readers like you.

Torrey House Press is supported by Back of Beyond Books, the King's English Bookshop, Maria's Bookshop, the Jeffrey S. & Helen H. Cardon Foundation, the Sam & Diane Stewart Family Foundation, the Barker Foundation, Robert Aagard & Camille Bailey Aagard, Kif Augustine Adams & Stirling Adams, James Allen, Diana Allison, Karin Anderson, Richard Baker, Patti Baynham & Owen Baynham, Klaus Bielefeldt, Joe Breddan, Karen Buchi & Kenneth Buchi, Rose Chilcoat & Mark Franklin, Linc Cornell & Lois Cornell, Susan Cushman & Charlie Quimby, Lynn de Freitas & Patrick de Freitas, Betsy Gaines Quammen & David Quammen, Laurie Hilyer, Phyllis Hockett, Kirtly Parker Jones, Susan Markley, Kathleen Metcalf & Peter Metcalf, Donaree Neville & Douglas Neville, Katie Pearce, Marion S. Robinson, Molly Swonger, Shelby Tisdale, the Utah Division of Arts & Museums, Utah Humanities, the National Endowment for the Humanities, the National Endowment for the Arts, the Salt Lake City Arts Council, and Salt Lake County Zoo, Arts & Parks. Our thanks to individual donors, members, and the Torrey House Press board of directors for their valued support.

GREAT SAND DUNES MASSACRE

A National Park Mystery
By Scott Graham

Coming next in the National Park Mystery Series

TORREY HOUSE PRESS

Salt Lake City • Torrey

TWO MONTHS AGO

He would be watched.

Frank Cameron had warned Chuck Bender he would be.

Which explained the glimmer of sunlight on glass that caught the corner of Chuck's eye as he knelt on the rocky slope in the northern quadrant of Great Sand Dunes National Park. And why the glint did not necessarily surprise him.

Though it did piss him off.

He stared at the round wooden object in the shallow hole in the ground before him. Over the preceding thirty minutes, he had scooped dirt and small stones away from the object with a trowel, then swept soil and pebbles from its top and sides with a soft-bristled paintbrush to fully uncover it.

The reflected glint came from higher on the hillside, revealing the location of his observer at the base of a small grove of piñons a couple hundred yards up the slope. The shimmer most likely was the reflection of the sun's rays off a pair of binoculars trained his way.

But it could just as well be that of sunlight flashing off a rifle scope.

He hunched his shoulders, his back growing stiff. He was alone, out in the open and exposed, with only knee-high sagebrush growing between him and the stand of trees.

The afternoon sun shone down from the clear blue sky overhead. Wind whipped across the slope, the sage branches shivering with each gust. Below, the pan-flat floor of San Luis Valley stretched away from the foot of the hill, the fifty-by-hundred-mile expanse in southern Colorado walled by the San Juan

Mountains to the west and, directly above him, the granite peaks of the Sangre de Cristo Mountain range barricading the east side of the valley.

He leaned forward, studying the object. It was wholly out of place here in the far corner of the tract of land recently added to the national park.

Who had buried it here? Why?

He tugged his ball cap lower over his short graying hair, shielding his eyes from the sun. He was torn. He wanted nothing more than to photograph the object in place, then remove it from the hole and closely examine it. But he was damned if he'd continue working while someone spied on him—particularly if his spy was armed.

He climbed to his feet while looking sidelong up the hill. The glimmer winked out, the binoculars hastily stowed in their case or the gun quickly lowered.

He pivoted and glared at the trees, jaw thrust out, hands braced on the hips of his brown cotton work pants.

Though the fact that someone was watching him, perhaps through the scope of a gun, angered Chuck, it didn't necessarily worry him. Armed or not, his observer wouldn't dare assault him here in the national park, where he was backed by the full weight of the federal government.

At least, that was what he told himself.

He dropped his hands to his sides and strode up the slope toward the piñons, leaving the object behind.

As chief resources officer for Great Sand Dunes National Park, Frank Cameron had hired Chuck to conduct an initial archaeological survey of the huge new tract of land north of the sprawling dune field at the center of the national park. The park's namesake sand dunes were the tallest in the world, rising more than seven hundred feet above the valley floor.

Chuck was to record and assess the cultural significance of

any and all human-made objects he discovered in the course of his survey of the land tract. He would perform the survey on foot, walking a grid pattern across the eight-thousand-acre parcel mile after mile, day after day. Objects he discovered might be ancient, left by Native Americans who'd lived in and passed through San Luis Valley over the preceding thousands of years. Or they might be of more recent origin, abandoned by those who visited or settled in the valley over the preceding four hundred years—Spaniards who arrived in the so-called New World beginning in the 1600s, followed by the hordes of Americans drawn to Colorado in the mid-1800s by the discovery of gold in the Rocky Mountains.

"There's a bunch of anti-government types living in the valley who are fired up about the park expansion," Frank told Chuck when they met in his cluttered office to finalize the contract. "And not in a good way."

Frank's office occupied a corner of a small clapboard building adjacent to the dune field. The dunes rose outside his office window, towering tan waves arrested in midair, the hulking pyramids of sand as out of place here in the Rocky Mountains, a thousand miles from the nearest ocean, as a polar bear in a rainforest.

Despite their motionless appearance, the dunes were anything but. Winds surging constantly across the valley floor sculpted and re-sculpted the dunes while marching them eastward to the base of the Sangre de Cristos. Creeks running out of the mountains carried the sand back around to the west side of the dune field, where the prevailing winds reconstructed the dunes once more, a ceaseless process underway for millions of years that would continue only because of the land acquisition by the national park.

Frank jabbed his finger at the newly added acreage outlined in blue on the oversize park map covering the wall of his office above his scarred oak desk. "The water hogs in Denver were itching to buy the land to get their hands on the groundwater beneath it. They were going to drill wells and drain the aquifer dry, which would've lowered the water table in the valley and killed the surface streams that carry the sand around the dune field. With the streams gone, the sand would have blown away into the mountains, leaving nothing behind."

Frank was in his late fifties, a decade older than Chuck, nearing the end of an illustrious career with the National Park Service. His hearty laugh and twinkling blue eyes belied his dead-serious devotion to the Great Sand Dunes. Frank's thinning black hair was pasted to his scalp and a bristly mustache jutted from his upper lip. His shiny brass ranger badge shone on the left breast of his gray uniform shirt.

Chuck sat forward, studying the map. "You'd think the anti-government folks would care about the future of the dunes."

"They only care about one thing: freedom from governmental tyranny—their idea of freedom, anyway."

"Wasn't the land owned by some other governmental entity before the park took it over?"

"Sort of. The Nature Fund gave the land to the park after acquiring it from its previous private owner through a tax-write-off program."

"The anti-government people should be mad at the Nature Fund, then, not the park."

"They're mad at everybody who had a hand in the deal."

"How mad are they?"

"They say they're willing to kill for what they believe in." Frank tsked, waving a dismissive hand. "But that's when they're online, hiding behind their fake names like FreedomFighterForever or KillerForAmerica. In real life, I seriously doubt it."

Now, Chuck would find out if Frank was right.

He climbed the slope, winding his way through the low

sagebrush. No movement showed at the edge of the trees above, no more glimmers off glass.

He was fifty yards from the piñons when a man stepped out of the grove and stood facing him. The man was skinny and stooped, his head canted forward on a noodle-thin neck. He wore a flannel shirt, faded jeans, and sneakers. And he clutched a hunting rifle at his side.

Chuck's heart raced at the sight of the gun. But he didn't stop walking.

The man put the rifle to his shoulder and aimed down its barrel at Chuck, his eye to the scope.

Heart thumping, Chuck hooked his hiking boot on a sagebrush branch and stumbled. Righting himself, he continued up the slope.

The man held his position, gun raised.

Chuck kept walking, noting as he drew nearer that the man was young, in his early twenties, with a straggly beard and stringy hair twisting in the wind beneath a stained yellow ball cap that sat low on his forehead.

The man's pale gray eyes glinted with fear. He lowered his gun to his side.

Chuck exhaled, still approaching.

The man licked his lips, his tongue darting between gapped teeth. He pivoted and strode downhill through the sage, angling away from Chuck. He swung the gun over his shoulder and broke into a jog, the gun bouncing against his back on its leather sling.

Chuck followed, maintaining his walking pace. After less than a hundred yards, the man slowed to a walk as well, his thin shoulders heaving. He headed toward the far northwest corner of the park's new tract of land, glancing back at Chuck every minute or two.

A barbed-wire fence ran along the north edge of the tract,

marking the national park's newly established northern boundary. At the corner of the park, the wire fence met a six-foot-high wood-slat fence set along the park's new western boundary.

Beyond the wire fence, dirt roads cut the private land on the valley floor into five-acre residential parcels. The large lots ran north to the town of Crestone, its tight grid of streets visible in the distance. Between the park boundary and town, faded aluminum house trailers, ancient RVs resting on flattened tires, and plywood shacks topped with rusted tin roofs sat in the middle of the rural lots. Detritus surrounded the crude homes—broken-down cars and pickup trucks, abandoned household appliances, collapsed metal sheds, and piles of weathered lumber, the boards bent and useless beneath the withering sun.

The wooden fence guarded a commercial enterprise of some sort immediately west of the park. On the far side of the fence, sunlight shimmered off the surface of a pond. The pool of water extended to a large greenhouse walled and roofed with alternating panels of olive and clear glass.

The man veered west, aiming for the slatted fence and the business behind it. He reached the fence and turned to Chuck.

"Stop!" he hollered, his voice high and reedy. "Please, stop!"

Chuck halted a hundred feet away.

"Leave me alone, won't you?" the man pleaded, his back to the fence.

"You're the one who was spying on me," Chuck reminded him.

"You weren't supposed to see me."

"But I did." Chuck stepped forward.

"Don't." The man swung his rifle off his back and aimed it at Chuck, threatening him.

Chuck raised a hand placatingly. "I just want to know why you were watching me."

The man stood, rifle raised, silent and unmoving. Seconds

passed. The gun began to wobble in the man's grip, rocking up and down and side to side. He lowered the weapon, pointing its barrel at the ground.

His shirt was tattered and torn. Greasy fingerprints smudged the bill of his cap.

The wind spun strands of his thin hair into the corner of his mouth. He tugged the strands free from his cracked lips with his free hand. "I don't want no trouble with you."

"Put down the gun and you won't."

"It's not mine."

"I don't care whose it is. Just put it down."

Chuck again stepped forward. Paused. Took another step.

The man crouched and rested the rifle on the ground. Straightening, he raised both hands in the air. "I told you, I don't got no problem with you."

"Just tell me why you were spying on me."

"Ain't no law against watching somebody." The man pressed his hands, on either side of his head, toward Chuck. "Just stay back and let me get the hell out of here."

The center of the man's right palm evaporated in an explosion of red mist. The bullet that pierced his hand continued on, plugging a dime-sized hole in the fence behind him. He screeched and pressed his wounded right hand to his chest and covered it with his left.

The deep bass reverberation of a sniper-rifle blast echoed in Chuck's ears a full second after the bullet pulverized the man's hand, the bellow of the big gun coming from the slope behind. Chuck ducked and charged toward the fence. A bullet whizzed past his left ear and tore through the fence, leaving another hole. A third shot missed him on the right side of his head. That bullet, too, drilled a hole through the wood.

Ahead of Chuck, the man stood in front of the fence, wide-eyed, face blanched white. Blood from his shattered hand soaked his shirt, staining it red.

Two more gun blasts trailed the pair of missed shots, thundering past Chuck.

The man spun, grabbed the fence with both hands, and, cursing with pain, slung his body sideways. He hooked one of his sneakers over the the top of the slats, hauled himself upward, and teetered on the fence for a moment. Then he toppled over the far side, disappearing from sight.

Chuck sprinted to the wooden fence and swung himself upward. He lay horizontally atop the fence, the slats digging into his chest, and looked over the other side.

At the foot of the fence, the pond lapped against a narrow shoreline of round river rocks. Tendrils of steam curled off the murky green water. The opposite side of the pool disappeared beneath the greenhouse wall, which ended a few inches above the water's surface.

Ten feet from shore, the man flailed neck-deep in the pond. He swung his arms across the surface of the pool, fighting to stay afloat, blood pulsing from his right palm.

Ripples appeared, arrowing across the pond toward him. He spun, paddling his hands, and faced the approaching wavelets, the water around him turning red with blood.

The ripples disappeared a few feet from him. He swiveled his head, staring all directions.

Suddenly, he shot across the surface of the pool. He screeched in terror, the water roiling behind him. He stopped moving in the center of the pond, and the underwater force that had propelled him forward drew him downward. He clawed desperately at the water, his fingers scrabbling, as first his shoulders disappeared into the depths, then his neck.

He threw back his head when his chin met the surface of the pool. For a moment, only his face remained above water, the bill of his cap aimed at the sky. He locked eyes with Chuck, his mouth open in a silent scream.

Then his face vanished into the depths of the pond, his body dragged from below. Ripples spread outward in silent circles from the point where he disappeared, and a stream of bubbles rose from the pool, breaking the red skim of blood on the surface.